Not Far From The Tree

A Gangster Story

M. J. Feinauer

Michael Feinauer

Copyright © 2023

All Rights Reserved

Dedication

To my brother **'Frosty'**

Table Of Contents

About the Author

Michael started his writing career in late 2017, just a few months before retiring from a rewarding professional career in manufacturing. He has published three novels since then, Neptune's Chalice and Neptune's Chalice: The Reckoning and Confession of the Lord. Each has had modest success and have a five-star rating. He enjoys writing fictional stories and giving readers an opportunity to immerse themselves in his 'page turning' novels. He lives in the United States, in the tiny sprawling town of Braselton Georgia, where in his 'Me' time enjoys target shooting, playing golf, playing the drums, and watching a wide range of movies and sports.

The mob is a man voluntarily descending to the nature of the beast.

- Ralph Waldo Emerson

Chapter 1

(Tampa, Florida, 1954)

It is 1:15 a.m., Sunday. Michel Santoro and his associate, Salvatore Carducci, sat quietly in Michel's car across the street from the Empire Theater. Neither of the men attempted a conversation while the late spring Tampa deluge mercilessly pummeled the hallow steel roof of Michel's new Ford hardtop sedan. They didn't want to let out their frustration, so they chose silence to keep them company. But the thing about silence is that it's always deafening when you have something to say but can't.

The two men had been sent by their Underboss, Thomas Califano, to visit theater and nightclub owner, Bert Marlow. This was not a social visit. Marlow had been short on payments to the Barzetti crime family for two consecutive months. Bert Marlow needed to have this month's payment in full along with the balance of the two previous months, with interest or else, things would go South quickly.

Sal Carducci was always a fidgety, impatient soul. The waiting only aggravated his contemptible demeanor. He reached inside his overcoat and pulled out a pack of cigarettes. Although Michel was looking out of his driver-side door window, he knew exactly what Sal was about to do.

"You're not going to smoke that shit in my brand-new car." Sal paused momentarily, then proceeded to put the cigarette in his mouth. He flipped the cover of his Zippo open and said,

"What was that? I didn't hear you!" He ignited the lighter and slowly brought it to the end of his cigarette. Michel turned his head sharply toward Sal then snatched the cigarette from the lips of his defiant associate.

"I said no," asserted Michel. He rolled down his window and tossed the forbidden cig out. But this didn't deter Sal. He pulled out the pack of cigarettes from the inside of his overcoat once again. Before he could remove another cigarette from the pack, Michel seized it, then crushed the pack and tossed it out the window into the rain. Now Michel's blood was boiling. Self-control is a finite resource and Sal was wearing his patience thin.

"You tend to forget who the hell I am, Santoro," exclaimed Sal as he stared into the eyes of Michel. What he saw wasn't fear but rather someone whom he secretly feared himself.

Michel's tolerance for Sal had begun to wane over the past few months since the rumor that Sal was being considered for a promotion in the Barzetti crime family. Moving up the ranks in the family wasn't something that interested Michel. He didn't want the responsibility that came with the titles. Being a loyal 'soldier' was more than enough for him, if he didn't have to answer to 'power drunk' psychos like Sal Carducci.

Michel and Sal became part of the crime family when they were teenagers. It wasn't something new for them, having been introduced to crime and violence at a very young age. The neighborhood they lived in was known for housing criminals, so this was the norm for them.

They would make a few dollars after school running errands for Thomas Califano when he was a young new Capo—or Captain—for the family. You could say the two boys were raised by organized crime. Eventually, by the time they were juniors in high school, both had decided that going to school interfered with their ability to make lots of money. Their mothers knew what they were doing and felt powerless to stop them simply because their fathers encouraged and supported them. They believed it was extra income coming into their families and that no one would get hurt if the boys didn't kill anyone. After all, power is power.

The boys did well for themselves. They were happy being used in small truck heists and store burglaries.

They were never put in harm's way and were paid very well for their efforts, until one day when Sal turned nineteen years old and felt like he was old enough to move stolen merchandise on his own. He decided to sell a stolen gold watch to an off-duty detective. As the story goes, the detective knew he had Sal on the 'Sale of stolen property' charge, and when he flashed his badge and attempted to put handcuffs on the young hoodlum, Sal pulled the detective's pistol from his holster and shot the detective at point blank range, sending a .38 caliber slug into his heart. To this day, the authorities have no clue who committed the murder. Sal's ability to do whatever it took to reach the top impressed their Underboss.

From that point on, competition between the two men brought each of them to the point where there was nothing they wouldn't do if that brought them one step ahead of the other on the scale of brutality. This behavior was expected from the crime family's soldiers. As the years passed, Sal created a name for himself as one of the family's most feared enforcers. Whereas Michel was considered more diplomatic. Just as dangerous, mind you, but his techniques limited the blood he had to spill to get what he wanted.

As Michel looked toward the theater through the pouring rain to see if there was any sign of Marlow, he could only imagine what his life will be like when Sal becomes a Capo and has his own crew. In that moment, he knew the day would come when he just had to leave the Barzetti crime family or kill Sal. The latter would be fine with him. Over the years, he stopped caring about his comrade and started thinking of him as a frenemy than a friend.

The marque lights of the theater were being turned off. It was what the two men had been waiting for. Marlow would be making his way to the front doors shortly.

"Alright, Sal, we are going to do this my way."

"How is that?" quipped Sal. "You going to say pretty please and start begging?" Sal reached inside his coat, pulled out his .45 semi-auto pistol, and racked one into the chamber. "This is how we handle this, my soft-hearted friend. We put a bullet in his kneecap. It saves a lot of time talking."

"If you blow his kneecap off, how is he supposed to work, you moron!" snapped Michel. His frustration had now started becoming apparent. "Put your gun away. I told you I will handle this." Sal sat there staring at Michel with a grin and a look of contempt on his face as he slowly pointed his gun at Michel and then said,

"How about I handle this my way, and you just stay in the car."

"I don't have time for this shit," Michel said as he turned up the collar on his coat, opened the door, then climbed out. Sal chuckled, put his weapon back into the holster under his coat, opened his door, and climbed out of the car. Once out, he closed the door, turned to look from over the car's roof, and delivered another antagonistic comment toward his associate. To his surprise, his gaze was met with Michel's arm stretched across the car's roof, holding his .45 caliber weapon and pointing directly at Sal's head.

"You point a gun at me again, Sal; I'll take it away from you, shove it up your ass, and pull the trigger."

"I'm going to remember this, Michel," said Sal.

"This is nothing, Sal; here's something to remember." Michel moved his gun a fraction to the right and pulled the trigger. The bullet passed by Sal's cheek, grazing the skin enough to produce a small amount of blood, then slammed into the brick wall behind him. "I could have killed you, Sal; remember that too." Sal was more angry than surprised. He touched his cheek and saw the blood on his fingers. He immediately reached inside his trouser pocket and pulled out a handkerchief to dab his wound. As Sal stood speechless and angry, Michel holstered his weapon, turned away, and started walking toward the theater's front doors. After taking a few steps, a single bolt of lightning accompanied by a loud clap of thunder tore through the night sky, startling Michel. As tough as he looked, there were some things that frightened even the likes of him. He quickly turned around as he reached for his weapon inside his coat, mistaking the thunder for a gunshot, only to find Sal laughing at him. Sal was still standing in the same spot dabbing his cheek.

"Get used to it, Michel; you're going to be looking over your shoulder a lot more after tonight," commented Sal.

There it was, the threat Michel knew was coming. He released his grip on his weapon that remained in its holster.

"You coming in, or will you stay out here and bleed all over my car?" shouted Michel.

"Fuck you!" shouted Sal. He dabbed his cheek again and no longer saw any blood on the handkerchief. He angrily walked around the car catching up to Michel just as he reached the front entrance to the theater.

Michel peered through the double glass doors looking for Marlow. The timing couldn't have been any more perfect. Marlow came through the lobby with his keys in one hand, looking for the one he would need to lock up. He was just a few feet away from the doors before he looked up and saw the dark silhouettes of two men in long coats wearing Fedoras. Startled, Marlow stood frozen. He knew who it was, considering what time it was. Normal patrons wouldn't be at the door this time of night. His pulse quickened, and he began to sweat. This was a business visit which more than likely would not turn out well for him.

Marlow managed to present a nervous smile as he unlocked the door.

"Gentlemen, please come in," he cautiously invited them. "What brings you out on such a miserable night like this?" he asked, directing his question to Michel. Bert Marlow always dealt with Michel. He had never met Sal, which only fueled the terror that streamed through his body.

"Cut the shit, Bert; you're the one that brings us out on a night like this. I could be home right now, nice and warm, snuggled up in bed with my wife."

"I apologize, Mr. Santoro, I had planned to come and talk to you tomorrow," explained Marlow.

"About what, Bert?" asked Michel. Marlow suddenly was at a loss for words. Michel and Sal could see he was becoming increasingly nervous.

"What were you going to come and see me about Bert?" asked Michel once again.

"Well, I was going to bring you some of the money I still owed you and to ask you…."

Sal knew what would come out of Bert Marlow's mouth next. He unbuttoned his overcoat to give himself easier access to his weapon. The move didn't go unnoticed by Michel. He looked into Sal's eyes and without speaking a word, indicated that there would not be any violence. Sal understood. However, it didn't stop him from exposing his weapon to Marlow when he pulled his coat open ever so slightly. Michel patted Marlow's shoulder as he slowly turned him away from the entrance doors. The two men slowly began to walk back toward the lobby. Sal quietly followed a few steps behind.

"Bert, you know I can't go back to my boss and tell him what you just told me."

"Mr. Santoro, I am telling you the truth, I don't have it all yet."

Michel stopped walking but kept his hand on Marlow's shoulder. Marlow couldn't look at Michel any longer simply out of fear.

"Look at me, Bert," ordered Michel. "Do I look like a fuckin' idiot to you?"

Too frightened to look up, Marlow continued to look at the floor.

"I said, look at me, Bert." The tone of Michel's voice became demanding. Marlow raised his head and looked into the eyes of the enforcer. "Do I look like a fuckin' idiot to you?"

"No, Mr. Santoro," responded Marlow.

"That's right; I'm not an idiot. Neither is my boss, so don't give me this shit about not having the money. I know the size of crowds that come in here to watch the movies. So don't tell me you don't have it."

"Mr. Santoro, I can show you the receipts; people aren't coming to watch the movies." Michel looked around the lobby to see posters of what was playing and upcoming releases.

"Well, no wonder Bert," exclaimed Michel. "Look at the films you're showing…Godzilla, Baby Buggy Bunny, and Dixieland Droopy, for Christ's sake! What is that shit!" Marlow managed to conjure an ounce of bravery to defend his movie selections,

"The kids seem to like those kinds of movies."

"You should be showing films like Rear Window, The Caine Mutiny, or On the Waterfront. Show movies that adults like; they are the ones with the money! Am I right?" At this point, Marlow would no longer defend his choices. No matter what he said, it did not change the fact that he still owed them money. All he wanted to do was leave this meeting with all his extremities and air in his lungs. Once again, he bowed his head in a humbling manner. Michel took a deep breath and said,

"Alright, Bert, here's what I'm going to do. I know some good movies are coming out in the next week. I will give you two more weeks to get the money together." Marlow raised his head smiling and replied,

"Thank you, Mr. Santoro; I promise I will have all your money by then." Michel could see the relief on Marlow's face. Truth be told, he was relieved as well. This made things easier.

"That's what I want to hear, Bert because if you are one dollar short, I'll kill your whole fuckin' family." Michel's threat had suddenly erased the joy and relief experienced by Marlow just a moment ago. Michel looked at Sal, gestured, and said, "Let's go." Sal could not believe what he had just witnessed and wanted Michel to know it.

"That's it?" asked Sal. He had come here hoping to get his hands dirty. Michel looked at him, nodded, and replied,

"Yes, that's it, let's go." Michel walked past Sal, who stood there astounded at his associate's leniency toward Marlow. The entire situation was unacceptable in Sal's eyes, and he was not about to let it ride if he could inject his opinion into the matter. He briskly walked toward Marlow as he reached inside his coat and retrieved his gun. Bert Marlow's eyes opened widely, filled with terror. He had no time to react as Sal swiftly and forcefully hit him on the side of his face with his pistol, leaving a three-inch cut across his cheekbone. Michel heard the strike immediately and turned around quickly, only to see Marlow fall to the floor, holding his cheek as blood poured through his fingers. Sal holstered his weapon, turned around, and quickly walked past Michel.

The two men exited the theater leaving Bert Marlow writhing in pain on the floor. The rain had stopped, and Sal pulled a cigarette out from a new pack and lit it. Michel grabbed Sal's arm and stopped him.

"What the hell was that? I told you I would handle it."

"You handled it alright, that little shit was playing you for a fool, so I made damn well sure he understood."

"Why did they send you with me anyway?" asked Michel. Sal looked at him, took another drag from his cigarette, and chuckled.

"You don't know, do you?" asked Sal.

"Know what?"

"I chose to come with you. I wanted to see how you worked these days."

"What concern is that of yours?" a puzzled Michel asked.

"I got the word this morning. I am being considered for promotion; they want to make me a Captain, and I wanted to see what kind of men would work for me. Ain't that a kick in the balls!" Sal could not help but laugh at the expense of Michel. He was right; it was a kick in the balls. It took the breath from Michel. The last thing he ever wanted was to have to answer to Sal for anything. This turn of events could seal Michel's fate with the family.

Michel could not let Sal see how the news upset him. He had to change the subject quickly. He had to be discreet about his emotions. There was no room for vulnerability.

"Let's go have a drink to celebrate," Sal knew exactly what Michel was up to.

"No Michel, I won't be drinking with you anytime soon, not after this." pointing to the fresh wound to his cheek, compliments of the bullet from Michel's gun.

"I could have made it worse," Michel replied, hoping to bring humor into the conversation.

"Fuck you, Michel. This I will never forget," pointing to the wound.

Sal walked past the car, and onto the sidewalk. Heading for a bar just a block away. Michel watched him every step of the way until he was a distant shadow. He knew he would hear about this from Thomas Califano, the Underboss. One positive thing came from all of this; he would have a much more enjoyable ride home to Gulfport without Sal in the car.

Chapter 2

onnie Santoro slowly opened the master bedroom door, where Michel remained asleep. She lightly rapped on the door, hoping not to startle her husband.

"Honey?" she called softly. Michel rolled over on his side to face the bedside clock, then opened one eye to see what time it was. It was ten o'clock.

"What?" he mumbled. Bonnie walked over to the bed, sat next to her husband, placed her soft, warm hand on Michel's arm then said,

"Honey, Thomas is downstairs. He's here to see you." Michel opened both eyes this time to peer at the clock again, hoping it would have read something different than before, like eleven o'clock perhaps.

"Did he say what he wanted?"

"He just said he had to discuss an important matter with you." The slumber fog cleared quickly from Michel's mind. He knew exactly why his Underboss came to his house so early in the morning. It was to talk to him about what happened last night with Sal. Michel sat up immediately, nearly knocking Bonnie off the bed.

"Christ Michel, give me a chance to get off the bed!" scolded his wife.

"Did Thomas appear to be angry or upset?" asked Michel.

"No, not at all. He was nice, like he always is. Why, is something wrong?" asked Bonnie.

"No, no, nothing's wrong." Michel saw the worried expression on his wife's face. It always appeared whenever one of Michel's associates came to the house. She knew enough about what her husband did for a living to have him locked up for a long time. She constantly prayed for that day never to come, so until then, she never asked him about his business. She knew she didn't marry a nine-to-five sort of guy, but still worried about him until he came home, and she could feel him crawl into bed next to her no matter what time it was.

Michel ran his hands through his thick black hair and asked,

"Did you give him some coffee?"

"Of course, I even offered him some breakfast, but he didn't want anything."

"Keep his coffee cup filled, and I'll be down in a couple of minutes." Bonnie leaned forward, kissed her husband's forehead, and approached the door.

"Will you be wanting breakfast?" she asked.

"No, I'll just have some toast and coffee." As soon as Bonnie stepped out of the room, Michel's feet hit the floor. He quickly showered and dressed and made his way downstairs to the kitchen.

"Good morning, Thomas," greeted Michel as he stepped into the kitchen. Thomas rose from his chair as Michel approached him. The two men embraced and greeted each other with a traditional kiss on each cheek.

"Sleep well Mikey?" asked Thomas.

When he first started working for Thomas, Mikey was the nickname given to Michel. Michel was just a young teenager when Thomas gave him the nickname. The Underboss thought it was a fitting name for his young Italian/American soldier. However, Thomas was the only one Michel would allow to address him by that name. Others had made the mistake and paid a painful price to learn never to use it again, at least not in his presence.

"Like a rock," replied Michel. "What brings you out from the city so early on a Sunday morning, shouldn't you be in church or something?"

he asked as he took a seat across the table from his boss. Bonnie placed a hot cup of black coffee on the table before her husband and turned away to retrieve the toast that had just popped up. With Bonnies back to both men, Thomas motioned for Michel to wait.

"Did you get any rain here last night?" Thomas asked.

"Did we ever!" stated Bonnie. "It just poured for about ten minutes. No thunder or lightning, just a hard rain.

"We didn't get a drop. It's like we have this dome over the house. Everything seems to go right around us," complained Thomas. Michel knew his boss didn't have time to sit around talking about the weather, but he knew Thomas was his usual cordial self around Bonnie and wanted her to engage at the breakfast table with the two men. That was one of many things Michel admired about his Underboss. He wanted people to be relaxed and comfortable around him.

Thomas slid his chair out away from the table, looked at Bonnie, and said,

"I would love nothing more than to sit here the rest of the day drinking coffee, my dear, but I must be getting to work." He stood from his chair, leaned over, and kissed Bonnie on the cheek. "Thank you for the coffee, love."

"You're very welcome, Thomas, anytime." Michel stood from his chair and took one more bite of his toast,

"I'll walk you out, Thomas," he said as he wiped his hands and mouth, then tossed the napkin on the table.

Michel retrieved Thomas's hat from the coat tree next to the front door. Before handing it to Thomas, he noticed the look and feel of the Fedora.

"Is this new?" he asked as he handed it to him.

"Yes, it is. I had to replace my old brown one. I was at the peer yesterday, and a goddamn seagull shit on it and stained it. The bad thing about it was I walked around for hours with bird shit on my hat! No one bothered to tell me!" Michel couldn't help but laugh at his boss's misfortune. As Michel opened the door for Thomas, he continued to chuckle. "It's not fuckin' funny, Mikey."

"I'm sorry, boss, you're right. It's a terrible thing."

"Goddamn right it is." Michel closed the door behind them. The two men began a slow walk toward Thomas's car, which was parked in the driveway. Nothing had been said until they reached the car. The two men always took precautions when business was discussed around their homes and when the family were nearby.

"I heard you had an incident last night with Sal," began Thomas. Michel nodded as he stared down the street looking over Thomas's shoulder, then muttered, "It was nothing."

Thomas quickly became upset in response to Michel's unconvincing reply. He stepped closer to Michel. When he did, Michel looked into the eyes of his boss and immediately knew he was pissed.

"Nothing? It was nothing? Let me tell you something, Mikey. Sal went directly to the 'Old Man' about this.

He was referring to Vincenzo Barzetti, the head of the family. Barzetti had been made head of his own family with help from long-time associate and friend Franco Di Stasi, who had close ties to Santo Trafficante Jr.

Barzetti insisted internal squabbles were dealt with straightaway by the Family's Underboss. Any delay in reaching an equitable conclusion to any matter would result in the intervention of Barzetti and his Consigliere. The Underboss in this case, Thomas Califano, would be looked upon as weak and unworthy to advance in the 'Family' hagiarchy. Thomas had worked too long and hard for something like this to interfere with his climb to the top.

Unfortunately, with Sal going over Thomas's head and directly to the boss, produced one strike against Thomas before he even got out of the gate.

"I might have gone a little overboard with Sal, I just wasn't in the mood for his shit," confessed Michel. Thomas was fuming inside and paused a moment before speaking.

"I don't give a damn what kind of mood you were in, Mikey. You don't go shooting at a made man unless it's authorized. You know that. What the fuck is wrong with you?" Michel had no response. He knew the ass-chewing wasn't over and remained quiet until he felt Thomas was finished with his reprimand. "I don't know if you have heard, but they are looking at making Sal a Captain."

"Yes, I heard," said Michel.

"You knew this, yet you shot him?" asked Thomas.

"I only grazed him, he would be dead if I wanted to kill him," replied Michel, unable to keep silent which he would soon find out was a mistake.

"You getting smart with me Mikey?" asked Thomas as he short-handed the back of Michel's head. "You getting smart? Let me tell you something, Mikey, I must make things right with this, and I don't need your smart-ass sense of humor. You understand?" Michel nodded. "Let me tell you right now, my friend, whatever I come up with to resolve this thing, you are going to agree to it, capito?" Michel once again silently nodded. "Good," responded Thomas as he patted Michel's cheek just like he used to when Michel was a boy. "I've arranged a sit down with Sal this afternoon I will call you when it's over. In the meantime, stay home today. Spend some time with your family."

"Sounds like good advice Thomas, I will do that." The two men embraced, each patting the other on the back. Michel stepped back from Thomas to allow him to open his car door and said,

"I'm sorry about all of this Thomas."

"I know you are Mikey, let's hope it doesn't happen again."

"It won't boss; next time I'll kill the son-of-a-bitch." The smile on Thomas's face quickly disappeared. He was about to scold Michel once again until the front door of Michel's house swung open, exposing the smiling faces of Michel's two children who ran out to greet their 'Uncle' Thomas, who didn't mind the title even though he was not related to them.

Giovanni or 'John' as everyone called him, was Michel's seventeen-year-old son. His younger sister Angela or 'Angie' was the apple of Michel's eye. She adored her father. He was her hero. Both Giovanni and Angela were well mannered and respectful. Each had their own personal goals in life, which made their parents exceptionally proud. Giovanni had his sights set on possibly becoming a priest. His strong religious conviction and the admiration of the family's priest, Father Angelo Bernardi, appealed to Giovanni's sense of worth. He could see himself helping the downtrodden and those suffering spiritually.

Even though she was only twelve years old, Angela demonstrated ambitions to become the world's greatest chef. She was front and center in the family kitchen to assist her mother with preparing the evening dinners. Her mother would have to shew her out of the kitchen for breakfasts and sit-down lunches, when they had them. She wanted her aspiring young chef to also enjoy being a kid, and play. She knew her daughter would have plenty of time to learn her craft. So, for right now, her mother wanted her to also enjoy the life of being a child.

The scowl on Thomas's face quickly disappeared when the children began to run toward him.

"Uncle Thomas! We didn't know you were here!" shouted little Angie. She was the first to greet her Uncle Thomas with a warm hug.

"Hello, my little princess, how are you?" he asked.

"I'm fine," she replied sweetly.

"And who is this strapping young man, Michel? You must have hired a new partner because this can't be Giovanni," exclaimed Thomas as he extended his hand in greeting. At times, Giovanni couldn't tell if Thomas was joking or not. This was one of those times.

"No, it's me, Uncle Thomas, Giovanni," he said embarrassingly.

"What are you feeding these kids, Michel? They are growing so fast!" Michel's response was short. He had the issue with Sal weighing heavily on his mind.

"Yes, they are, just good home cooking." Thomas could see his most reliable soldier was troubled. The last thing he wanted to do was to draw attention to it in front of the kids.

"Have you started driving yet Giovanni?" asked Thomas.

"No sir, but Pop has been letting me drive once in a while on the back roads of the orange farms." The admission sparked the curiosity of little Angie. She looked up at her father and asked him a surprisingly direct question that caught Michel off guard.

"Does Momma know about that, Daddy?" Suddenly all eyes were on Michel,

"Of course, she does sweetheart, I tell Momma everything." Thomas and Giovanni smiled, knowing the answer Michel gave wasn't entirely truthful. On the other hand, Angie believed her father and thought nothing more about it. To help rescue his loyal soldier Michel from the unsympathetic line of questioning from his twelve-year-old daughter, Thomas reached into his front trouser pocket and pulled out a folded wade of cash held together by a thick rubber band. The action did not go unnoticed by the two youngsters. Thomas peeled a crisp fifty-dollar bill off the top and gave it to Giovanni. The tall young teenager's eyes lit up like a flare.

"Fifty dollars! Thank you very much, Uncle Thomas." Michel was just as surprised as his son at Thomas's generosity. He had witnessed Thomas give less to a young soldier who ran drinks to Thomas all night during a marathon poker game.

"That isn't necessary, Thomas," said Michel.

"Sure, it is he has to start saving for his own car," commented Thomas.

"That's right, Pop, this will be a great start," agreed Giovanni hoping his father wouldn't insist he give it back. He was relieved when his father made no further comments.

Even at the tender age of twelve, Angela knew the value of the bill handed to her brother and wanted her fair share. She was not shy to ask Thomas either.

"Where's mine?" she asked with her hand held out.

"Angela, is that how to ask?" reminded Michel.

"May I have one too please, Uncle Thomas?" Without hesitation, Thomas peeled another fifty-dollar bill from the wad of cash and handed it to Angela.

"She's not saving for a car Thomas," commented Michel.

"Perhaps not, but it would buy a real nice bicycle, wouldn't it sweetheart?" he asked as he directed the question to Angie. Her face lit up like a Christmas tree at the thought of a new bike.

"Thank you, Uncle Thomas," she squealed while giving him a big hug.

"Yes, thank you, Uncle Thomas," said Giovanni as he too drew close to hug Thomas.

"Alright, you two, Uncle Thomas needs to get going," commented their father. The two extremely grateful children said their goodbyes and ran back to the house anxious to show their mother what their uncle had just given them. Thomas watched their hasty retreat every step of the way with a warm smile.

"That was a bit much, Thomas," said Michel.

"Perhaps, but I enjoyed every minute of it," replied Thomas. He resumed climbing into his car. Michel closed the door for him once he was completely inside. Thomas started the car and put it in reverse.

"My meeting with Sal is at one o'clock; I'll call you when it's finished," assured Thomas. Michel nodded in acknowledgement.

Chapter 3

Thomas Califano sat at a small table toward the back of the modest Cuban coffee shop, Café Baracoa, sipping his espresso and eating one of his favorite Cuban pastries, Pastelitos de Guayaba. A flakey puffed pastry filled with cream cheese and Guava jelly.

He glanced at the clock on the café wall, then at the entrance door. Sal Carducci had less than five minutes to sit across from Thomas for their meeting to discuss what had happened between him and Michel the night before. If there was one thing Thomas insisted on his men, it was to be on time. Those who found the courage to test the Under Boss' patience and show up late never did it again. For Thomas to maintain control of his men, he would make examples of those who broke the rules. The harshness of the punishment depended on whether you were in good standing with the family. His form of management stood the test of time and was condoned by the head of the family, Don Vincenzo Barzetti.

With one minute remaining the front entrance door swung open, ringing the tiny bell attached to the door's frame. In stepped Sal Carducci. It was easy to find Thomas in the back of the shop because that was where he always sat. As Sal walked past the waiter who came out from behind the counter, he ordered coffee.

Sal glanced at the wall clock and saw he had fifteen seconds left before he was seated. To annoy Thomas, Sal took his time removing his hat, glancing at it as he held it and meticulously removing tiny pieces of lint. Once he finished, he slowly sat down. It was exactly 1:00 P.M.

"You test my patience Sal," stated Thomas. It was exactly what Sal intended to do. He knew he was getting upped, which meant Thomas would have to show him a little more respect than he would if he were just a soldier. Sal decided to get a taste of things to come.

The waiter delivered Sal's coffee and placed it in front of him. Sal spun the cup around in the saucer so the handle could be picked up with his right hand. He brought the cup to his lips and took a small sip.

"That's damn good coffee, and hot too." He returned the cup to the saucer and asked Thomas, "Did you talk to Michel?"

"Yes, I did. He agreed that he overreacted and assured me that everything would be fine," replied Thomas.

"That's it? Everything is going to be fine. That's all he had to say?" Thomas shrugged his shoulders slightly and said,

"In so many words, yes. That's all he said." Sal seemed agitated and squirmed in his chair.

"That's not good enough, Thomas. Michel must pay for what he did."

"What did you have in mind Sal?" asked Thomas.

"For one thing, I don't want him to be a part of my crew when I'm captain. If he ever looks at me sideways, I'll cut his fuckin' heart out."

"Done," responded Thomas. "What else?" Sal could see he was being offered a blank check over the incident. All he had to do was name his price.

"I want that bastard to pay me a hundred grand for all the aggravation he's caused me." Thomas sat back in his chair and raised his brow at the high compensation price tag.

"That's a lot of money," commented Thomas. He knew Michel would not be able to come up with that kind of money, especially not immediately. He thought a moment then replied,

"What if I have him give you a percentage of his action coming out of Pinellas airport?"

"How much of percentage and for how long?" asked Sal giving the impression he was interested. Thomas sipped his espresso as he contemplated the amount and length of time.

"How does 15% for two years sound?"

"I'm still listening," quipped Sal.

"20% for two years," said Thomas. This time Sal didn't comment. He sat silently, staring directly at Thomas. Thomas realized padding the offer any further would infuriate Michel. He had no choice. Despite how he personally felt about Sal, he knew Sal needed to be well compensated. "25% for three years; that's the final offer." Thomas believed he struck an agreeable amount with Sal just by his facial expression. Knowing Sal, however, Thomas knew he would try and squeeze more out of the deal. He was right. Sal took a deep breath, then began to make his counteroffer.

"How about…" Thomas cut him off mid-sentence.

"Take it or I'll let you two kill each other and I won't have to deal with either one of you." Sal didn't give it anymore thought then displayed a sheepish grin and replied,

"Alright then, I accept." Thomas immediately slid his chair back and stood up from the table. "Where are going?" Sal asked. Thomas put his hat on and responded,

"I'm going to make a call and close this deal. I would appreciate you get the check."

"Sure, no problem boss. By the way, is that a new hat? What happened to the old one?" Thomas was in no mood to tell the story of the bird and the hat, especially to Sal.

"Never mind, I'll see you later." Thomas made his way out of the café and to his car. He decided to call Michel from his home, giving him time during the drive on how to approach Michel with the news.

***

The Santoro family were enjoying themselves having Michel home on a Sunday afternoon. Typically, he rarely spent time at home during the day because of work. It felt a bit strange, but Bonnie didn't give it much thought. Over the years she knew not to ask Michel about his business if she liked to keep the peace around the house. The kids, John and Angie, took advantage of the situation and spent as much time with their father as possible. John and Michel washed the family car while Angie helped her mother in the kitchen preparing the Sunday afternoon lunch. It was Angie's first attempt to make potato salad, with her mother's supervision of course. Angie was very focused on making sure she followed her mother's recipe to the letter.

"I hope Daddy likes my potato salad," commented Angie as she struggled to mix the dense potato mixture in a large wooden bowl and equally as large wooden spoon.

"I know he will love it honey," replied Bonnie. "If he doesn't, then there will be more for you, me, and your brother. The comment from her mother struck Angie in a funny way. She couldn't help but giggle.

John was undertaking the final stage of the car washing project. Cleaning the white wall tires and hubcaps was the one part of the process Michel never liked. Fortunately, he had help from his son this time.

"Take your time and do a good job on those tires son," said Michel. "I want to be able to see myself in the chrome hubs."

"Yes sir," replied John. Michel watched his son work on the first tire. From where he stood it looked like he was doing a good job. He could not understand why John was spending so long scrubbing the hubcap. Michel knew they weren't that dirty. He didn't remember driving through any mud last night. The extra effort John was putting into cleaning the tire had now become a mystery that Michel needed answers to. He walked up behind his son and peered over his shoulder.

"What's giving you so much trouble, son?" he asked. John stopped scrubbing. He rinsed off the tire and hub with the hose he had on the ground in front of him, then dropped the sponge into the bucket, appearing to be exhausted and a little bit frustrated. Once again, his father asked, "What's the problem?" John glanced over his shoulder at his father then looked back at the shining hubcap.

"You told me you wanted to see your face in the hubcaps. I've been scrubbing like crazy and all I see is my face." At first, John's comment didn't register in Michel's brain because he was so intently studying the hubcap and looking for the cause of his son's problems. Then it hit him. John looked over his shoulder again and saw his father's toothy grin.

"I have a wise guy for a son," chuckled Michel.

"Gotcha Pop!" remarked John, but the gag wasn't quite over. Michel suddenly noticed the spray nozzle on the end of the hose was pointed at him from under John's right arm. Before Michel could react, a blast of water hit him square in the face. John did not wait around for any form of retaliation from his father. He sprung up as quick as a rabbit and took refuge on the other side of the car. Michel was now armed with the water hose, but the youthful John was too quick on his feet and easily eluded his father's retaliatory assault. Suddenly the watery dual was interrupted when Bonnie came out onto the porch to inform her men that lunch was being served.

"Tell him to quit, Mom!" shouted John. Bonnie simply shook her head. She could see that her son got the best of her husband, and he was not about to call a truce. As he continued to take unsuccessful shots at his son, Bonnie could see she would have to intervene and bring the battle to an end. She came off the porch and walked over to the water spicket and turned it off, totally disarming her husband.

"Thanks, Mom!" shouted John as he quickly ran onto the porch past his mother and into the house laughing the entire way. With his head and shirt soaking wet, Michel followed behind John but at a much slower defeated pace. He stopped when he reached Bonnie and attempted to give her a kiss. She coyly pushed him away and teasingly said,

"I don't kiss losers; my winner is in the house."

"How quickly they turn on you," said Michel laughing then joined shortly by Bonnie. "Let me run upstairs and change my shirt, I'll be right down."

Bonnie returned to the kitchen where she found Angie holding the large bowl of potato salad waiting for her father to take his seat at the table.

"Daddy will be down, honey, right after he changes his shirt. You can put that on the table."

"No, I want to bring it to Daddy and tell him I made it."

"Okay, I'll see you in a few minutes then." Bonnie left the kitchen and stepped into the dining room, only to find John sitting at the table waiting for everyone else. He helped himself to a serving tray of sweet pickles.

"Save some for the rest of us John."

"Yes ma'am." He took one more and set the tray back to the center of the table. Bonnie took her seat and placed her napkin on her lap. The sound of footsteps coming down the staircase at a quickened pace announced to Angie that her father would soon be seated at the table. The sound of his voice would be her que to begin her presentation.

"Rueben sandwiches, my favorite," exclaimed Michel. He looked at Bonnie and asked, "Where's Angela?" Suddenly, the kitchen door swung open. Smiling from ear to ear and carrying a wooden bowl nearly half her size, Angie presented her father with her first masterpiece. "Well, what do we have here?" asked the proud father smiling.

"It's potato salad, Daddy! I made it!"

"You did? I bet it's delicious. Can I have some?"

"Of course," replied Angie. She remained standing next to her father making sure he took a healthy portion. Michel passed the bowl to John as Angie stood there patiently waiting for her father to take his first bite of her culinary work of art. Michel quickly noticed his daughter remained at his side. He knew what she was doing, so he deliberately took his time and did anything he could to avoid taking his first fork full. Angie watched his every move. When he picked up his sandwich to take a bite, Angie looked at him as if to say, *"Don't you want to taste my potato salad, Daddy?"* He could not continue with the charade. The puppy dog eyes of his little girl nearly broke his heart. Just as Michel was bringing his sandwich to his mouth, he stopped and said,

"What am I doing? I want to taste Angie's potato salad first." His daughter's eyes brightened, followed by a joyous smile. Michel set the sandwich back down on his plate, picked up his fork and scooped up a heaping mouthful of potato salad. He closed his eyes as he chewed and moaned savoring his daughter's work of love. He peeked at Angie out of one eye only to see her face gleaming with pride.

"Do you like it, Daddy?" she asked.

"Like? Well, let me tell you, I think I will give your brother my sandwich and I'll keep this potato salad all to myself." He picked his plate up and acted as if he was going to trade his sandwich with John for the bowl of potato salad, until Angie spoke up.

"No, Daddy, I made it for everybody!"

"Oh, well then, I guess it's nice to share, right?" Angie nodded her head in agreement and confirmed it with a resounding,

"Yes." Michel set his plate back down in front of him and passed the salad back to John.

"How's that sweetie?" he asked her.

"Good," she replied, climbing onto her chair and taking a bite of her sandwich.

The delightful family moment suddenly ended when the phone rang. Michel glanced up at the wall clock to see what time it was. His appetite seemed to disappear when his instincts told him it was Thomas. He stood up from the table and motioned to Bonnie that he would answer the call in the kitchen. Before he picked up the receiver, Michel waited for the kitchen door to completely close.

"Hello."

"Mikey, I just finished my meeting with Sal. I need to talk to you."

"You're talking to me now, what is it?"

"I didn't want to do this over the phone. I wanted to talk to you in person." Michel knew Thomas was stalling.

"Is what you're going to tell me change if you do it in person?" Thomas paused before he answered.

"No, it's not."

"So, tell me. Quit fuckin' around." Thomas knew Michel was expecting unsettling news just from the tone of his voice.

"I told Sal you would be giving him 25% of your action from Pinellas airport."

"For how long, Thomas?"

"Three years." There wasn't any response from Michel. Thomas was not sure he was still on the line. "Mikey, you still there?" There still wasn't any response. A few more seconds passed before Thomas finally received Michel's response.

"I don't think so," said Michel as he hung up the phone and returned to the Sunday afternoon lunch with his family.

Chapter 4

It was Monday morning, the beginning of another week of school for John and Angie.

Bonnie prepared the children's breakfast, which normally consisted of cold cereal, jelly toast, and orange juice. This time of the morning was the 'quiet before the storm' before the children would be running down the stairs to boast of being the first at the breakfast table. It was a little contest played between the two ever since Angie reached the age of being able to challenge her older brother at feats of speed and agility. John would never admit his little sister was a formattable opponent, especially to his parents, but John would always compliment Angie when it took everything he had to beat her in a foot race. At times, he would also let his little sister win at some challenges. As a big brother, he believed his younger sister should have as much confidence in herself as he had in her.

Bonnie poured the children's orange juice into their glasses, then glanced at the wall clock. It read 6:50. The first steps could be heard descending the stairs. Bonnie recognized the lightness in each step and knew that her daughter was about to win the Monday morning dash to the table. Angie rounded the corner into the kitchen when Bonnie suddenly heard the thumping of her son's size eight shoes scrambling down the stairway.

"Mom, Angie cheated!" shouted John as he rounded the corner into the kitchen, only to find Angie already eating her cereal. Bonnie glanced at her daughter, who immediately shrugged her shoulders, silently proclaiming her innocence.

"Good morning, John," greeted Bonnie. "How did she cheat?" she asked. At this time, Angie had focused her attention on the back of the cereal box in order not to have to look at her brother or mother. Chances were, if she did, she would start to giggle, demonstrating a clear admission of guilt.

John acted as if he was upset, but he really wasn't. In fact, he admired how clever his sister had become in her effort to win their morning table dash.

"Good morning, Mom," replied John.

"So, how did your sister cheat?" Bonnie asked. John looked at his sister, whose eyes remained focused on the cereal box.

"She hid my shoes."

"Now, how would she know what shoes you were going to wear. You probably left them somewhere and forgot where you put them," explained Bonnie. John looked at his mother, knowing she did not know the entire story before making her comment.

"Mom, she hid all of my shoes!" John exclaimed. Bonnie could see out of the corner of her eye that Angie quietly and slowly slid the cereal box directly in front of her to be able to hide the expression on her face from her mother. Bonnie quickly took a sip of her coffee to keep herself from laughing. To maintain her impartial standing with her two children, she could show no favoritism no matter how impressed she was by her children's imagination or ingenuity to gain the advantage.

"Did you do that, Angie?" asked Bonnie.

"Yes," answered Angie, still hiding behind the cereal box. Even Bonnie thought the move was ingenious and struggled to remain neutral.

"You shouldn't hide your brothers' things. You wouldn't like it if he did that to you, now, would you?"

"No, Ma'am."

"Alright then." As far as Bonnie was concerned, Angie had won this battle. She removed the cereal box in front of her daughter, only to find her sweet girl smiling with the face of an angel and the crafty mind of a mob boss.

"Good morning, everyone," greeted Michel as he entered the kitchen, still in his pajama bottom and robe. Bonnie's initial response was,

"What are you doing up so early?" however, the children's response was shared,

"Good morning, Daddy, and good morning pop." Michel leaned into Bonnie and gave her a kiss on the cheek as she poured her husband a cup of coffee.

Bonnie glanced at the wall clock and was surprised at how time that morning had quickly slipped away.

"Alright, you guys, put the dishes in the sink, get upstairs, and brush your teeth. It's almost time to get to school." The children immediately responded, and both quickly climbed the staircase to their upstairs bathroom to brush. Bonnie sat next to Michel at the table and asked,

"You have something important this morning? Is that why you are up so early?" Michel took a sip of his morning brew and said,

"Yes, I have something important to address this morning."

"Does it have anything to do with Thomas' visit yesterday?" Michel set his coffee cup down and put his hand on top of Bonnies and spoke.

"I love you, honey, and you know better than to ask me about my business. So why are you asking now?" Bonnie placed her other hand on top of Michels and looked her husband straight into his eyes, and replied,

"You didn't sleep well last night, for one thing."

"And the other thing?" he asked.

"I can see it in your face. You have a lot on your mind." Michel turned his eyes away from his wife and stared at the table to hide what was apparently written on his face.

"We may have to leave Florida," stated Michel. Bonnie was confused about why and began to ask Michel what he was talking about but was suddenly interrupted by John and Angie as they re-entered the kitchen and headed for their lunch bags. Bonnie stood from her chair and responded to the children's sudden return.

"That was a pretty fast brush job if you did, in fact, brush your teeth and not just rinse your mouth."

"We brushed! exclaimed John." He was immediately defended by his sister,

"We brushed, Momma." Suddenly, there was a knock at the kitchen back door. It was John's close friend and schoolmate, Dante Carducci, the son of Sal Carducci, the person Michel now owes monthly payments to.

Michel liked Dante despite the disdain he held for his father, Sal. Dante and John practically grew up together. They met when their fathers, Michel and Sal, were first brought into the Barzetti crime family. The two boys were inseparable. They did everything together. Every morning Dante would stop at John's house to walk with him and his sister to school. The walk to school was just over a quarter mile from where John lived. It gave the two boys time to talk, just as long Angie was not trying to listen to their conversations. Most of the time, the two boys would let Angie walk ahead of them. That way, John could do what all big brothers should do watch out for their sister.

Michel motioned for Dante to come in.

"Good morning, Mr. and Mrs. Santoro," greeted Dante. Bonnie was the first to reply.

"Good morning, Dante, and you know it's alright to address us as Michel and Bonnie. You've known us long enough to do so."

"Thank you, Ma'am, but if my father were to hear that, he would tan my hide for showing disrespect." Michel captured the opportunity to inquire into Dante's father's well-being even though he just saw him the night before last.

"So, how's your father, Dante?" Dante smiled and shook his head.

"You should see the cut he has on his cheek Mr. Santoro. He told me he got in a fight in a bar in Tampa. My dad came out on top, but I know if you were there with him, he probably wouldn't have gotten a scratch." Michel knew the cut to his father's face was not from a bar fight but from the .45 slug he grazed Sal's cheek with.

"Thank you for the compliment, Dante, but your father has always been able to take care of himself," assured Michel. Dante exhibited a proud smile and said,

"I suppose you are right, sir; he is a pretty tough guy."

John and Angie grabbed their lunch bags and schoolbooks, then gave their parents a kiss on the cheek and headed for the door.

"Have a good day, kids," said Bonnie as the trio went out the door. After the door had been closed, Michel continued to stare at it. Bonnie could see his thoughts were elsewhere. She returned to the table and sat next to her husband. She placed her hand on top of his and then asked,

"What's happened, Michel? Why did you say we may have to leave Florida?" He looked at Bonnie and saw the concern in her eyes. Michel hesitated to answer her question. Rarely did he discuss his business with her, but in this case, since she would be involved, he made an exception.

"Thomas gave Sal 25% of my business from the airport."

"Why did he do that?" she asked.

"The scratch Dante was talking about that was on his father's cheek didn't come from a fist fight. I grazed his cheek with a bullet." Bonnie sat quietly for a moment taking in what had just been disclosed to her and what the consequences might be for her husband's actions.

"We are going to have to leave Florida because you hurt Sal Carducci?" Michel shook his head and replied,

"No. We are going to have to leave because I will probably be answering to Sal very soon. They are planning to make him a Captain. They don't take kindly to soldiers killing their Captains."

"You're going to kill Sal?" asked Bonnie. She really did not want to know the answer to that question, but her anxiety prevented her from holding back.

"I don't know yet," responded Michel. Bonnie was somewhat relieved to hear her husband say that. It meant she had time to change his mind before he did something he would regret.

Michel patted the back of Bonnie's hand and asked her if she would make him some eggs and toast while he went upstairs to shower. She realized that was her husband's way of saying, "End of discussion."

***

John, Dante, and Angie reached their school with plenty of time before the day officially began. The middle school wing of the massive building was the first they came to on their morning trek. Angie broke away from the two boys and ran toward the building, joining several of her classmates who were standing outside. Now that John's little sister was no longer nearby, the two teenage boys were free to talk about what most boys their age talk about…girls.

"I saw you talking to Rebecca Stone last Friday at lunch. You a little sweet on her buddy?" asked Dante.

"I don't know D (A nickname John had given Dante when they were six years old). She asked me if I would like to go to a youth retreat with her in a couple of weeks."

"A retreat? Like off into the woods without parents for several days kind of thing?" inquired Dante.

"No, it's just a one-day religious getaway for teens. It starts in the morning and ends early evening."

"What are they going to do there?"

"They are going to have people come and talk to us."

"That sounds wonderful, buddy. Are you going to sit there and have a bunch of old people lecture you all day? That sounds like it would be a great first date," sarcastically quipped Dante. "Where are you going to take her to dinner? Wait, let me guess, they are going to give you fishing poles so you can catch your supper." The sarcastic remark made John think for a moment. *Maybe he's right!*

"I don't think it will come to that D. The speakers are going to be people our age, maybe a little older. They going to talk about learning how to teach younger people about God. It sounds like something I might like to do."

"You are a better man than I, Giovanni Santoro. Just promise me one thing. Just bring some mosquito repellent with you when you and Rebecca wander off into the woods to make out. Don't want you two getting your asses bit," joked Dante as he put his arm around the shoulders of his friend."

"Piss off, D, what an asshole." The two laughed as they reached the steps to their school entrance. Once inside, the two made a couple of turns around hallway corners until they reached a bank of lockers that contained their individual lockers spaced about ten feet from each other. As the two stowed their books, they continued their conversation concerning the girls who had recently caught their eye. "I heard you and Anna James were caught passing notes to each other in history class. What's that all about?" asked John.

"You heard right, my friend. She's cute, and she thinks I'm cute too."

"I didn't know Anna was blind, D?" ribbed John.

"Fuck you, Santoro," responded Dante in a joking manner. "Fortunately, there wasn't anything in the note that would have gotten us in trouble."

"What did it say?" asked John.

"I just asked her if she liked what we were learning about the Civil War."

"What did she write?"

"She wrote that she did, as long as I was there to help her study about it!"

"Sounds like she has it made in the shade with that."

"How is that?" questioned Dante.

"We all know you are a walking encyclopedia when it comes to Civil War history. No better way to a girl's heart than through her brain!"

"Indeed, my friend," agreed Dante.

The bell sounded, notifying the students that it was time to head to their first class. The boys closed their lockers and proceeded in opposite directions to their first class.

***

Bonnie walked her husband out to their car, parked in the driveway. She gave him a kiss and said,

"Be careful today." He nodded and climbed into the car. As he did, his suitcoat opened, exposing the double-shoulder holster he was wearing. It did not go unnoticed by Bonnie. Michel rolled down the window and reached out to squeeze his wife's hand. As she held his hand tightly, she asked,

"Packing heavy today, are we?"

"I want to make sure I have their attention," he said, giving Bonnie's hand a gentle squeeze. She wasn't sure who he was referring to. The only thing she cared about at that moment was that she would see her husband again later that day. It wasn't the first time Bonnie burned the last images of her husband into her brain in the event he never came home again. The sickening feeling deep in her stomach always started at this moment and never ended until she held him in her arms once again.

He shifted the car into reverse and backed down the driveway. Bonnie blew him a kiss and slowly made her way back into the house, thinking about where she might want to move to in case they had to leave Florida.

Chapter 5

Michel decided to park a half block away from the corner grocery store that supplied the front needed for the crime family's local operations.

Bay Street Grocery was owned and operated by a friend of the Barzetti crime family, Georgy Kharkov. Georgy came to the United States when his parents smuggled him and his two sisters out of Russia during World War II to escape from the death grip of their nation's leader, Joseph Stalin. It was an educational experience for Kharkov, but he learned quickly how to make friends with the right people and quickly make money by any means he could. His store was very successful despite its appearance. Georgy believed to remain anonymous and out of the watchful eye of law enforcement, he would never put any large amount of money into the store that would draw attention. The store portion of the building looked old and run down. The back portion of the building was kept clean, updated, and orderly. This area was, for all intent and purposes, the office for Thomas Califano.

It was relatively early for the locals to do their grocery shopping. Michel realized that and closely watched everyone who entered the store. Most of the men going in the store he recognized, all except two men dressed in dark clothes, who arrived shortly before Thomas Califano did. His head count was six. Once again, his intuition to bring more firepower with him this morning paid off. He waited five more minutes, then checked behind him through his rearview and side mirrors. Believing it was as safe as it was going to get, Michel opened the car door and climbed out. He straightened his lightweight linen sport coat and made sure his two .45 caliber handguns were well covered. Michel closed the door and began his walk toward the store. As he approached the front of the store, he decided rather than walk in using the front door, he would enter through the rarely used side door. It was just another added precaution he took in case Sal or even his old friend Thomas had a surprise waiting for him. He quietly stepped up onto the small porch and stood off to the side of the door and peered in through the window. It didn't come as a surprise when he spotted one of the men he didn't recognize earlier standing in the entryway outside of Thomas' office, looking through a partially opened door at Thomas. Michel reached inside his sport coat and retrieved one of his handguns. He pulled the slide back slightly to confirm there was a round in the chamber. He then reached down and turned the doorknob. To his delight, it was unlocked. Michel stepped in completely undetected by the stranger.

He knew exactly where to step to avoid the creaking planks on the floor. He knew because he was in the same exact spot a month earlier when he was assigned to assassinate a man that had insulted Thomas' daughter in a Tampa nightclub. The man was brought to meet with Thomas and pay restitution, but Thomas didn't want the man's money. He wanted him dead. That was Michel's job, and he was very good at his craft.

Michel was close enough to the man that he could have taken a bite out of his ear, but instead, he put the barrel of his weapon against the man's head behind his right ear.

"Now, who the hell are you?" whispered Michel as he quickly removed the man's weapon from his shoulder holster, stuffing it in the front of his slacks. Michel nudged his gun into the back of the man's head and said,

"Open the door slowly and walk in. You make a sound. I'll put a bullet in your brain. Do you understand?" the man did not respond in any manner. "Are you deaf?" asked Michel. The man stood silent and motionless. "What's wrong with you? Don't you understand English?" The man replied,

"Nessun inglese."

"Jesus Christ, did you just get off the boat?" whispered Michel.

"Che cosa?" asked the man.

"Never mind, walk." The man didn't move. "Walk, camminare," ordered Michel nudging his pistol against the back of the man's head. The man opened the door slowly and quietly, then stepped in. Michel briefly surveyed the room as he entered. A round conference table was directly in front of him. Thomas was sitting there alone with his back to Michel. The other man, whom Michel did not recognize, was at the bar with his back also to Michel, preparing a cup of coffee for Thomas.

"Good morning, Michel," greeted Thomas.

Perhaps it was a sixth sense, a change of temperature in the room, or having the hearing capabilities of a dog, but Thomas knew Michel entered the room. Michel wasn't all that surprised. You don't live long in this business unless you develop acute survival traits. It was apparent Thomas had mastered his.

The man at the bar quickly spun around. Without hesitation, Michel removed his second pistol with his left hand and pointed it directly at the man's chest. He began to make a slow, deliberate move to retrieve his weapon from inside his jacket, which was quickly noticed by Michel.

"No!" shouted Michel shaking his head from side to side. "Metti la tua pistola sul bancone," The man reached inside his coat and removed his gun from its holster, showing Michel that his finger was not on the trigger, and placed it on the bar. Michel then motioned for both men to sit at the table. The two sat next to each other across from Thomas. Michel walked over to the other entrance door to the room and locked it, keeping his guns always pointed at the three men.

"What are you doing, Michel?" asked Thomas.

"Who are these fuckin' guys?"

"They're from a crew on the north side. They will be working for Sal. I brought them here today so that both you and Sal could meet them," explained Thomas. Michel nodded as he looked at each man,

"Bullshit, you brought them here to persuade me to accept the deal you made with Sal."

"C'mon, Michel, what the hell are you talking about? I'm helping Sal build a crew."

"Is that right? Where are you from?" Michel asked the two men. The two looked at Thomas, then at each other.

"They don't understand fuckin' English, Thomas! "Di dove sei?" Michel asked again, only this time in Italian.

"Palermo," said one. "Messina," replied the other.

"Just some local boys, Thomas?"

"Alright, alright," muttered Thomas. "They were brought in just in case things got a little ugly with you and Sal.

"You planning on having me whacked, Thomas?" The Underboss and long-time friend couldn't look Michel in the eye. If he had, he would have seen disappointment and hurt on his most loyal soldier's face.

Normally in this business, if someone were betrayed, they weren't alive long enough to feel the heartache of betrayal. For Michel, this wasn't the case. He felt like he had just lost one person who always had his back and the only one he could trust in this cut-throat line of work.

"So, what now?" asked Michel.

"Lasciaci, leave us," said Thomas to the two men. Before they made any move whatsoever, both looked to Michel first for his consent. Michel nodded, giving his consent. The men rose from the table, walked to the main door to the office, unlocked it, and stepped out, closing the door behind them. Michel walked over to the bar and brought Thomas the cup of coffee that had been prepared for him earlier. He then sat down next to Thomas, facing both doors to the room. He laid both of his pistols and the one he had stuffed in his waistband on the table, placing them directly in front of him.

"What do you want me to do, Mikey?" asked Thomas as he took a sip of the coffee. "Christ, it's ice cold!" He sat the cup back on the saucer and pushed it away.

"What I want you to do, is kill the deal you made with Sal concerning my airport business. Then I want you to keep that sick fuck off my ass."

"I can't do that, Mikey. There are rules we must follow. You broke those rules, and now you must pay." Michel slammed his open hand on the table and shouted,

"Pay! Do you know how much money he will be taking out of my pocket for three years?!" Thomas sat silently. He didn't know off the top of his head what the dollar figure would be. Apparently, it was a large sum for Michel to be this upset.

"Two hundred and fifty thousand dollars!" shouted Michel. Thomas couldn't help but raise a brow after hearing the amount.

"So, what are you going to do, Mikey?" There were a hundred different thoughts running through Michel's brain, and he started to verbalize some of them,

"I'll just quit this thing; I'm getting tired of this shit anyway," Thomas responded immediately,

"You know you can't just walk away, Mikey." He knew Thomas was right."

"I'll just disappear then, move somewhere out west." Thomas didn't respond verbally to his comment. He only shook his head. Michel began to get frustrated and angry.

"Then I'll kill the piece of shit!" shouted Michel. Thomas slid his chair away from the table and picked up his cold cup of coffee, then walked over to the bar, where he made himself a fresh cup.

"That's the second time you suggested killing Sal. Let me remind you, Mikey if you kill Sal without it being sanctioned, the family will come after you, and I won't be able to stop them. In fact, they will probably want me to handle it, and I don't want to have to do that." Thomas returned to the table with his fresh cup of coffee and sat down. Michel stared into Thomas' eyes, looking for an answer until it came to him. The idea was not something he could share with Thomas; in fact, he would not be able to share it with anyone. Michel was never one who did well hiding his emotions. He no longer had the look of rage in his eyes, and Thomas could see his best soldier calming down. Most people would be relieved at the sight, but not Thomas. He knew when something was brewing in the brain of his friend, and it scared him to death. Michel took a deep breath and smiled.

"You're right, Thomas. There are rules," he stated as he stood from the table. "Don't worry, Thomas, everything is going to be alright." He patted his long-time friend on the shoulder, picked up his pistols from the table, holstering two of them, and tucked the third in the waistband of his pants. As he started to make his way to the door, Thomas asked,

"I will tell Sal everything is settled then?" Before he opened the door, Michel looked back at Thomas and said,

"Sure, you can tell him that."

Michel exited the office and walked through the store, and headed for the front door passing the two Italian men whose eyes were fixed on his every move. When he reached the front of the store, he was met by the owner, who was setting up a produce display outside on the sidewalk.

"Good morning, Georgy."

"Michel, good morning. How are you?" Michel stopped and replied,

"I'm still above ground." Georgy thought the response was peculiar and said nothing more. He just nodded and grinned uncertainly.

"Catch you later, Georgy," said Michel. He began to walk toward his car that he had left parked down the street. With every step, his plan on how to deal with Sal became clearer. He muttered to himself when he reached his car and opened the door, looking back at the store, "fuck 'em."

***

The school day ended. The mad scramble of the children headed to their school buses, bicycles, and cars lined up to pick up the pampered few, was on. The chaos was not part of John's, Dante's, or Angie's after-school routine. They liked being able to walk leisurely home. Angie would walk with a few of her friends while John and Dante would stay a watchful distance behind her.

"Guess what, D? I told Rebecca I would go to the retreat with her this Sunday," commented John.

"Have you worked out a plan to sneak away while you are there?" the mischievous Dante asked.

"No! We are going there to listen to the speakers."

"Really?" the surprised and disappointed Dante asked.

"Yes really. There's nothing wrong with that D. I have all the time in the world to make out with girls. I'm really interested in learning about Bible instruction." Dante could see how serious and passionate John was. Nevertheless, it still didn't keep Dante from making light of his friend's desire.

"Forgive me, Father Santoro, for I have sinned by suggesting you partake in a carnal activity with the extremely sexy Rebecca Stone." Dante maintained a sincere expression on his face to make his mock repentance get a laugh from John. It only managed to get a slight grin from his friend.

"Knock it off, D," responded John. He quickly moved the focus of attention to Dante. "How was history class with Anna? Did you pass any notes?"

"We sure did. I'm going to her house tomorrow after school, so don't wait for me to walk home. In fact, I won't be by your house in the morning. I'll be riding my bike tomorrow."

"Why are you going to her house?"

"To study." John looked at Dante to see if he was joking. It was clear to see Dante had mischief written all over his face.

"Study my ass. What are you doing, D?"

"Alright, I'll tell you. Anna's parents are leaving town tomorrow right after she gets home from school, and she's not going with them."

"Why not?" asked John.

"Because they are going to Orlando. Her father has an early morning appointment there, so they are going to stay the night there. Anna will be home by herself. Pretty sweet, hey!"

"What are you going to tell your parents?" inquired John.

"I've already told them I was going to come to your house to help you with your history assignment. Pretty good, right?" asked Dante, seeking his friend's approval.

"Sounds pretty good," agreed John. "What's the history assignment about?" Dante laughed as he opened a folder he was carrying and pulled out a sheet of paper with writing on the front and back.

"What's that?" asked John. Dante handed it to him. John read the title at the top of the page aloud, "General Stonewall Jackson, the Man." John began to hand it back to Dante when he said,

"Keep it. I'll lose it. Remember, it's evidence," remarked Dante with a wink and a smile.

The boys and Angie reached John's house. John and his sister darted to the side door that entered the kitchen, and Dante continued down the sidewalk alone, headed to his house. Bonnie greeted her children with a kiss on the cheek.

"How was your day?" The response was as repetitive as the question,

"Fine," they replied as they made their way up the stairs and to their rooms. John placed his stack of books on the desk in his room. The paper Dante gave him remained on top. He picked it up and quickly looked at it. He turned the paper over to read how Dante ended the brief profile of the Confederate General. It was Jackson's last words from his death bed…

"Let us cross over the river and rest under the shade of the tree." John folded the paper and placed it inside the cover of his history book.

51

Chapter 6

The evening passed quickly after dinner. The children were asleep, Bonnie and Michel were also in their room preparing for bed themselves. Bonnie sat on the edge of the bed, brushing her straight, long raven hair, while Michel was shuffling and moving things around inside their closet. Bonnie could hear her husband mumbling to himself. That was the first indicator that Michel had difficulty finding whatever he sought. She patiently waited until he began to swear before asking what he was doing.

"Goddamn it! Where the hell is it!?" shouted Michel, loud enough for Bonnie to hear but not loud enough to wake up the kids.

"What are you looking for?" asked Bonnie as she chuckled, realizing how well she knew the man she loved.

"A small wooden box with a gold latch and hinges."

"Did you look in the corner on the shelf?" Michel moved to his right and began to take things off the shelf. "The other corner," directed Bonnie. Michel tossed what he had in his hands back to the right corner of the shelf and took items off the left side. He lifted the end of what seemed to be an overnight case that felt like it contained bricks. It was heavy.

"What in the hell is in this damn thing?" he grunted. Bonnie leaned in to see what he was referring to,

"My books are in there," said Bonnie.

"What books? You have books all over the house! Why are there books in the closet?" inquired Michel.

"I swap them out when I get tired of the ones that are on the shelves," she replied. Michel paused from what he was doing for a moment. He needed clarification on what Bonnie just told him.

"Let me get this straight; you have read every book in this house, correct?"

"Yes," confirmed Bonnie.

"You swap them out. Why?"

"So, guests don't always see the same old books." Michel shook his head and whispered, "Of course; what was I thinking?"

He returned to his search, and within a minute, he found what he was looking for.

"There you are!" he exclaimed. He pulled the small wooden box out from under the overnight case, then sat next to Bonnie on the edge of the bed. Bonnie stopped brushing her hair and watched her husband flip the latch upward and slowly open the box. Bonnie had forgotten all about it or didn't know the box contained a shiny nickel plated .22 caliber revolver.

"When did you get that?" she asked.

"I bought it for your 30th birthday, don't you remember?" Michel could see it in his wife's face; she really didn't remember.

"Why are you showing it to me now?" she asked.

Michel removed the pistol from the box and disengaged the cylinder, popping it out to the left side to see if it was still loaded. It was. He re-engaged the cylinder and handed the pistol to Bonnie.

"Do you remember how to use one of these?" he asked. Bonnie took the pistol from her husband and answered,

"I think so."

Once the weapon was in her hand, everything Michel taught her how to use a handgun came rushing back to her.

Michel taught Bonnie how to shoot many years ago. He assured her that she would never have to use a gun if he was around. However, if he was not there for her, she would need to know how to use it to protect herself and the children.

Bonnie ejected the cylinder to the side, saw it was loaded, and popped the cylinder back in place with a flick of her wrist. She then placed her index finger inside the trigger guard and spun the pistol around her finger until the grip faced her husband. Then she handed it back to him and asked, "Why are you showing this to me, Michel?"

"I'm not showing you; I'm giving it to you. I want you to start carrying it in your purse."

The color in Bonnie's cheeks vanished. She was suddenly pale as a ghost, and her eyes widened with fear.

"What's happening, Michel? Why do you want me to carry a gun?" Bonnie quickly stood up and walked to the dresser, where she gently set the weapon down. The terror she felt was quickly replaced with anger as she spun around to face Michel and to show him, she did not like what she had just been told.

"Why Michel? Why do you want me to carry a gun?" she asked, insisting on an answer.

"I don't want to get into all that right now, Bonnie. Will you, for just once, trust me and do what I ask you to do?"

It was clear to her now that her husband was worried. It didn't make sense to keep pressing him for a logical answer. Her anger was beginning to get the best of her. All she ever wanted was to have a normal life, watching her children grow up to be good people and one day have their own children.

"Just to let you know, Michel, I will not stand by, and watch Giovanni get into your business!"

Michel didn't see that comment coming. It surprised him since the children were not a part of the conversation. To calm Bonnie down, he quickly responded, "I totally agree. I don't want him involved in any form. Giovanni is too good of a kid to get into this; he deserves much better."

Michel could see he had said the right things. Bonnie was beginning to calm down.

A light tapping on their bedroom door suddenly paused their conversation. They looked at one another in hopes that the children hadn't been listening. Michel opened the door.

"Sorry to have interrupted, Pop, but I needed to ask you and Mom something," said Giovanni. Michel opened the door wider, welcoming his son inside.

"No problem, son, come in."

Giovanni walked in and stood just a few feet inside the room.

"Are you feeling alright, honey?" asked Bonnie.

"I feel fine, Mom; I just needed to ask you and Pop something." Both Bonnie and Michel held their breath, waiting for their son to ask them to explain what it was they were talking about.

"I wanted to ask you if I could go to a retreat for youths this Sunday at Lake Tarpon?"

"What kind of retreat is it, son?" asked Michel.

"They are going to have several speakers talking about a youth ministry program that is starting in the area this summer. I thought this was something I wanted to do and wanted to see what it was all about."

"How did you hear about this?" his father asked.

"Rebecca Stone told me about it."

"Who is Rebecca Stone?" asked Bonnie.

"She's a girl from school."

"Will she be going too?" Michel asked. Giovanni nodded. He and Bonnie kept from grinning not to embarrass their son. It was the first time their son had mentioned anything about spending time with the opposite sex.

"And how will you get there, son?" resumed Michel.

"We will be taking a bus from Clearwater Methodist Church over on Hammel Drive." Bonnie was surprised to hear that the Methodist Church was sponsoring the program. Their family had been devout Catholics for decades. However, the more she thought about it, the more she liked the thought of her son getting involved more deeply with the church, no matter what denomination it was.

"When did you say this was?" asked Bonnie.

"This Sunday. I'll need to be at the church at 8:00 a.m. Rebecca said we should be back by 7:00 p.m. She said her father could pick me up and bring me home since it would be on the way."

Bonnie looked at her husband and waited for his decision.

"It sounds fine to me, son. Have a good time," said Michel. An ear-to-ear smile emerged on Giovanni's face.

"Thanks, Mom; thanks, Pop!" exclaimed Giovanni. "I can't wait to tell Rebecca!"

He turned and bolted back to his room. Michel closed their bedroom door quietly and turned to face Bonnie.

"There you are honey; there's no need to worry about Giovanni following in my footsteps."

"Alright, Michel, I'll do it."

"Do what?" he asked.

"Don't worry; I'll be fine." She placed her hand on his arm, then leaned in and kissed him on the cheek. She spun around, retrieved the weapon from the top of the dresser, walked over to her purse on the chair next to the door, and placed the gun inside, making sure Michel could see her do it. Michel approached her and wrapped his arms around her, holding her close.

"Thank you," he whispered. "I love you."

Bonnie gave him a quick kiss on the mouth and said, "I love you too; let's get some sleep." The two discarded their robes and placed them at the foot of the bed, then climbed between the sheets. Michel reached over and turned out the bedside lamp.

Michel began to systematically relax himself by clearing his mind and resting every muscle in his body. If done properly, he could send himself into a deep sleep within minutes. Bonnie didn't have any sleep issues. She would typically fall asleep as soon as her head hit the pillow, and tonight wasn't any different.

Suddenly, the telephone began to ring. The disturbance sent Michel quickly reaching for the receiver and answering the call. But Bonnie remained fast asleep.

"Hello?" answered Michel, softly.

"Mikey! How the hell are you?"

At first, Michel thought it was Thomas since he was the only one Michel would allow referring to him as Mikey, but the voice wasn't right.

"Who is this?" Michel asked.

"It's your new boss, Sal! Who the fuck did you think it was?" It was obvious to Michel that Sal had been drinking. He had to do all he could do to keep from hanging up on him.

"What do you want, Sal?"

"Sounds like you want to get straight to the point. Don't you want to chat?" asked the annoying Sal.

"It's late, Sal; what is it?"

"Is it late? What time is it anyway?"

Michel could hear Sal shuffling what he assumed were glasses and a bottle of booze. Sal was looking for his watch. "Oh, here it is! Hell, it's only 5:30, Mikey!"

"It's 11:00 at night, dumbass; you're looking at your watch upside down." Sal took offense at being called a dumbass.

"Hey! Now you listen to me; you can't talk to me like that. Furthermore, you must do what I say; I'm a captain now." The ceremony to make Sal a captain had occurred earlier that evening, and Thomas was still waiting to inform Michel. He had heard enough and responded in kind, "Fuck you, Sal."

Michel's insubordination was pissing Sal off.

"Now wait just a goddamn minute, you son-of-a-bitch! You work for me now, and you will do what I say or else."

Michel realized talking to this guy when drunk was futile, so he decided not to fuel the fire and asked Sal why he called.

"Alright, Sal, what do you want," asked Michel calmly and respectfully. His approach worked.

"Now, that's better." Sal had calmed down. "I called because I want to see you at the store tomorrow around noon. We have a few things to discuss."

"Is that it?" Michel asked.

"Yeah, that's it," replied Sal.

"Alright, I'll be there, Sal. Just one more thing, if you call me Mikey again, I'll fucking cut your tongue out." Michel hung the phone up quietly so he wouldn't wake up Bonnie and then rolled over to face his wife. Bonnie lay there facing him with her eyes open and asked, "You're going to kill him, aren't you?" Michel softly caressed her cheek and said, "Go to sleep."

Chapter 7

It was 11:40 a.m., and Michel arrived twenty minutes early at the Bay Street Grocery store. Once again, he parked half a block down the street to survey who was going in and out of the store. His scheduled meeting with Sal could be less than pleasant, and he wanted to get the best head count of who was in the building when he entered. Nothing appeared out of the ordinary.

He was surprised to see Sal driving up to the store unaccompanied, which was very peculiar because Sal was now a captain. Most captains in the business always have someone with them for security purposes. Nevertheless, Michel suspected Sal had some of his soldiers planted inside. Knowing Sal, the way he did, they probably spent the night there.

It was now 11:55 a.m., time to make his way into the store. This time Michel decided to enter the store through the front door. He was carrying both .45s, a .38 strapped to his ankle and a six-inch switchblade knife. If Sal was going to take him out, it wouldn't be without a fight.

As Michel reached for the door handle of the store, the storefront glass reflected a black four-door vehicle stopping directly in front of the store. Both doors on the passenger side swung open. Two large men in dark suits emerged from the vehicle and headed straight for Michel. His instincts told him he was about to be killed.

He released his grip on the door handle, crossed both arms as he reached into his coat, and pulled out both .45 caliber weapons. He then spun around and dropped to one knee, pointing a gun at each of the two men. The men immediately stopped and held up their hands. To Michel's surprise, it was the same two non-English-speaking Italian men he met the other day at the store when he had the meeting with Thomas. He watched both very closely to ensure they would not try to make a move for their weapons.

A quick glance into the back seat of the vehicle revealed someone remained; it was Thomas.

"Wound a bit tight these days, Mikey?" shouted Thomas. Michel slowly stood and holstered both of his weapons.

"No thanks to you," he replied. He walked over to the car, leaned over, and peered inside.

"C'mon, get in, Mikey," invited Thomas.

"I can't; I have a meeting with Sal. He's inside waiting for me."

"No, you don't; I postponed it. Get in; I have something I want you to do." Michel was a bit irritated. He wanted nothing more than to get the meeting with Sal over with. He knew Sal wasn't going anywhere. He also knew the longer Sal had to wait for anything, the bigger a prick he would become. And that was something he didn't look forward to.

Michel got into the back seat with Thomas. One of the men who he had just kept at gunpoint closed the door behind him. The two men stood outside the vehicle while Thomas and Michel spoke.

"I have a situation, Mikey, that needs immediate attention. This is coming from the top, and Don Vincenzo Barzetti wanted me to put my best man on it."

"Sal is inside the store," retorted Michel.

"Don't be a smartass; this is fuckin' serious," scolded Thomas. "The Don wants you to take care of a potential problem. Florida State Senator, Charles Meeks, is scheduled to appear in front of the grand jury in two days with his attorney." Thomas handed him a black and white photo of the Senator.

"What for?" Michel asked.

"A witness has come forward, claiming she witnessed the Senator at the home of Don Barzetti gambling, drinking, and consorting with hookers on several occasions.

We believe his attorney, Donald Patterson, has convinced the Senator to disclose everything he has seen and heard at Barzetti's home, for a mild reprimand and keeping his seat in the State Senate."

Thomas handed Michel a black and white photo of Donald Patterson. The State doesn't want Meeks, they want the Don, and we can't let that happen."

"Who's the witness?" asked Michel.

"It's a high-class hooker they hired for the Senator. She goes by the name of Kate." Thomas handed Michel a black and white photo of the woman. Michel committed all the photos to memory and handed them back to Thomas. Thomas then handed him a piece of paper with writing on it.

"This is the attorney's address. We've learned both he and Meeks will be there tonight." Michel memorized the address, then tore it up and tossed it out of the window of the car.

"Anything else I should know?" Michel asked.

"Only that you have until the day after tomorrow to clean this up."

"Understood," replied Michel. "I'll get right on it." He opened the door and stepped out. He saw the two men and realized this was the second time he had the drop on them. Before closing the door, Michel looked inside the car at Thomas and said, "These fuckin' guys are going to get you killed."

Michel backed away from the car and looked at the two men standing close by. He grinned and said, "You two better go back to Italy before you get yourselves killed."

Both men stood motionless, not understanding a single word he said. Michel could see his message did not get through to them,

"Torna a casa in Italia." The two understood Michel this time and replied by each of them giving him the middle finger. The gesture struck Michel in a humous way.

He turned away and started to laugh as he walked back to his car.

Standing inside the store, watching what had just taken place, was Sal Carducci. He saw Thomas talking to Michel. By reading the expressions on each of the men's faces, he knew it wasn't a social visit. The one thing that bothered him was that Thomas hadn't spoken to him about appointing Michel to do a job, and it irritated him because he was now Michel's captain. Sal watched Thomas' car pull away. He dropped his cigarette on the floor and then ground it into the hardwood directly in front of Georgy, the store owner.

"What an asshole," thought Georgy. Sal felt disrespected by Thomas and stormed out the front door of the store with his bodyguard chasing after him.

***

Bonnie stood at the kitchen sink, rinsing the vegetables she was planning to use in the salad for that night's dinner, when she heard a car door close. She turned off the water and dried her hands with her apron. Believing that the car door she heard came from her driveway, she walked over to the side door in the kitchen. Before she could peer out, the screen door was snatched open and in stepped Michel.

"I thought I told you to start keeping this door closed and locked when you are home alone," stated Michel.

"You never told me such a thing," replied Bonnie. Michel tried to remember when exactly he told her but could not recall making the statement. He approached Bonnie and kissed her on the cheek.

"Maybe I didn't, but I am now."

"What are you doing home?" she asked as Michel hurriedly descended the basement stairs.

"I need to get some tools!" he shouted from the bottom of the stairs. Bonnie knew it differed from the tools you would find at a hardware store. Michel was referring to the tools he mostly used in his profession… guns.

Michel kept the tools of his trade securely locked in a heavy oak cabinet, tucked away inconspicuously in an area of the basement that the previous owners once used as a wine cellar. He told his children his private things were in the cabinet, and not to go there. With it practically hidden from sight, Angie and John had forgotten the cabinet even existed.

Once the cabinet was unlocked and opened, Michel removed a few items. A sawed-off 12-gauge shotgun and box of shells, a wallet size case of lock picks, and four additional magazines of .45 caliber bullets for the two handguns he was already carrying. He placed the shotgun in a case. The ammunition and lock pick set were placed in a small leather duffle bag.

Michel closed and locked the cabinet door and scurried back up the stairway to the kitchen, where Bonnie had finished rinsing the vegetables. He didn't set any of the items he had just brought up from the basement down. He walked over to Bonnie, kissed her on the cheek again, and said, "I may be home late tonight, don't wait up."

"Why don't you take a few minutes and have some lunch with me?" suggested Bonnie as she seductively pressed herself against Michel. He knew exactly what kind of lunch his wife was referring to, and it didn't involve bread. Bonnie could see and feel through her husband's light-weight pants; the lower portion of his body was keen on the idea. Michel kept both of his hands on the shotgun and the bag. He knew if he were to set them down, he would not be leaving for at least an hour. He kissed Bonnie on the lips and said, "Hold that thought; I'll be home as soon as I can."

He headed for the door. Bonnie could see he would need assistance in opening it and scampered ahead of him to do so.

"You might want to hold the bag in front of you until you get in the car," she suggested. Michel glanced down and saw the effect her attempted seduction had on him.

"I guess so," he said and moved the bag to cover the erection protruding from his pants.

"I'll see you tonight," he said while Bonnie held the door open for him. She watched him place the items he retrieved from the basement in the trunk of the car. He looked back at her as he walked to the driver's side door and held his arm out to his side, and shouted, "All better!"

She understood what he meant by the comment and looked down at the front of his pants. The erection had subsided. She knew her husband was now in a "business" frame of mind.

***

Michel sat in his car watching the 5:00 p.m. working crowd file out of the building where the attorney for Senator Meeks would be holding the meeting. The attorney's office was on the fifth-floor corner office, facing the street. Michel wanted to wait until sunset before paying a visit and give the streets a chance to clear out.

How he was going to get into the building after hours was still uncertain. Watching any activity in and around the building would be key to his gaining access. He didn't worry about it; an answer to any dilemma always presented itself.

Ninety minutes had passed. The sun had nearly set, and the tall shadows from the buildings made it darker than it really was. A few random office lights facing the street indicated there were still a few people in the building, but the one that concerned Michel was the one located on the right corner of the fifth floor.

He would occasionally see a dark silhouette pass in front of the window. It wasn't clear if both the Senator and his attorney were in the office; it was a call Michel had to make. He waited a few minutes more, then decided now was the time.

He exited his car and crossed the street. As he reached the sidewalk, a car pulled up in front of the building. The driver climbed out of the car and surveyed the street.

Michel recognized the driver from Thomas' photo; it was Senator Meeks. Michel quickened his pace to be at the entrance of the building before the Senator. When Michel was just a few steps away, he began to stick his hands into the front pockets of his pants, acting as if he was searching for something. The Senator approached and asked, "Lose something, friend?"

Michel gave the Senator a convincing look of desperation, "I can't find my keys; I may have left them on my desk." The Senator smiled and pressed the button for the Patterson Law Office.

"We can fix that," assured the Senator. The door buzzed, accompanied by a loud click from the door unlocking. The Senator opened the door and cordially let Michel enter first.

"You're a lifesaver; I'm already running late," thanked Michel.

"No problem at all. Have a good evening!" bid the Senator as he walked to the elevator. Michel saw a flight of stairs leading to the basement and took them. He stopped halfway down and waited to hear the elevator doors close. Michel ascended the stairs and walked over to the elevator, watching the floor indicator stop on the fifth floor. He walked over to the ascending staircase and began a slow, deliberate climb as he attached a silencer to the end of one of his handguns.

Once Michel reached the fifth floor, he stopped for a moment to catch his breath.

"I need to exercise," he muttered to himself. He looked around to make sure there was no one else roaming the hallway.

After locating the front of the building, he quietly walked through the hallway, reading the nameplates on the doors. It wasn't long before he reached the law office of Donald Patterson.

He brought his ear close to the door and heard two men speaking. It was then that he was totally satisfied and ready to carry out this portion of his assignment. Michel reached down and turned the doorknob slightly and quietly. The door was unlocked.

He opened it slowly with his weapon held out in front of him. The location of the attorney's desk was deep in the room and next to a window where Patterson stood looking out. The Senator sat in a leather-bound chair across from the desk.

Michel was able to walk in slowly and as quiet as a mouse. The only light in the room came from a lamp on the attorney's desk, leaving the rest of it in shadowed darkness. It wasn't until he was about ten feet away from the two men that the Senator noticed him. The Senator smiled, recognizing Michel from moments earlier, until he noticed his gun; his smile quickly vanished.

"What's the meaning of this?" questioned the Senator. His attorney turned away from the window and was now facing the Senator. He looked at the Senator, then followed his gaze toward Michel.

"Step away from the window," ordered Michel. The attorney reacted with a quick move toward his desk to retrieve a pistol he kept in the top left drawer of his desk. He managed to open the drawer but was immediately stopped when Michel placed a bullet precisely in the side of his head, just above his right ear. The bullet's impact threw the attorney against his chair, then dropped onto the floor.

The Senator was frozen with fear and remained sitting in his chair. Michel quickly approached the Senator and shot him once in the chest, followed by one shot to the forehead.

To ensure the attorney was dead, Michel walked around the desk and shot him once again in the head. He stood there for just a moment to admire his work. But now it was time to leave. Michel walked out of the office door and closed it behind him. He took out a handkerchief and wiped off the exterior doorknob, then made his way to the stairwell and exited the building the way he came in through the front door.

***

Michel drove to the 'red light' district of Tampa and parked his car a few blocks away. He thought it best to be on foot to mingle with what seemed to be an endless amount of people patronizing the sex trade business. He casually walked on the sidewalk, looking at every prostitute standing on the corners and curbs in hopes of spotting 'Kate.' He didn't limit his search to just prostitutes.

He would also stop and look at the pictures of featured strippers posted on club marques. He made it a point not to take much time looking at the photos. He did not want any of the street promoters of the clubs getting a good look at his face. The mile-and-a-half-long 'red light' district was becoming a grind for Michel.

Prostitutes constantly approached him and rubbed against him to encourage him to buy their favors. The heavily perfumed street walkers had transferred their seductive scents to Michel's sport coat. He knew he would have some explaining to do as soon as Bonnie caught a whiff of it.

"That's just fuckin' great," he thought to himself.

After working his way back toward his car from the other side of the street, Michel was nearing the end of his search when a car pulled up to the curb several feet before him. The front passenger door swung open, and to his delight, stepped out Kate. Michel stopped to observe what she would do and where she was going. She first walked up to a darkened pane of glass in the front of a bar to apply some lipstick. She smacked her lips a couple of times, then fluffed her hair. Once her appearance satisfied her, she walked over to the bar's front door, pulled the door open, and entered. Michel gave her about a minute to be seated, then walked in behind her.

He wasn't impressed with the establishment when he stepped in the door. Jazz music blared from the jukebox. He hated jazz. He felt it had no structure and was nothing but rambling noise. The bar was dimly lit, and smoke filled the air. The occupants appeared to be mostly men, with a few female 'bar flies' mixed in, along with a couple of prostitutes and their Johns. As Michel made his way halfway down the bar, he spotted Kate sitting alone at the far end. It appeared there was an empty stool next to her as well.

Just as he reached the end of the bar and turned the corner, another male patron approached Kate and immediately sat next to her. The man sat with his back to Michel and was focused entirely on her. Michel could see by the expression on Kate's face that this guy was cringeworthy. Kate caught a glimpse of Michel over the man's shoulder. Their eyes quickly met, and Michel could see her roll her eyes, indicating she would rather have his company than the one currently sitting next to her. Michel read the distress call ideally, approached the man, and slapped him on the back.

"Alright, pal, I'll take it from here." The man swiveled his chair around to see who had just interrupted him.

"What did you say, buddy?" asked the man as he straightened up in his stool, trying to project his strength and defiance.

"I said, this is my wife, so get the fuck out of here." The man's quick assessment of Michel's physique and the possibility that his statement was true changed his opinion of the situation. Without any further delay, the man slid off the bar stool and left.

"Very clever," said Kate.

"May I sit?" asked Michel.

"Absolutely," replied Kate. The bartender made his way to the end of the bar to see if Michel needed anything.

"Welcome to Bailey's," greeted the bartender as he gave the portion of the bar top directly in front of Michel a quick wipe with his bar towel.

"What will it be?" Michel looked at Kate and asked,

"What are you drinking?"

"Bourbon," she replied as she tossed down the remainder of her drink. Michel held up two fingers, indicating he would have one as well.

"You from around here?" she asked.

"Nope, just stopped on my way to Miami."

"A little off the beaten path for a drink, aren't you?"

The bartender returned with two empty glasses and a bottle of bourbon. Michel placed a twenty-dollar bill on the bar and said, "Keep it."

The bartender snatched it up and replied, "Thank you, sir; let me know if you need anything else."

Kate noticed the generous tip and suspected that there was probably more of the same where that came from. She scooted her stool closer to Michel. He placed her glass in front of her and opened the new bottle of bourbon. As he poured their drinks, Kate asked, "What did you say your name was?"

"I didn't," responded Michel. He lifted his glass to toast. Kate responded by doing the same. They touched their glasses together and then tossed their drinks down in one motion.

"Oh, that's good," stated Kate. Michel poured her another but did not refill his glass, which didn't go unnoticed.

"You done already?" asked Kate.

"Just want to pace myself; this may turn out to be a long evening," he replied. Kate giggled and assumed her new acquaintance was taking a liking to her. Besides, it looks like he may have a lot of money on him, and she would like nothing more than to get her hands on some, if not all, of it.

"You spend much time in this place?" asked Michel. Kate shrugged her shoulders and looked around,

"Yeah, I guess so." She pointed at the bartender, "Carl keeps an eye on me and makes sure no one gives me any grief, not to mention the music they have on the juke is the best!" she exclaimed as she bobbed her head to the rhythm of another jazz song.

"You actually like this shit?" asked Michel.

"Yeah! Don't you?"

Michel shook his head. He poured her another drink and one for himself.

Kate began to sense that her new friend was losing interest and was ready to get back on the road. She reached into her purse and pulled out an empty pack of cigarettes.

"Carl!" she shouted over the music, who was at the other end of the bar. Carl heard the call and looked at her. Kate held up the empty pack of cigarettes in front of her. Carl nodded, acknowledging her request.

Little did Michel know that the cigarette request signaled to Carl that he was now a target for Kate and her accomplices to roll and steal his money. Carl reached under the bar where the cigarettes were kept and retrieved a pack. As he did, he also pressed a button that alerted a former heavyweight wrestler, Bruno Chase, who stayed in the bar's back office until he was needed to roll those passing through with money, or to bounce unruly patrons out of the bar.

Carl delivered the cigarettes to Kate. Michel tossed a five-dollar bill in front of Carl and nodded, signifying for Carl to keep the change again.

"I gotta pee," said Kate. "Don't go anywhere, okay?" Michel nodded. Kate put the cigarettes inside her purse and held onto it as she slid off her stool and proceeded to the lady's restroom, located behind where Michel sat.

On her way to the restroom, she stopped at the office door and lightly knocked. Bruno Chase opened the door and stepped out. Kate pointed Michel out to him and then continued to the restroom. Bruno stepped back inside the office and closed the door.

Kate returned to the bar and stood next to Michel. He poured her another drink and slid it toward her. He could see that she had reapplied her lipstick and freshened her perfume. Michel knew the invitation to leave the bar was about to be presented shortly. Kate took just a sip of the drink he had just poured for her then asked,

"When do you have to be in Miami?"

"Not until tomorrow afternoon."

"Why don't we take the rest of that bottle back to my place and finish it there?" Michel glanced at the bottle and grinned, "I was about to suggest the very same thing."

"We'll go out the back and cut through the alley; It's shorter that way."

"Lead the way," he replied. He corked the bottle of bourbon and picked it up from the bar, holding it by the neck of the bottle with his left hand. Kate led the way, past the office and restrooms, then straight out the back door.

Bruno exited from the office as soon as he heard the back door slam shut. Kate and Michel walked down the dark alley side-by-side, until Kate stopped and pulled Michel toward her, as she backed up against the brick wall from an adjacent building. The last thing Michel wanted her to do was kiss him and was relieved when she reached down and began to rub his penis through his pants. Michel reached inside the hip pocket of his coat and retrieved the switchblade he was carrying. With a press of a button, the six-inch blade darted out. With the precision of a surgeon, Michel thrust the blade into Kate's throat, severing her vocal cords. He retracted the knife and then slashed her throat, cutting in deeply. Kate slowly slid down to the ground. Suddenly, Michel's right arm was grabbed from behind. It was Bruno. He spun Michel around, causing him to lose hold of the knife. The momentum of being spun around aided Michel in smashing the bottle of bourbon he had been carrying in his left hand against Bruno's face, severely cutting his cheek. The burley Bruno grabbed Michel by the lapels, lifting him up and slamming him against the brick wall. The neck of the bottle remained in Michel's hand. He had no choice but to thrust the sharply jagged edge that remained into the side of Bruno's neck, opening his jugular vein. Blood began to pour out with tremendous force from Bruno's neck. He maintained his grip on Michel for just a few more seconds before releasing him. Bruno grabbed the side of his neck and staggered away. After taking just a few steps, he dropped to his knees and then fell to the concrete face first.

Michel quickly located his knife. He pulled a handkerchief from his back pocket and began to wipe the spattered blood from his face. He gave one last look at his victims to confirm they were dead. He then continued down the alley, making sure he was not being followed. The alley ended; he was now back on the street. Fortunately, the street it emptied onto was practically deserted. All except for a rag-tagged old man who was sitting on the sidewalk against a building. Michel was about to just walk past him when he saw the old man hoist a bottle of alcohol to his lips. Michel approached him and said, "Hey, pops, I'll give you fifty dollars for the rest of that bottle. Michel held the fifty-dollar bill in front of the man so that he could see it clearly. Without hesitation or speaking, the old man gave him the bottle and took the money.

"Thanks," said Michel.

The walk back to his car gave Michel a chance to clean more blood off his face and hands with the help of the alcohol and the handkerchief. He smelled like he had been bathed in alcohol and heavily perfumed hookers. The last thing he needed was to be pulled over by the police on his drive home. But it didn't matter; he had already decided if he was, he would have to kill them too.

Chapter 8

At 2:00 a.m., Bonnie found it difficult to sleep. She feared for her husband's life that evening for some unexplainable reason. She waited for him to return home by sitting on the living room sofa beside a table lamp, browsing home décor magazines. The children had been in bed for hours sound to sleep, so she thought.

John had heard his mother go downstairs. Her not sleeping that time of night concerned him. She never stayed up late to wait for his father, but tonight she did. His mother's actions intrigued him enough to find out what was going on, so he lay in his bed until he heard his father's car pull into the driveway. Thirty minutes had passed, and John began to struggle to stay awake. Just as his eyelids began to close to end his well-intentioned attempt to stay awake, the sound of a car door closing produced a sudden adrenaline rush. His eyes were wide open as he climbed out of bed and crept toward his partially opened bedroom door to get a glimpse of his father and ease his mind. He heard the kitchen door open and close and his mother hurrying to greet him.

John's blood ran cold when he heard his mother call out his father's name in horror,

"Michel! What happened?" Bonnie was not prepared to see her husband standing in her kitchen at 2:35 in the morning with a heavily bloodstained shirt and coat. Her first reaction was to run toward him and hold him. Michel halted her approach, keeping her from getting any blood on herself.

"I'm fine honey, I'm fine."

"My god Michel, what happened, and why do you smell like a cheap drunken whore?"

"Not now, honey, not now," he replied. John began to worry just as much as his mother. He wanted to see his father for himself before he would even think about sleeping that night. Opening his bedroom door further and sticking his head out slightly gave John the best opportunity to see and hear what was happening.

"Why not now?" questioned Bonnie.

"Let's not talk about it right now, alright?" requested Michel of his concerned wife. "This is not my blood." Bonnie's heart rate began to return to normal from the comforting news.

"Let's get you out of those things. I'll run you a bath,"

"That sounds wonderful," John heard his father say. He was not expecting his father to suddenly appear at the bottom of the stairs looking up toward his room. John had a clear, unobstructed view of his father's bloodied clothes. He would have given anything to not have seen what he did. His father also regretted his son's misfortune of seeing him like that.

Michel's eyes locked onto his sons. It didn't matter that the stairway was dimly lit; Michel saw the alarm and confusion on his son's face. John was speechless as Michel began to ascend the stairs, all the while keeping his eyes fixated on John; he began to think of how he would explain it all to him. As he neared the top of the stairs, Michel watched John slowly close his bedroom door. That didn't bother Michel; he understood how his son reacted to what he had witnessed. He didn't understand when he heard his son lock his door when he walked by.

***

Bonnie awoke after getting about four and a half hours of sleep. It was Saturday. Her daughter Angie always enjoyed helping her mother cook breakfast for everyone, provided they didn't sleep until noon. As she walked past John's bedroom, his door was open. She was surprised to see he was already up. She looked at the end of the hallway and saw that Angie's door was also open.

As Bonnie entered the kitchen, she wasn't surprised to find Angie pouring her mother a freshly brewed coffee.

"Good morning, sweetheart," she said as she kissed her daughter's cheek.

"Good morning," replied Angie as she handed her mother a piping hot cup of morning brew.

"Have you seen Giovanni this morning?" asked Bonnie.

"Just for a second. He was heading out when I came down," described Angie.

"Did he say where he was going?"

"He said he was going to Dante's house, then over to Rebecca's later on." At first, Bonnie didn't recognize the name Rebecca. She looked at Angie and asked,

"Rebecca?"

"Yes, Mom, Rebecca. The one who's taking him to that religious retreat tomorrow."

"Oh, yes, of course, Rebecca," recalled Bonnie.

John rode up to Dante's house on his bike. He stopped on the front lawn and laid the bike on its side as he ran up to the front door. He knocked on the door, then peered inside through the small window of the door. He saw no one coming to answer the door. He knocked again, using a bit more force than the first time. He peered through the small window again to see if his second attempt stirred anyone inside. His gaze was met by a hand with an extended middle finger. John couldn't help but laugh; he knew Dante was at the door. He heard the deadbolt unlock and the small door chain being disconnected. The door swung open to reveal Dante in his underwear and nothing else.

"What the fuck are you doing at my door this early on a Saturday morning," asked Dante as he rubbed his eyes and face to help stimulate blood flow.

"Let's go to your room," recommended John as he walked briskly past his friend heading straight to Dante's bedroom. Dante did not copy his friend's pace and lazily shuffled his feet back to his room.

"Close the door," ordered John once his friend entered the room.

"What's going on?" asked Dante as he quietly closed the bedroom door behind him, grabbed a pair of jeans draped over the back of a desk chair, and quickly slipped them on.

"My dad came home last night covered in blood."

"Is he okay?" asked Dante.

"That's just it; he's fine," explained John.

"Did you ask him what happened?"

"No. But I heard him tell my mom the blood wasn't his." Dante's eyes widened.

"Well, whose blood would it be?" John sat down on the end of his friend's bed as he shook his head, and replied,

"I don't know." Dante began to think of other possibilities of why his friend's father would have come home covered in blood.

"Maybe he was in an accident, or maybe he got in a fight," suggested Dante.

"I checked the car this morning; it looked fine. A fight? Maybe, but if it was a fight and it wasn't his blood, he must have killed the guy he was fighting."

An eerie silence fell between the two friends. John continued to think of other possibilities, but Dante struggled to keep his thoughts to himself, and his friend could see the conflict in his eyes.

"Did you think of something?" John asked. Dante shook his head and searched for a shirt to put on.

"What is it?" Again, Dante shook his head and continued his search for a shirt. "C'mon, D, what do you think?" Dante ended his search for a shirt by simply opening his dresser drawer and pulling out a clean white tee shirt. He sat on the bed next to his friend and said,

"Do you remember Billy Wyman? He was a senior last year." John nodded slightly as he tried to put a face to the name.

"I think so. Wasn't he always in trouble and wore a black leather jacket?" asked John.

"Yes, that's him," acknowledged Dante. "I was in the bathroom one-time last year when he and a couple of his friends came in to smoke a cigarette. They were talking about something they were going to steal and who they were going to sell it to.

"What does that have to do with my dad?"

"The person they were going to sell it to was your dad." John didn't believe what he had just been told.

"What were they going to steal?" asked John.

"A supply truck full of guns from the armory." John wasn't one to regularly use vulgar language. However, this time, he couldn't hold back,

"Get the fuck out of here!" he exclaimed.

"That's not the funny part," continued Dante, "They were going to deliver it to my father." John sat speechless, not believing what he was being told.

"You mean to tell me these guys were talking about all of this in front of you? Bullshit!"

"No, they didn't talk about all of this in front of me. I was in a stall taking a shit. They didn't know I was there."

"Why didn't you tell me this last year when it happened?" John asked.

"I wanted to do a little investigating of my own before I said anything to you."

"Apparently, you haven't found any proof, or else you would have told me something by now," assumed John. Dante placed his hand on John's shoulder and replied,

"I wish that were true; I've found plenty of evidence that would put both yours and my father in jail for a long time." John stood up from the bed quickly. His face began to turn red from the rise in his blood pressure.

"Fuck you, D, you're lying!" Dante remained calm despite his friend's growing anger. He needed to make his friend understand that their fathers were not the men they thought they were.

"John, our fathers are in the Mafia." The information rendered by his lifelong friend was difficult to comprehend. John was speechless. Memories of the fun and loving moments John had shared with his father raced through his mind. The images of his father being a gangster began to overshadow the fond memories he had.

"It can't be true! How can you be so sure?" shouted John.

"I did a little snooping last summer when my parents were visiting my aunt in St. Louis. I found a secret compartment in the floor of their bedroom closet. Do you want to know what was in it?" John hesitantly nodded. "Guns, ammunition, money…"

"That doesn't mean anything, D; many people hide that kind of thing in their houses."

"Perhaps, but I bet they don't keep payment schedules."

"What's that?" asked John, who began to listen a little more intently to what his friend was telling him.

"It was a list of businesses and payment amounts and what day of the month they needed to pay." John was slowly digesting every word but still had doubts about his father's involvement.

"That isn't proof that my father is involved in any of that," declared John.

"You didn't let me finish," said Dante. "Your father's name was next to half of the businesses. I'm assuming he was the one that collected their payments." John began to feel sick to his stomach and quickly left Dante's bedroom and went outside onto the front lawn. He rested his hands on his knees, preparing himself to vomit. Dante stood outside by the front door to make sure his friend would be alright and was shortly joined by his mother, who saw John running out the front door.

"Dante, is John alright?"

"He'll be okay, Mom; he said he wasn't feeling too good this morning." To John's relief, he didn't get sick. He stood up straight and took a few deep breaths.

"Are you alright, honey?" called out Dante's mother. John rested his hands on his hips and walked to Dante and his mother.

"I'm fine, Mrs. Carducci; it might have been something I ate last night."

"Well, you probably need to go home and rest; you'll probably feel better tomorrow."

"You're probably right, Mrs. Carducci; I'll do just that."

"Let me get back inside; I have something on the stove. Say hi to your mom for me!"

"Yes, ma'am, I will," assured John. Dante made sure his mom was well on her way back to the kitchen before he spoke.

"You going to be alright?" asked Dante. John nodded. "Listen, you can't say anything about what I told you, especially to your father." John was confused and didn't understand his friends' pleas.

"Why not? He is my father. I have a right to know what he does for a living."

"Sure, you do if your dad was a car salesman," quipped Dante. "But he's not; he's in the Mafia, dumbass. People get killed for knowing too much when it comes to organized crime. No matter who they're related to."

John knew Dante was right. His friend was obsessed with the law and crime. He read about it as much as the American civil war. He also had firsthand information on a mafioso who he called father. Now that John's trust in his father had been shattered, he had no one else but God and his friend. His anger and physically sick feelings were replaced by hurt and sorrow. He had all he could do to keep from crying in front of Dante. He turned his head away from Dante to keep him from seeing his eyes well up with tears.

"You're right," he said. "I won't say anything." Dante could see a tear stream down his friend's cheek. He put his hand on John's shoulder as John tried his best to calmly wipe the tears away. John gathered himself enough to bid his friend goodbye.

"Let me get going; I'm headed over to Rebecca's house. We're going to the youth retreat tomorrow."

"That's right," replied Dante. "Behave yourself now, don't do anything I wouldn't do." John forced a smile on his face and said,

"I won't. I plan on praying. I'll see you later." John stood his bike up, hopped onto it, and sped down the driveway onto the street, headed for Rebecca's house.

***

away, John pulled into the driveway of his friend Rebecca Stone. She was sitting on the front steps of her house talking to her friend Cindy when she saw John ride up. She smiled and waved at John as he approached. Cindy stood up and said,

"I'll talk to you later, hi John!" she shouted. John smiled and waved. Rebecca briskly left the steps and greeted John as he got off his bike. She reached for his hand. John grabbed it firmly and asked,

"Can I trust you?" Rebecca wasn't prepared for such a direct question. She smiled and let out a slight chuckle.

"What do you mean, John?" she asked.

"Can I trust you? It's a simple question," snapped John. Rebecca could see that he was not playing or teasing. He was serious. Her smile disappeared quickly, then she replied,

"Of course, you can, John." He stared deeply into her eyes and saw what he was hoping for…the truth.

Without hesitation, John wrapped his arms around Rebecca and gave her a heartfelt embrace.

"John, is everything alright?" He let her go but held onto her upper arms as he once again looked deep into her eyes.

"Yes, everything is alright now." He smiled, prompting her to smile as well. "I have to go. I'll be here early tomorrow, okay?"

"Okay, I can't wait," remarked Rebecca. John climbed back on his bike, giving Rebecca one last smile before riding off. He decided to take a longer route home to collect his thoughts about what he witnessed last night. He was uncertain what he would do if his father decided to talk to him about it. If he had a choice, it would be not to go home at all.

Chapter 9

The tension around the Santoro dinner table that evening could be felt by everyone except Angie. Everything was right with the world in her eyes. Her parents carried on delightful conversations with her throughout the course of the meal. When they directed any questions or comments to John, his responses were short and direct. He declined to carry any conversation any farther than was required. This only added to the level of tension in the room but also validated the need for Michel to have a serious conversation with his son.

The meal ended as it normally did. Bonnie and Angie cleared the table, with Michel and John assisting by bringing their own plates to the kitchen to be washed. Michel and John found themselves alone for just a moment in the kitchen while Bonnie and Angie gathered more items from the table.

"I'd like to talk to you, son, about last night," said Michel. John kept his head down, still unable to look his father in the eye, and nodded.

"Let's go in the backyard where we can be alone." They set their plates in the sink and walked out of the kitchen door that led to the backyard.

"Let's sit awhile," Michel said, pointing to the bench swing that hung under an enormous live oak tree. It was one of the more tranquil areas used by everyone in the family most often.

The two sat quietly for a few minutes, enjoying the coolness of the shade and a refreshing northeast breeze. Michel spoke first,

"I can imagine how you felt seeing my clothes covered with blood last night; I'm sorry for frightening you. There is a simple explanation, and I wanted to ensure you understood." John couldn't hold back any longer; he looked his father in the eyes and asked,

"Are you in the Mafia?" The question was unexpected and extremely direct. Michel heard the question clearly, but couldn't help but reply by asking,

"What?" Michel could see the steely look in his son's eyes. It reminded him of himself and how he dealt with uncooperative people in his business.

"You heard me," replied John.

Michel looked away to take in more of his serene surroundings, hoping it would calm his nerves. He knew that he would have to reveal his occupation to his children one day, but he didn't imagine it would be this soon. He took a deep breath before he spoke.

"When your uncle Thomas and I were overseas fighting the Nazis, we were stationed in Belgium. We had done our fair share of fighting throughout Europe, and after France was liberated, we were rewarded by being transferred to a supply depot in Cherbourg on the French coast of the English Channel. Thomas got involved with smuggling things out of France and sending them back to the ports in New York. He told me all about his operation and asked me several times to become his partner, but I didn't want any part of it. He made a lot of money and made some very influential friends back here in the States. When the war ended, we were brought back to the States. Our first stop just happened to be New York City. Your uncle Thomas couldn't wait to meet those who he had been dealing with, so he had me tag along. I didn't have anything better to do."

"Thomas set up a meeting. We jumped in a cab and headed to Brooklyn. We had yet to learn who we were meeting. All Thomas cared about was getting paid for the last big shipment he sent to New York. I remember when the cab came to a stop, we were sitting in front of an old empty warehouse. I told Thomas I didn't like the look of the area and tried to convince him to reschedule the meeting in a more public area. He wasn't listening to what I said and told me I had lost my nerve working at the supply depot in France."

"We paid the fare, and the cab left us there. I asked Thomas if he had brought a gun with him. He showed me he had a .45 tucked in his waistband. I told him to let me have it because he would be distracted with taking care of business, and I would be able to watch his back. He called me a 'nervous Nelly' but handed it to me anyway."

"We didn't have a clue as to where the meeting was to take place, so we walked around looking for anybody who might look like the men Thomas was to deal with. Finally, a guy in a long coat appeared out of nowhere and called us over to a doorway on the side of one of the empty warehouses. He asked Thomas if he was there to meet with Carmine Martino. Thomas told him he was, but neither one of us saw anyone else. The man motioned for us to follow him deeper into the empty warehouse. At that point, I believed we were being set up. I pulled out the .45 Thomas gave me and grabbed the man from behind and put the gun to his head. Thomas opened the man's coat and removed the pistol he was carrying. Suddenly from behind Thomas, another man appeared, pointing a Thomson machine gun at us. I shouted for Thomas to get down, and he dropped to his knees; I held the other man in front of me by the back of his collar and used him as a shield, then fired one round, striking the man with the machine gun in the head. I put my gun to the back of the man's head that I was holding in front of me and pulled the trigger."

The expression on John's face indicated to Michel that his baby boy had just lost his innocence, and he would never look at his father again in the same light.

"That is how it all began, son. It's my job. It's what puts a roof over your head, clothes on your back, and food on the table. It gives you and your sister an opportunity to go to college if you want to and advantages in life that many people won't have."

"Does mom know what you do?" asked John. Michel looked toward the house and spotted Bonnie through the window above the sink doing the dishes. He suddenly recalled the day he told his wife what he did to earn money. He could remember the fear that streaked across her face as if it had happened yesterday.

Michel knew he had lost a portion of his son's love if not all. He wanted to be careful in how he needed to reveal Bonnie's knowledge of his occupation to John. The last thing he wanted was for John to hate his mother for something she had no control over. Michel looked back at John and answered,

"Yes, she did, but it was when we had been married for several years. I want you to understand something. When I told your mother, she was so upset; she wouldn't speak to me for a month. She told me to leave."

"Did you?" asked John. Michel grinned, thinking about those difficult days.

"You bet I did. When an Italian-blooded woman gets angry, you can either stay and learn to sleep with one eye open or find a safe place to stay until she calms down." John liked that his mother wasn't the subservient type and stood up to his gangster father. John wanted to hear more about his newfound hero and asked,

"What happened then?"

"After she started talking to me again, I gradually let her into my world, but I never told her anything that would put her life in danger. I have never told her what I had just told you. She didn't need to know that, and to this day, I have never given her any details about anything that had made me come home in the condition I did last night."

John sat quietly, taking everything in. He started the bench swing to sway gently. It helped keep him calm and think clearly.

"I don't want to frighten you, son," stated Michel. "But I can't say this enough; you can't tell anyone about what I do or anything I've told you." John chuckled, thinking his father was beginning to be a little overdramatic. The lighthearted attitude John appeared to take angered Michel. He stood up quickly from the bench and stood directly in front of his son.

"What's so fucking funny, boy?" John wanted to melt into the wooden bench swing he was sitting on. His father had never spoken to him in that tone of voice or used that kind of language toward him. "This isn't a fucking game. Not only do I have to worry about this family more than I already do, but I now must also make sure I don't get clipped for talking to you about it. To ask me if I'm in the Mafia took a lot of balls, I give you that. Now that you know, it will take a bigger man to keep them."

Michel turned away and took a few steps from side to side to help him quiet his anger.

"How did you ever conclude I was in the Mafia?" Michel asked. Without thought or hesitation, John blurted,

"Dante told me."

"Oh, Jesus Christ," muttered Michel. "How did he know?" he asked, but at the same time could picture Sal telling Dante everything.

"He said he found some things in his father's closet."

"Such as?" inquired Michel. He had to hear just how careless his associate had been.

"Guns, money, documents."

"Documents?"

"Some had your name on them," stated John.

Michel looked up at the beautifully colored sunset and decided he had heard enough. It was time for him to take his family and leave Florida. It had now become too dangerous for all of them. He wanted to trust his son, but the slightest slip would cost all of them their lives. John assumed since his father had finished speaking, their talk was over. He stood from the bench and took a couple of steps toward the house, then stopped and turned around to face his father.

"I never want to be like you. You kill people. I can't do that."

"I'm glad to hear that, son; I prayed that you would become a better man than I am. That's the truth."

"I'm glad you decided to tell me the truth, Pop; you've been a lie to me my entire life," stated John with a heavy heart.

"Those words pierced Michel's soul. He would have rather been tortured and killed than listen to his son refer to his father's life as a lie. John stood looking into his father's eyes and seeing only a stranger. Tears began to run down John's cheek but could not be seen by his father because the light of dusk had forbidden it.

Angie realized it was becoming dark outside and walked to the back door window to see if John and her father were still in the backyard. She was able to catch a glimpse of both standing and facing one another.

"What are they doing, Mom?" Bonnie knew exactly what they were doing and hoped each of them would come to an understanding.

"They are speaking man to man," answered Bonnie. "One day, you and I will speak, woman to woman.

***

4:00 a.m. the following morning, John sprung from his bed and wasted no time getting ready. Today was the day to go with Rebecca to the youth retreat. John walked the few short blocks to her house in just a few minutes. To his surprise, he found several lights on at the Stone residence and observed Rebecca helping her father load the trunk of the car. As he approached the house from the sidewalk, he glanced at his watch to assure himself he wasn't late. He had ten minutes to spare.

Out of the corner of her eye, Rebecca caught a glimpse of John walking toward the house. She smiled and struggled to contain her enthusiasm from seeing John. She walked briskly to greet him. John was just as pleased to see Rebecca's smiling face,

"Good morning," greeted John as Rebecca took his hand and led him towards her father to introduce him.

"Daddy, this is John." Mr. Stone extended his hand and said,

"Good morning, John, a pleasure to meet you."

"Good morning, sir; nice to meet you," said John as they shook hands.

"Hope you're up for a long day?" asked Mr. Stone.

"Yes, sir, I've been looking forward to this."

"It shouldn't be too bad of a drive; this old girl should get us there in comfort," stated Mr. Stone as he patted and caressed the car as if it were a magnificent show horse.

I thought we were supposed to ride on the bus?" asked John.

"I gave up our seats for another family; I hope you don't mind?"

"No, not at all, sir." John was overjoyed with the change in transportation. He looked at the situation as an excellent opportunity to get to know Rebecca even better.

"Becky (Her father's nickname for his daughter) tells me you're Catholic."

"That's correct, sir, but only on my mother's side," quipped John. Mr. Stone found the comment humous; he chuckled and replied,

"Humor at five o'clock in the morning, excellent." Rebecca's mother approached smiling, extending her hand,

"Hi, I'm Rebecca's mother," she greeted. John shook her hand,

"Good morning, Mrs. Stone; happy to meet you."

"It looks like we have everything," said Mr. Stone. "I'll run inside and turn off the lights and lock it up."

"Well, let's climb in, shall we, kids?" suggested Mrs. Stone. Rebecca cringed every time her mother referred to her as a kid. She hoped John wouldn't be offended by the comment. Mrs. Stone walked around to the front passenger side of the car and climbed in while John opened the left rear passenger door to allow Rebecca to get in. As she passed in front of him, he whispered,

"Kids?" Rebecca could only respond by mouthing the word "Sorry". The chivalrous gesture of opening her daughter's door for her delighted Rebecca's mother. Her first impression of John was a positive one. John walked around the back of the car and took his seat behind Mrs. Stone. As soon as he was in the car, she turned around smiling and said,

"Rebecca tells me your Catholic."

Chapter 10

Michel hastily made his way down to the kitchen. As he passed John's room, he noticed the door was wide open, and his bed had been made. The aroma of freshly brewed coffee mingled with the unmistakable scent of fried bacon, was a pleasure to his senses.

Buttoning the cuffs of his shirt as he stepped into the kitchen, Michel was greeted by two enthusiastic "Good morning" salutations. He walked to the stove to kiss Bonnie, then leaned down to kiss Angie on the forehead as she sat at the table waiting for her father to be seated so she could pour him a small glass of orange juice.

"Good morning, sweetheart, and thank you for the juice." Michel noticed there needed to be a place setting for John.

"Where's John?" he asked.

"He had the youth retreat he was going to with his friend Rebecca," declared Bonnie. Michel thought a moment, then replied,

"Oh yes, youth retreat." Bonnie placed his plate of two eggs, bacon, and toast in front of him.

"Thank you, honey." He picked up a piece of bacon and took a bite after dipping it into the yoke of his egg.

"What do you suppose this retreat is about?" he asked Bonnie. Before she could answer, Angie injected her thoughts on the matter,

"I think it's about Giovanni spending all day holding Rebecca's hand and trying to kiss her." Before Michel could agree with his daughter's comment, Bonnie revised Angie's perception of her brother's activities at the retreat,

"Giovanni is going to the retreat to learn how to talk to kids his age about Jesus." Angie just shrugged her shoulders and took another bite of toast. She wasn't the least bit interested in what her brother was doing that day.

"Does he want to be a priest or something?" asked Michel.

"No, not a priest," replied Bonnie. "He thinks Catholics lose the real message in all of their rituals." Surprised, Michel asked,

"He told you that?" Bonnie nodded. Michel picked up his cup of coffee and took a sip, "So, my son wants to be a preacher."

"I wouldn't go as far to say that he just wants to belong to something he strongly believes in," added Bonnie. "Not to change the subject, but why are you dressed to go to work? I thought we could maybe go to the beach today and take a long walk on the shore."

"That sounds a lot better than what I have to do today," commented Michel. Bonnie was struck with a sense of dread at her husband's remark. All she could picture was him coming home covered in blood once again. Michel could see Bonnie was worried and quickly put her mind to rest,

"I need to talk to Sal," he said. Bonnie removed the empty plate in front of Michel and said,

"That's supposed to make me feel better?"

"It will be fine, I promise." Since Michel appeared to be calm and displaying no anxiety, Bonnie believed him.

"I tell you what, when I get home, we'll take a drive to the beach, get our feet wet, and maybe get some fresh seafood down by the peer; how does that sound?" Angie didn't hesitate to submit the verbal vote.

Sounds good to me!" she exclaimed. Bonnie smiled and said,

"Sound good; try not to be too late; the kids have school tomorrow." Michel stood from the table to head back upstairs to finish getting ready. He stopped at the kitchen sink, where Bonnie began to clean the breakfast dishes.

"I won't be long, I promise," he said, giving Bonnie a gentle kiss on her cheek.

***

Michel arrived at the store and parked directly in front of it. To his delight, he spotted Sal's car parked along the side of the building. He would be showing up unannounced, and it couldn't have been a better situation to confront Sal.

"Good morning," greeted Georgy as Michel stepped through the door and walked directly toward the back of the store.

"Good morning. Is Sal back there?" asked Michel as he pointed toward the door to the back room of the store.

"Yes," Georgy replied.

"Is he alone?"

"Yes, he's alone."

Michel grasped the door handle and opened it without missing a step. The natural light emanating from the front of the store illuminated the extremely narrow hallway leading to the open office area.

The hallway was designed purposely that way to force anyone, friend or foe, to enter single file. It would make it easier for those in the office to defend themselves if necessary.

When Michel reached the end of the hallway, he saw Sal sitting in the chair typically used by Thomas, reading the Sunday morning paper. When Michel entered, Sal didn't put the paper down and assumed it was his bodyguard, Marco.

"Get me another cup of coffee, would you, Marco?" requested Sal. Michel stood still and looked around the room. There was no one else there. A few seconds passed as Sal realized he heard nothing from Marco, no footsteps, or acknowledgment of his request. Sal turned the paper down to see what Marco was doing.

"Get your own fuckin' coffee," uttered Michel. The look on Sal's face was one of surprised disdain.

"What are you doing here, Michel?" asked Sal. "Did Thomas call you in?" Michel removed his hat, then walked slowly to a chair that was placed in the corner of the room, approximately twelve feet away from where Sal was seated. The corner chair also allowed Michel to see all the entryways into the room with a single glance, but more importantly, it placed Sal in Michel's preferred killing range.

"No, Thomas didn't call me in; I came to see you." Sal folded the newspaper, placed it on the table in front of him, and scooted his chair closer to the table so he could rest his arms on it.

"You should have called me; we could have arranged a time to meet," advised Sal.

"That's precisely why I didn't call you. I didn't want you to arrange anything."

"What the hell is that supposed to mean?" asked Sal.

"Enough with the bullshit, Sal. I'm here to give you your cut of the airport take this month." Michel reached inside his coat pocket and retrieved an envelope. Michel's sudden move reaching inside his coat unnerved Sal. He reacted by beginning to reach for his pistol from his shoulder holster, which didn't go unnoticed by Michel.

"Relax, Sal, if I wanted to kill you, I wouldn't do it here." Michel tossed the envelope on the table. "It's twenty-five-thousand dollars." Sal stood from his chair and reached across the table for the envelope. He opened it and peered inside. A smile quickly streamed across his face,

"Nice," he said as he stuffed the envelope into the inside pocket of his coat and sat back down.

"There's one other thing I wanted to talk to you about," said Michel. "This coming week on Friday, there's a plane coming into Pinellas. I won't be able to be here when it arrives. I was hoping you could make the pick-up for me."

"Where are you going to be?" asked Sal.

"I'm driving Bonnie to Orlando; she's seeing a specialist."

"For what? Is she sick?"

"She's having female problems; she might have to stay the night. We won't know until they see her."

"Ah, female problems, well good luck with that shit. Besides, she already has a couple of kids; look at it as a blessing in disguise."

Sal's callous comment made Michel want to pull out his gun and shoot Sal in the head, but what Michel had planned for Sal would justify his self-control.

"You need to understand something, Sal; This isn't going to be some shipment of Italian shoes or some other bullshit like that. This is going to be big, and I don't want you to send one of your goons to make the pick-up. If I were here, I'd do it myself."

"What is it?" asked Sal.

"It's a shipment of uncut diamonds from Zimbabwe." It was clear to see by the expression on Sal's face he had no idea where Zimbabwe was. "Is that in New Mexico?"

"No, you dumbass, it's in Africa," replied Michel.

"How do you know people in Africa?" asked Sal.

"Never mind that. Will you make the pick-up or not?" Sal's thoughts were racing. He could see nothing but dollar signs after taking his more than fair share of the hall. This was a deal he certainly could not pass up, especially since Michel would not be there to watch his every move.

"Alright, Michel, I'll be there. Here, write down the details, so I know where to go." Sal tossed a tablet of paper and a pencil across the table. Michel rose from his chair, walked to the table, and proceeded to write down the information Sal would need.

As Michel wrote, he reiterated the importance of being on time.

"Two more things, don't fuck it up, and don't try to rip me off."

"Remember who you are talking to; I'm your fucking boss!" shouted Sal. Michel finished writing, tossed the pencil on the table, and said,

"I know exactly who I'm talking to; that's why I said it."

"Fuck off!" barked Sal. Michel put his hat back on and said,

"I'll see you when I get back from Orlando." He turned away and headed back down the narrow hallway and through the door from which he entered. Sal picked the notepad up as soon as Michel left the room. He read what Michel had written. The more he read, the bigger the smile on his face became. He knew he would be making some easy money from this job, but even more when he cheated Michel of his fair share.

Suddenly, the expression on Sal's face went from one of joy to anger when he read what was at the bottom of the paper, a parting sentiment left by Michel.

It read: "Fuck you."

***

Later that evening, John and Rebecca fell asleep in the back seat of Rebecca's parents' car on their way home from the retreat. As soon as the car drove onto the slight bump at the beginning of the driveway, the two awoke from their much-needed sleep.

"We're home, kids!" announced Rebecca's father.

"We know, Dad," replied Rebecca feeling a little embarrassed about her father acting like a porter on a train.

Before John opened his door, he asked Mr. Stone,

"Can I help you bring some things into the house for you, sir?"

"Nice of you to offer, John, but we will get it all tomorrow." Everyone began to exit the vehicle. John and Rebecca walked to the rear of the vehicle and were immediately followed by Rebecca's parents.

"It was a pleasure meeting you, John," said Mr. Stone as he held out his hand. "I hope you enjoyed the day."

"The pleasure was all mine, sir," replied John as he shook Mr. Stone's hand, then smiled and gave Rebecca's mother a gracious nod.

"Have a blessed evening, young man; sweetheart, don't be too long; you have school tomorrow," instructed her father.

"Yes, Dad, I'll be in shortly," responded Rebecca. As Rebecca's parents walked toward their front porch, John and Rebecca stood silently gazing into each other's eyes, speaking not a word. Rebecca looked over her shoulder to confirm her parents were inside the house before she spoke.

"I really liked spending the day with you, John." He immediately reached for her hand and held it between his.

"I liked being with you too, Rebecca," responded John. It was the only thing he could think of saying since his mind and his heart were racing. Both found themselves in the moment when fear kept them from moving or speaking. This is when you find breathing difficult, you want to jump out of your skin. It is soon replaced with warmth and desire, and your heart aches to hold and kiss the one who has created this emotional chaos. It is exactly what John and Rebecca did next.

The kiss was short and gentle, but it was enough. At that moment, John and Rebecca knew they had something special that would remain with them for the rest of their lives.

The porch light began to turn on and off. It was Mr. Stone's signal to Rebecca to say goodnight.

"I have to go; I'll see you tomorrow?" she asked. John smiled and said,

"I hope so." He released Rebecca's hand, stepped backward, and said, "See you tomorrow." He turned away and suddenly broke into a fast-paced jog, running the entire way home. To this day, when asked if he "Remembered his feet touching the ground the entire time he ran home?" He would respond with a contemplative "No."

***

The voices of Angela and Giovanni shouting,

"Thanks, Mom, see you after school!" woke Michel from a disturbing dream. One that involved Sal threatening to kill Bonnie and the children. Although he knew it was only a dream, he didn't hesitate to go downstairs to see them.

"Well, there's Mr. Restless," greeted Bonnie as Michel made his way into the kitchen. He sat at the kitchen table while Bonnie poured him a cup of coffee.

"Kids gone already?"

"Yes, dear, they left fifteen minutes ago."

"How was Giovanni's retreat? Did he have a good time?"

"I don't know; all he talked about was Rebecca." Michel gave Bonnie a look of confusion. "Rebecca, the girl who invited him…" explained Bonnie. Michel nodded,

"Yes, of course, Rebecca," acknowledged Michel.

"What on earth were you dreaming about last night? You were flopping around like a fish out of water," Bonnie asked. Michel took several sips of coffee before answering.

"I don't remember," he answered, knowing Bonnie would know he was lying. Bonnie sat at the table next to Michel.

"Don't give me that; you remember your dreams." She held Michel's hand and caressed his face, "What do you want to tell me?" she asked. He looked at her and replied,

"We are going to leave Friday morning. I need you to discreetly begin packing things for us and the kids. Pack light, we will take only what we need. We can always buy the rest." The expression on Bonnie's face was one of fear and confusion.

"What's happened?" she asked. Michel stood from the table and went to the coffee pot to pour himself another cup.

"Nothing has happened yet. Just be ready to leave on Friday."

Chapter 11

The week's schedules and activities pass without any interruptions. It was 8:00 p.m. Thursday evening. In twenty-four hours, the Santoro family will have l eft the Tampa area, heading to an unknown location.

Michel exited his bedroom and passed by both of his children's rooms on his way downstairs to the kitchen to speak to Bonnie. He first passed Giovanni's room. The door was open, and all the lights were turned off. Michel wanted to confirm that his son wasn't in the room. He stopped at the open doorway and reached inside to flip on the light switch. He wasn't surprised to see his son wasn't there. The faint scent of men's cologne verified Giovanni was at Rebecca's house, or out on a date. The two had been inseparable the entire week. Michel had observed the light-hearted giddiness that had befallen his son, and knew it was all because of the fondness his son held for his friend, Rebecca.

Michel dreaded what was to come when he revealed to Giovanni that he probably would not see Rebecca again. Michel sighed, then quickly replaced the vision of him and Giovanni arguing, with cheers of delight from his daughter Angie. He was confident Angie would look upon the news as a new adventure, and an opportunity to meet new people and make new friends, no matter where they lived.

Michel passed by his daughter's room and peered in through the open door. He found Angela lying on her bed, working diligently on her cursive writing. Angela spotted her father watching her and greeted him,

"Hi Daddy!"

"Hi honey," responded Michel. "Don't stay up too late, okay? You still have one more day of school this week."

"I know I do; I won't, Daddy," Angela replied as she continued writing. She didn't even look at her father during the entire conversation.

Michel was relieved to know his children would not be nearby when he spoke with Bonnie in the kitchen.

Bonnie was sitting at the table in the breakfast nook, looking at several individual items on the counter and walls throughout the kitchen. Her most sentimental items were those drawings stuck to the front and side of the refrigerator. The artistic display was created by Angela when she was a preschooler, but also when she was in the 1st and 2nd grade. Bonnie knew her husband had clearly stated that she was to pack light, and bring only the things they would need. As she stared at her daughter's works of art, the more determined she became that when the time came, she would gather all the drawings and put them in her suitcase, even if it meant leaving some of her own items behind.

Michel entered the kitchen unnoticed by Bonnie.

"You okay?" he asked. Bonnie was so deep in thought; the sound of her husband's voice did not startle her. She found it difficult to generate a smile, but she did anyway.

"I'm fine," she replied softly.

Michel had been married to Bonnie long enough to know, when she said she was fine in a soft tone of voice, she was the exact opposite.

"Do you have all of us packed?"

She nodded, then said,

"I think so; I just have a few more things yet."

"That's great, honey. Where are the suitcases?"

"I put them behind the cabinet next to the workbench in the garage."

Michel briefly paused to envision as to where the suitcases were located, then he nodded and said, "Sounds good. I have a couple of things I want to add to mine as well."

"You don't have much room left," advised Bonnie.

"It's not much, just a couple of handguns, a knife, and some ammo. It will be fine." Bonnie looked at Michel and began to stare as she started to lose herself in thought.

She wanted to make sense of it all. She wanted dearly to be able to justify what they were about to do to their children without giving them any notice. She loved her husband to the ends of the earth. She loved her home. It was her labor of love for her family. She loved south Florida and all the friends they had made throughout the years. But the reality of the situation wasn't something she could hide from. She married a man who provided everything a family could need, unfortunately, the means in which he obtained the money to do so was mostly illegal.

The most frightening aspect of his profession was that, sometimes, the money could only be obtained by spilling blood. She could only assume that in this case it would be theirs if they didn't leave. As soon as Bonnie realized that, she knew they were doing the right thing.

"What is it?" he asked.

"Where are you taking us Michel?"

Now, it was he who began to stare without saying a word. Finally, he shook his head and said,

"I'm sorry honey, I can't tell you. Please understand it's for your own safety, but you know what? Once we are on the road, I will tell you."

Bonnie stood up from her chair, walked to the refrigerator, and pulled out a bottle of beer. She retrieved the magnetic bottle opener that was stuck to the side of the refrigerator and popped off the bottle cap.

"More importantly," she continued, "You're going to tell me why."

Michel knew his wife could be tough as nails when she needed to be, but when she reached for a beer without offering her husband one, it was a clear sign she was gathering up courage to handle anything her husband was about to tell her. He stood up from his chair and made his way to the refrigerator and pulled out a bottle of beer for himself, opened it, then returned to his chair at the table. He took a refreshing sip of the brew, then sat the bottle on the table.

"Tomorrow," he began, "Sal Carducci will be going to the airport to make a pick-up for me, because I told him I needed to take you to a specialist in Orlando. When he begins to leave with the take, the police will be there to arrest him. That's why we need to leave Florida tomorrow. Sal's people will be wanting to talk to me after that happens."

"You mean, Sal's people will be wanting to kill you," responded Bonnie.

Michel silently nodded.

Bonnie and Michel sat there quietly, drinking their beer. Neither one of them spoke for several minutes. Both had been wrapped up in thought about what was to become of the Santoro family. Michel drank the last of his beer and said, "I have to leave to make a phone call."

"Why do you have to leave? We have phones right here," questioned Bonnie.

"I don't need this call traced to this house," stated Michel. That was all the explanation Bonnie needed. She finished her beer and made her way back to the refrigerator to get another. Michel walked over to her and gave her a kiss on the cheek then headed for the door.

"I'll be back in ten minutes," he said as he left the house.

***

Michel drove to the nearest phone booth which was about a mile from his house. As he exited his automobile, he surveyed his surroundings to see how many people were on the street. To his delight, he found that the streets were relatively empty. He wanted to be as discrete as possible to who and how many people saw him in the phone booth. As an added precaution, he left the phone booth door open to prevent the booth's interior light from coming on.

He deposited a nickel into the phone and proceeded to dial a number. He paused for a moment before dialing the last number.

Thoughts of abandoning his plan so that his family could remain where they were raced through his mind. This wasn't the first time he entertained the thought, but he knew that if he didn't go through with it, he would be constantly having to keep a close eye on his new boss, Sal Carducci. He quickly made his final decision and dialed the last number that connected him to the Tampa Bay Police, Robbery Division.

Detective Al Mosley had just finished his egg salad sandwich and the carrot sticks his wife packed for him. The diet his wife had put him on always left him wanting more for his evening dinner. He rose from his desk and headed for the vending machine that was located just outside the shared Robbery Division office.

But before he could reach the office exit, the phone on his desk began to ring. He stopped in his tracks and turned to look back at his desk, hoping after a few rings it would stop. After the fifth ring, he abandoned his visit to the vending machine and returned to his desk to answer the call.

"Mosley," he said answering the call. At first, there was no response to the greeting. The detective waited patiently for a response. It finally came when he was about to hang up.

"Are you a detective?" the unidentified caller asked.

"That's right, Detective Allen Mosley, at your service."

"I need you to listen to me very carefully, I'm not going to repeat myself, so get a paper and pen." The detective chuckled and tried not to be offended by the suggestion. He did as he was instructed and replied, "Okay, go ahead."

At this point, Mosley assumed this was going to be worthless information. More times than not, his instincts were correct. Nevertheless, he waited for the caller to continue.

"Tomorrow, at 3:00 p.m. a shipment of diamonds will be arriving at Pinellas International Airport. The shipment is going to be hit by a member of the Barzetti crime family."

"That's very interesting, Mr..... what was your name again?" asked the detective.

"I never gave it to you, just shut up and listen," responded Michel. "The shipment will be held in cargo hanger 17B; that is where the move will be made on it."

"So, who's the member you referred to?" asked Mosley.

"His name is Salvatore Carducci." Upon hearing the name, the detective stood up from his chair to look at the bulletin board located on the wall a short distance behind him. His eyes quickly scanned the entire board, looking at every picture and name of all the suspects in the mob family that have recently been placed on the Division's priority list. Once the detective located Carducci's name and photo, he recalled a run-in he had with Carducci over a year ago.

"Carducci, yeah, I remember that little piece of shit. He couldn't find his way around a bathroom stall, and you want to tell me he is going to pull off a diamond heist? C'mon, you have to give me more than that to take you seriously. That's a long-ass ride to the airport from here, don't be wasting my time!"

Michel didn't expect this kind of skepticism from the police. He assumed once he dropped Carducci's name, the police would be eager to hear what he had to say.

Just my luck to get a hard ass on the phone, he thought to himself. Michel didn't want to be on the call any longer than he had to, in fear of it being traced.

"Just one more thing, Detective," continued Michel. "Carducci isn't some mob hoodlum anymore. They just bumped him up to captain. I thought you might like to know." With that final bit of information, Michel ended the call.

Detective Mosley hung up the receiver from his phone and turned once again toward the bulletin board. There was nothing attached to the photo of Salvatore Carducci indicating his recent promotion. Mosley continued to stare at the board determining the legitimacy of the phone call he just received. He was about to dismiss the call as a meaningless prank, when Chief Detective Harold approached the bulletin board and pinned a slice of paper to the photo of Salvatore Carducci. It had just one word on it...CAPO.

The smirk that adorned the face of Detective Mosley through most of his phone conversation with Michel, suddenly disappeared. He immediately placed a call to the desk of the Chief Detective.

Chapter 12

Michel was just a few short blocks from his house when he noticed his son Giovanni walking on the sidewalk, heading in the same direction. Michel assumed Giovanni was on his way home from visiting Rebecca. He pulled his car a few feet closer to the curb so not to block traffic, and slowly crept up behind Giovanni.

Look at that, this boy has it bad, thought Michel as his son continued the pace in his step, oblivious to his surroundings. Michel sounded his horn with a quick short tap. Giovanni was suddenly brought out of his daydream and quickly turned toward the vehicle that was following him. He peered inside and realized it was his father. Michel stopped the car as Giovanni proceeded to walk toward him smiling from ear to ear.

He opened the front passenger's door and said, "Is this what you do in your spare time? Harassing pedestrians?"

"Only on Thursdays," quipped Michel. "Get in, I'll give you a lift home." Giovanni complied even though he had just another six hundred feet before reaching their house.

"Son, before you run off to your room, when we get home, your mother and I need to talk to you and your sister." Giovanni couldn't think of why they needed to talk to him. He had hoped it wasn't going to be an interrogation into what were his intentions with his newfound friend, Rebecca. He dreaded the thought.

The two entered through the kitchen door. There, Giovanni found his mother sitting at the breakfast nook table sipping wine. Oh shit, thought Giovanni. He always knew he was in big trouble if his mother needed a glass of wine before talking to him. Michel headed upstairs to bring Angela down to join them.

"Hi, Mom," Giovanni cautiously said as he pulled a chair out from the table and sat down.

"Hi, honey," replied his mother. I'm not in trouble, he thought, she didn't sound angry, but then again, she appeared sad. This could be bad, he speculated.

"Are you alright?" asked Giovanni just as his father and sister joined them at the table.

"She's alright, son, just a little blue," commented Michel. Angela looked at her mother expecting to see her with blue skin. The expression on her face prompted her father to explain,

"Being blue, sweetheart, means to be sad."

"Oh," responded Angela.

In Giovanni's eyes, she wasn't "alright". He couldn't recall the last time he saw his mother so sullen. Michel quickly moved the focus of their conversation away from Bonnie.

"Your mother and I have something to share. We hope you will eventually understand what we are about to tell you." Giovanni's heart began to race from the mysterious build-up his father made of the situation. He began to grow uncomfortably anxious and couldn't remain silent any longer.

"Just come out and say what you have to say, Pop. I'm a big boy, I can take it," Giovanni insisted. Michel picked up Bonnie's glass of wine and drank half of it. He set the glass down in front of Bonnie, looked at his son and said,

"Very well, here it is. Something is going to happen tomorrow concerning my work." The first thought Giovanni had was rooted in what his friend, Dante, had told him about their fathers. His assumptions ranged from the family having to go on the run because his father killed someone, to his father had stolen a vast amount of money. No matter what it was going to be, Giovanni knew he was not prepared to hear it.

"All of us will be leaving Florida early tomorrow morning. We won't be coming back… ever." Giovanni sat motionless and quiet. Angela either didn't comprehend what was just told to her or she really didn't care less. Giovanni wanted to hear more before he reacted, but he could see both his father and mother were waiting for his response. He sighed, looked at both and asked,

"Where in the hell are we going? What did you do, Pop?" Angela couldn't believe her brother was cussing in front of their parents. She sat dumbfounded with her mouth open.

"You will know where we are going when we get there. As for what I did is my business. All I can tell you is that I'm watching out for this family. I don't want anything to happen to any of us, so, we must leave. Your mother has packed a suitcase for each of us, we will be leaving before daybreak."

Giovanni instantly thought of Rebecca and his close friend, Dante.

"We can't leave like that, not that way! I won't be able to say goodbye to my friends!"

Michel knew of at least one of his son's friends he wanted to make sure his son didn't talk to, at least not yet. It was Dante, the son of the man he was setting up to take the fall for the diamond heist.

Before Michel or Bonnie could speak another word, Giovanni stood up quickly tipping over his chair behind him. He swiftly moved to the door before Michel realized what he was doing. Giovanni opened the door and sprinted out into the darkness.

"Where is Giovanni going, Daddy?" asked Angie who was a bit upset and frightened. She stood from her chair and walked over to her mother's open arms.

"He's probably going to say goodbye to his friends, sweetheart," answered Michel.

***

Giovanni never slowed his full out sprint to Rebecca's house. The thought of not being able to see her again after tonight broke his heart. The tears that welled up in his eyes made it almost impossible to see clearly. As he drew closer to Rebecca's house, he calmed himself enough to prevent Rebecca from seeing that he had been crying.

Once he reached her driveway, he noticed there were several lights on inside her house. He went straight to the front door and knocked. The porch light had illuminated, and Mr. Stone answered the door.

"Hello, John!" he greeted, "Let me guess, you're here to see Rebecca?"

"Yes, sir, if that's alright?" Mr. Stone unlocked the screen door and invited Giovanni inside.

"Let me go get her," said Mr. Stone.

"Hello again, John!" greeted Mrs. Stone who was relaxing on one end of the sofa watching television. "Did you leave something behind from earlier?"

"No ma'am, I needed to let Rebecca know something very important."

"I see, please don't keep her too long, you two have one more day of school left."

"Yes, ma'am. I will try not to." Rebecca appeared from down the hallway with her father close behind. Giovanni smiled when he saw her, as did she.

"Not too long, Becky," instructed Mr. Stone.

"I won't be, Dad," she replied. The two walked out of the front door, closing it behind them. Once they were alone on the porch, Rebecca sensed there was something Giovanni wanted to say. He held his head low and hardly looked Rebecca in the eye. She grabbed his hand, held it, and asked, "What is it, Giovanni? What's wrong?"

"Tonight, when I got home, my parents told me we were leaving Florida in the morning."

Giovanni raised his head, quickly glanced at Rebecca, then suddenly looked away. He didn't want her to see him cry.

"What?" she asked, completely surprised by the news. It didn't take long for Rebecca's heart to react. Her eyes began to water. She tried to speak, but her emotions didn't allow her to. Giovanni worked up enough courage to look at her. When he did, and saw the tears streaming down her face, it opened the gaping wound that had already torn into his heart.

"You can't leave," pleaded Rebecca. Giovanni put his arms around her and held her tight. The embrace spoke for itself. It was at that moment the two knew they were meant to be together.

"I'll be back for you, I promise," vowed Giovanni. He reassured her with a deep long kiss and an endless embrace. Neither one wanted to let go.

"I better let you get back inside before your father comes out," said Giovanni, even though that was the last thing he wanted to do. Rebecca silently agreed with the nod of her head. The two released their tender embrace but continued to hold each other's hands.

"Will you write me?" she asked.

"Yes, of course, and when we get settled, I will call you." The promise to call brought a smile to the tear-dampened face of Rebecca. She released her grasp of Giovanni's hands and grabbed the chest portion of his shirt and pulled him into her. Playfully, she tightened her jaw and attempted to sound tough,

"You better Mr., or I'll come looking for you." The two embraced and kissed one last time.

"I gotta go," said Giovanni.

"You take care of yourself Giovanni Santoro, I'll see you again soon," stated Rebecca with the confidence of someone who would do whatever she had to, to make it happen. Giovanni turned away and stepped off the porch. He turned back once more to take one last look at the girl he loved but had to leave, all because of his father. The more he thought about it, the angrier he became.

He had one more stop before heading home, and that was to his best friend Dante's house.

***

Meanwhile, Bonnie remained sitting at the breakfast table sipping on her second glass of Merlot, while Michel escorted their daughter, Angela, to bed. He returned to the kitchen and said, "It seems like Angela took the news well, don't you think?"

Bonnie nodded and replied, "I agree; I think she did. You know your daughter, I think she has a little gypsy in her. She won't have any problem adapting. She loves to travel and see new things and meet new people. Now, your son is a different matter."

Bonnie took a larger sip of wine and asked, "You do think he'll come back home tonight, don't you?" Michel sighed deeply and said,

"I sure hope so, honey. I would hate like hell to have to go out tonight to find him."

Suddenly, the phone rang causing Bonnie to jump and almost spill her wine. Embarrassed, she looked at Michel and said, "Sorry, I guess I need a little bit more." Michel smiled as he stood up from his chair and walked over to answer the phone. The two would admit later, they assumed it was Giovanni calling to tell them he wasn't going with them.

"Hello," Michel answered.

"Hi Mikey!"

It was Thomas Califano.

"Hello, Thomas," responded Michel. Bonnie overheard Michel's greeting, rolled her eyes, and mumbled,

"Now what the fuck does he want?" Michel heard just enough of what Bonnie said to convince him that she didn't need anything more to drink.

"Is it a bad time, Mikey?" asked his boss.

"No, Thomas, everything's fine. What can I do for you?

"Word has it, you have chosen Sal to make your pick-up at the airport tomorrow. I wouldn't question your choice, but since the items he's going to pick up are quite valuable, I thought I'd do you a favor and go with him." Michel's heart sank into his stomach, and he quickly replied,

"No, Thomas! There's no need for you to do that." Thomas was puzzled by Michel's response.

"Mikey, are you sure? Sal can be a real pain in the ass. I know the two of you are always butting heads. I thought I would keep an eye on him to make sure you get your fair share. I wouldn't want that son-of-a-bitch watching my money for me."

"It will be fine, Thomas; Sal knows if he tries to steal from me; he's going to have a very bad day."

"Alright, have it your way. I just wanted to save you a little heartache. How is Bonnie by the way?"

"Bonnie? She's fine."

"Sal told me you were taking her to a specialist in Orlando." Thomas' inquiry about Bonnie caught Michel off-guard.

"Oh, that!" responded Michel, forgetting what he had told Sal as to where he would be the following day.

"You know Bonnie, she's a trooper. She's one tough cookie."

"Indeed, she is, Mikey; give her my love, would you please?"

"I certainly will, Thomas."

"I'll let you go, Mikey. I'll see you in a couple of days."

"Take care, Thomas, see you soon."

Bonnie could see that her husband was not going to share what the phone call was all about. She waited patiently while her husband returned to his chair. He said nothing.

"What did Thomas want?" she asked. Michel grinned and said,

"He wanted to volunteer to keep an eye on Sal tomorrow. I told him it would be fine, and there was no need to worry himself.

"But is there?" asked Bonnie.

"Is there what?" he asked.

"A need to worry," said Bonnie.

"Always," responded Michel.

***

Twenty-minutes later, Giovanni was walking up the driveway of the Carducci family home. He was watchful of where he stepped. The only light that aided his approach to the front porch came from the lamp in the front bay window of the house. He didn't see that Dante was standing on the side of the house next to the driveway, smoking a cigarette.

As Giovanni was about to knock on the front door, Dante called out clearly but softly,

"John." Giovanni turned toward the sound of his friend's voice and suddenly caught a whiff of cigarette smoke. He quietly made his way over to Dante.

"Are you smoking?" were the first words from Giovanni.

"No dumb ass, I'm milking the cat." Dante's reply seemed strange to Giovanni, but he ignored it, he had bigger problems to deal with. Dante took one last drag from his cigarette and flicked the butt across the driveway onto the neighbor's lawn.

"What are you doing here?" Dante asked. Giovanni didn't respond right away. He kept his head down while he worked up the strength to keep from crying in front of his best friend.

The silence raised concern for Dante. He could see his friend was deeply troubled.

"John, what's wrong?" Giovanni raised his head but looked across the street away from his friends captivated stare.

"We are leaving Florida early tomorrow morning. We won't be coming back."

"What? Why are you just telling me now?" asked Dante.

"Because I just found out about an hour ago."

"Where are you moving to?" Giovanni's gaze was now on his friend,

"I don't know, my dad wouldn't tell me, he said we would know when we got there.

"That doesn't make any sense," pointed out Dante, "Unless it has something to do with his job." Giovanni had already concluded that it did indeed have to do with his father's profession, but he didn't want to mention it in front of Dante.

"Do you want me to ask my dad, he might know something," offered Dante. Giovanni shook his head and replied,

"No, you better not do that. If it is something to do with work our fathers wouldn't like us prying into their business." Dante gave it some thought, then said,

"You're probably right."

The two boys suddenly fell silent. Both boys began to reminisce of all the good times they had growing up together. At times their laughter recalling some of their antics grew louder as the stories were retold. At one point, Dante's mother came out onto the porch to see what all the laughing was about. The dim lighting didn't reveal Dante's location.

"Dante?" called out his mother. Giovanni stepped out from the shadows, with Dante directly behind him.

"Well hello John," she greeted. "Is Dante out here with you?"

"Right here mom, responded Dante as stepped into the dim lighting.

"Oh, there you are!" stated Mrs. Carducci. "It's getting late honey, you have one more day of school, so don't be too much longer."

"Okay mom, I'll be in shortly."

"Goodnight, Mrs. Carducci," said Giovanni.

"Goodnight John, don't keep him too much longer."

"No Ma'am, I won't." With those reassuring words, Dante's mom went back inside the house.

"I guess I'll let you get back inside," said Giovanni. Dante didn't want to go inside. He didn't want his friend to leave.

"This really sucks! You know that don't you?" he asked Giovanni. Of course, he knew. The two had been friends since they were two young boys. Dante needed to express his feelings through words. Giovanni did it through actions. He wrapped his arms around Dante and the two boys hugged. Dante was never the emotional one and had to make light of the situation.

"You better not get an erection, I'll tell my dad," Dante teased. Giovanni couldn't help but laugh, as he pushed Dante away.

"You asshole," he chuckled. As the two shook hands, Giovanni said,

"Take care my friend, we'll see each other again, I promise."

"And when we do, added Dante, we'll laugh about me giving you a boner." The two had their last laugh together. They looked at one another, each of them giving the other a nod, solidifying their friendship. Giovanni turned and began his walk back home, thinking of the two friends he was about to leave behind.

Chapter 13

At 4:30 a.m., Michel and Bonnie had loaded up the car and finished tying the larger suitcases down to the roof of their car. The cover of darkness provided the privacy they needed from curious neighbors. The only thing left to do was to wake the kids up. Bonnie went to Angela's room, and Michel to Giovanni's.

Bonnie slowly opened the door to her daughter's room and wasn't surprised to find her sound asleep. As much as Bonnie loved to watch her little daughter sleep, she understood completely that Michel expected the children to hit the floor running. Although she thought it cruel, Bonnie turned the overhead bedroom light on. The room was suddenly flooded with 100-watt incandescent light. Angela's eyelids closed tightly as she reached for the covers and covered her head.

"Good morning, sweetie," called out Bonnie. "Time to get up!"

Michel saw what his wife did as he passed the doorway to Angela's room and decided to do the same to wake his son. He slowly opened the door and flipped on the light. To his surprise, Giovanni was not in his bed, but rather, he was fully dressed sitting on the edge of the completely made bed. He held in his lap a small leather duffle bag.

"I'm up Pop, you can turn the light off," muttered Giovanni.

"Sorry son, I didn't know you were up." Giovanni stood up from his bed, turned, and slowly walked toward the bedroom doorway in which his father stood. Michel realized his son was ready to leave the room; so, he stepped aside. Giovanni walked past his father without saying a word and headed downstairs. Michel gave one last look at his son's room before turning the light off and closing the door.

Michel walked to Angela's room to check on his wife's progress with their daughter. Bonnie had just stepped out of the room, closing the door behind her.

"How's she doing?" asked Michel.

"She's getting dressed, she'll be down in just a minute," assured Bonnie.

Michel headed downstairs to try and have a few moments with his son, but when he reached the kitchen, he discovered Giovanni wasn't there. He looked out the window toward the driveway, there still wasn't any sign of him. Michel's imagination began to get the best of him. He could picture his son running out of the house, and down the street to get as far away from his family as he possibly could. Just to make sure he wasn't overreacting; Michel quickly checked every room on the main floor of the house. Still, there wasn't any sign of him. Bonnie and Angela reached the bottom of the staircase, only to find Michel walking through the house at a quickened pace.

"What's wrong?" asked Bonnie.

"I think Giovanni has left."

"Left. What do you mean left?" asked Bonnie.

"It means he's not here; I can't find him." It became apparent to little Angie, they were not leaving right away, so she sat down on the last step of the staircase and watched her panic-stricken parents search for her brother.

Bonnie and Michel met back in the kitchen after searching the entire house.

"Where do you think he's gone?" asked Bonnie. Michel thought a moment, then remarked,

"I haven't checked the garage." He opened the door of the kitchen and turned on the outside light illuminating the walkway to the garage. Out of the corner of his eye, he saw movement in the backyard. He stopped and squinted to see what it was that caught his attention. He slowly walked out of the light and into the darkness. The movement that caught his eye continued as he approached. Once Michel's eyes adjusted to the dark, he could clearly see Giovanni sitting on the bench swinging.

"Son? Are you alright?" Giovanni didn't respond. Michel raised his voice slightly. He didn't want to disturb the neighbors at such an early morning hour.

"Giovanni?" It was obvious to Michel that he was heard this time. Giovanni stood from the swing, looked at his father and asked,

"Is it time to go?"

"Very soon, why don't you get yourself a glass of juice. We will stop along the way to get some breakfast," replied Michel. The thought of a cold glass of orange juice sounded great to Giovanni. With a quickened pace to his step, Giovanni walked past his father straight to the kitchen with Michel just a few steps behind.

Bonnie and Angela made their way to the kitchen as well. Angela continued to struggle to completely wake up. She laid her head on the kitchen table with her eyes closed as she waited for her mother to bring her a glass of orange juice.

"C'mon honey, sit up and drink your juice, we need to leave soon," beckoned her mother as she tenderly rubbed her daughter's back.

Giovanni finished his large glass of juice and placed the glass in the sink. Angela quickly followed her big brother to the sink to also place her glass next to his. The Santoro family stood silent in the middle of the kitchen, with each one looking at the other. Giovanni began to pray, asking God to make his father change the plans to move, and for the family to stay where they were. It was the most heartfelt prayer he had ever made, and with his newfound path to God, he truly believed that the Almighty would listen to his plea and answer his prayer.

He didn't have to wait long for God's answer. Michel reached into his front trouser pocket and retrieved the car keys. He looked at each of the family members, then said,

"Let's go."

***

At 7:00 a.m. the same morning, Salvatore Carducci had finished his breakfast of coffee and toast and was about to head upstairs to finish getting ready for a very busy day.

He would spend several hours this morning in the back room at the store, counting the total 'takes' for the week from the crews in the north Tampa territory. He couldn't allow himself to be distracted in any way even with being on the verge of making the biggest score of his life, which would take place that afternoon at the airport.

Just as Sal made his way to the top of the stairs, he met Dante emerging from his room.

"Morning, Dad," he greeted his father with very little enthusiasm, causing Sal to stop and take notice of how depressed his son appeared.

"Everything alright?" asked Sal. "You look like you lost your best friend." Dante wasn't in any mood to discuss it with his father, and gave his father a dismissive "It's nothing," brush off.

Sal threw his arm around Dante's neck, putting him into a headlock and playfully rubbing his knuckles against his scalp.

"Girl problems, hey?" commented his father as he continued the roughhousing with his son. Suddenly, Dante realized he nearly revealed Giovanni's secret about leaving Florida, and quickly responded to his father's comment about girl problems.

"Yeh, Anna's been a real pain in the ass."

"I know what you mean," replied Sal. "What are ya gonna do? You can't live with 'em, and you can't kill 'em. Just remember, there are plenty of fish in the sea." Dante wanted to end the conversation, so he immediately agreed with his father's statements.

"You're right, Dad, I'll be fine. I'm gonna go down and get some breakfast before I go to school."

"It's your last day, right?"

"Yes, sir."

"Well, have fun, but not too much fun. Won't be able to enjoy the summer sitting in a jail."

"Yes sir," agreed Dante. He then quickly made his way downstairs and poured himself a cup of coffee, thinking about his friend Giovanni, who he began to miss already.

***

Michel pulled into a small breakfast and lunch diner just shy of the Georgia / Florida line, to get the family fed and to stretch their legs. The diner was clean and accommodating. Shortly after seating themselves, a middle-aged waitress wearing too much makeup and giving the chewing gum in her mouth a serious work out, brought the family glasses of ice water and menus. Michel picked up the menus and handed them back to the waitress,

"We are in a bit of a hurry, so all of us will be having the same thing."

"That won't be a problem," responded the waitress. She pulled her order pad and pen from her apron and asked,

"What will you have hon?"

"We'll have scrambled eggs, bacon, potatoes, and toast. Coffee for my wife and I, and the kids will have orange juice." Not only was Giovanni embarrassed that he couldn't order his own breakfast, but to have his father refer to him as a kid angered him. Once the waitress left the table to give the order to the cook, Giovanni addressed his father in a less than pleasant voice,

"I would really appreciate if you would quit referring to me as a kid." The look on Giovanni's face and the tone of his voice sent a clear message to his father. Michel sat back and looked at his son with surprise and a sense of respect.

"I'm sorry son, I didn't know you felt that way," replied Michel. "You're right, you're nearly eighteen and a young man. I promise I will not refer to you as a kid again." At that very moment, Giovanni felt he would now be able to converse with his father man to man.

"But," added Michel smiling. "Your mother may have a different opinion, and that, you will have to take up with her." Giovanni's gaze moved quickly to his mother, only to find her smiling and shaking her head.

"You will always be my baby boy," declared Bonnie. The victory Giovanni just captured with his father, was short lived. He sighed, knowing his mother would never change how she referred to him. This was one battle he would never have a chance to win. He knew it was in his best interest to just let it go.

The coffee and orange juice were brought to the table, followed shortly by the food. There was very little conversation while the family ate their breakfast. Once everyone finished, Michel and Bonnie enjoyed their last sips of coffee as the waitress placed the check on the table. Michel glanced at the total then retrieved a folded wad of money held together by a rubber band from the front pocket of his trousers. He peeled off a five-dollar bill for the tip and placed it on the table.

"Is everyone ready?" asked Michel. Verbal as well as affirmative nods of the heads answered Michel's question. All of them proceeded toward the cashier, including a tall, burley, unshaven man who probably hadn't bathed in a couple of days.

"Ya'll go on ahead and I'll meet you outside," said Michel. "I need to use the restroom after I pay the check." Bonnie, Angela, and Giovanni left and stood outside the car and waited for Michel.

Michel pulled out his wad of cash to pay the $8.75 check. He peeled off a ten-dollar bill and handed it to the cashier, all under the observance by the burly man who stood behind Michel. The cashier gave Michel his change. He slid it back into his trouser pocket along with the large cache of cash.

"Thank you, come again," said the cashier. Michel turned and walked past the burly man and headed to the restroom. The large man stepped up and presented his bill to the cashier. He noticed Michel had gone to the restroom leaving his family standing outside their car. He paid his check and left.

Michel had spent fifteen minutes in the restroom. He was sure his family would begin to get impatient waiting for him. He quickened his step to get to the parking lot before his family decided to leave without him. As he opened the exit door to the diner and looked toward their car, he saw the large man standing next to their car with Angela and Giovanni standing in front of him. Bonnie stood just a couple of feet to the man's right. Everyone stood facing Michel. No one was talking, the children appeared frightened. Bonnie however, looked pissed off and irritated. Michel stopped in his tracks, approximately ten feet from the group. He noticed the man held a large, fixed blade knife in his right hand.

"Can I help you with something friend?" Michel asked. The man raised the knife and pointed it at Michel.

"You sure can Mr., I want that wad of cash you have in your pocket."

"There must be an 'or else' in there, right?" asked Michel.

"You goddamn right there's a 'or else' replied the man. "Or I'll carve your kids and your bitch up, right here in front of you." Michel removed his hat smiling. He ran his hand through his hair and put the hat back on, then said,

Well, I think that is quite the plan friend, but I don't think my wife is going to go along with it." Suddenly, the man heard the distinctive sound of a hammer being pulled back on a pistol in his right ear.

"Drop the knife, or I'll put a bullet in your ear, asshole," ordered Bonnie.

Neither Bonnie nor Michel thought that she would have to use the .22 caliber revolver he instructed her to start carrying. Nevertheless, she made him proud of the way she handled herself. Not everyone was as gleeful as Michel. The would-be thief certainly wasn't happy, Angela was in shock after hearing her mother swear, and Giovanni could see that his mother was now acting like his father. God help me, he thought.

Michel walked up to the burly man and picked the knife up from the pavement. Michel gave the knife a closer look while his wife kept her gun inches from the man's ear. He was impressed by the bone handle and the extremely sharp edge it had on it.

"This is really nice," said Michel. "I think I'll keep it. I wouldn't want you to get yourself in trouble by carrying such an impressive weapon. I think you should thank me for that, what do you think?" The man nodded his head the affirmative.

"I'm sorry, what was that?" asked Michel as he leaned in toward the man, lending him an ear.

"Thank you," responded the man.

"You're welcome," replied Michel. "Alright family, time to get back on the road!" Without hesitation, Angela and Giovanni quickly made their way into the car. Bonnie gently released the hammer on her pistol and returned it to her purse. Michel removed the leather sheath from inside the man's waistband of his trousers and placed the knife in it.

"I'll be taking this with me," said Michel. The man nodded and said,

"Yes sir."

"Well, if you would excuse us, we will be on our way," announced Michel. He walked over to the car and opened Bonnie's door for her. She climbed in and Michel closed the door. He then turned and looked at the demoralized robber and asked,

"You still here?" The man took a couple of steps backward, turned, then slowly walked away. Michel climbed in behind the wheel and the

Santoro family were back on the road.

It was quiet inside the car as they resumed their journey. Michel assumed the children might have been in a slight shock. He knew Bonnie was alright when she gave him a reassuring smile that everything would be fine.

"I bet ya'll thought this was going to be a boring trip," stated Michel. Angela giggled, Giovanni rolled his eyes, and Bonnie reached over and gently squeezed her husband's hand.

Chapter 14

Sal Carducci impatiently waited in his car, which he had discreetly parked outside of cargo hanger 17B at the Pinellas International Airport. It was 2:48 p.m. There had been no sign of activity in or near the hanger for the past thirty minutes. The inactivity only fed Sal's cynical disposition. He started to believe Michel had sent him on a bogus heist.

That son-of-a-bitch, he thought to himself, and the more he thought about it the angrier he became. He glanced at his watch, it read 3:06. He engaged the clutch, shifted the car into neutral and started to reach for the ignition key, when suddenly, a short bed truck with a canvas cover pulled up to the bay door of hanger 17B and sounded its' horn. Nearly three minutes had passed before the hanger door was raised by the attendant on duty. Sal was able to get a good look at the attendant, and noticed he was a short thin kid who probably wasn't old enough to shave. Good, he thought to himself, he won't be a problem.

The truck pulled inside the hanger. Both doors of the cab swung open, as two taller heavier men climbed out of the cab and headed to the bed of the truck. The two men pulled the canvas back revealing the only cargo in the truck bed, one small wooden crate.

One the men slid the crate to the end of the truck bed; the other man lifted the crate from the bed and asked,

"Where to buddy?" The attendant led both men to where he wanted them to place it. Sal could no longer see any of them. He decided it was time for him to make his move to the hanger.

He left his automobile and quietly closed the door. He quickly and quietly made his way to the hanger door and peered inside. He could hear the attendant instructing the men as to where to place the crate.

The sheer size of the hanger almost made the voices sound extremely far away. Sal stepped inside and hid behind a stack of crates nearby.

The three men returned. As Sal had hoped, the two delivery men climbed back into the truck cab and promptly backed out of the hanger. Once they cleared the hanger, the attendant stood just inside the overhead door opening to watch the delivery men leave, and to see if there was anyone else outside the hanger.

He saw nothing and hoped the heist would be called off. In a way, he was relieved; he never liked dealing with gangsters. They paid well, but the price he had to pay if he screwed up made him a nervous wreck. After every job he was a part of, he would swear he would never do it again, but his mind and morals quickly changed when he would be handed hundreds of dollars to participate.

The attendant turned around to head back to his work, only to see Sal standing just feet away holding a revolver which was pointed directly at him. The attendant was startled. Not by the gun pointed at him, but by Sal suddenly appearing out of nowhere. He made no sudden moves and slowly raised his hands above his head.

"Relax, kid, I won't hurt you unless you do something stupid," assured Sal. "I'm here to pick up a shipment from Zimbabwe, which I assume has just come in.

"If the abbreviation for Zimbabwe is, ZWE, it's right over there," pointed the attendant with his hands still raised. Sal motioned with his pistol toward the direction the attendant pointed and said, "Show me, and put your goddamn hands down."

The attendant lowered his arms and slowly walked in the direction he indicated. The two passed several aisles of crates, some stacked five and six high. It seemed to Sal the two had walked to the very far reaches of the hanger.

"Christ, kid, what'd you do? Hide it in another state?"

"No sir, it's right down here," pointed the attendant down the second to the last row of crates. He led Sal near the end of the row, stopped and pointed to the 8" x 28" crate marked with the red stenciled letters, ZWE, along with a few identification numbers.

Sal holstered his weapon, knowing he had nothing to fear, and placed both hands on the crate. The lid was securely nailed down.

"You have a crowbar kid?"

"Up by the overhead door, I do," said the attendant. There were two handles made of rope on each end. Sal grabbed one of the ropes and lifted the crate.

"Is there anything in this?"

"Yes sir, I mean, I think so," remarked the nervous attendant.

"You better hope there is, sonny," replied Sal. He motioned to the attendant and said, "Pick it up and take it up front."

The crate did not weigh very much and wasn't a burden for the boy to carry. The walk back to the front of the hanger seemed to take half as long as the trip into it did.

"Set it down and get a crowbar for me," instructed Sal. It took no time at all for the attendant to retrieve the crowbar and place it into Sal's hand. Sal began to pry the nailed lid from the top of the crate. Before Sal completely removed the lid, he looked at the attendant and said, "Turn around, you don't need to see what's in here." The attendant complied. Sal lifted the lid and began to comb through handfuls of shredded wood moss.

He was expecting to find a significantly larger box inside the crate and was somewhat disappointed when he discovered the container the diamonds were in was no larger than a tin of band-aids. Sal continued to feel through the shredded wood moss hoping to find another container or two. When he came to the realization the container he was holding in his hand was the only one there was, he dropped it in the crate and was livid.

"That prick sent me all the way out here for this shit!" he grumbled. Sal needed to vent his anger and disappointment. He stood up quickly and walked over to the attendant who still had his back to Sal, and grabbed him by his collar, shaking him violently.

"Where's the rest of it!" he shouted.

"The rest of what?" screamed the young man.

"Don't give me that shit, boy! Where is it!"

"I don't have anything else!" pleaded the attendant. As always, Sal never liked any excuse for an answer. He pulled his pistol out from the inside of his coat and pressed the barrel up to the boy's head.

"No! please mister, don't kill me, I didn't do anything!" cried out the boy.

"Shut the fuck up! Where's the rest of the diamonds!" Sal pressed the end of the barrel of his pistol harder against the boy's skull and placed his finger on the trigger.

"Hold it right there, Sal!" shouted Detective Al Mosely, as he pointed his revolver along with four police officers at the head and back of Sal.

"We're going to do this nice and easy, Sal. Release the kid!"

Sal didn't hesitate and released the grip he had on the boy's shirt collar and raised his hands in the air. When he did, the boy sprinted away and ran toward the police. Sal still held his revolver in his right hand, but had it pointed to the sky. "Alright now, Sal, I want you to slowly place your weapon on the floor and step away from it," ordered Mosley. Sal stood motionless as he contemplated his options.

Unfortunately for him, every scenario that ran through his head ended with him dying.

"C'mon now, Sal, you've been doing good so far, don't fuck it up now," stated Mosely. Sal knew the detective was right and slowly lowered his weapon to the floor, then stepped away from it. Two of the police officers advanced cautiously toward Sal with their pistols pointed directly at him as Mosely and the other officers lagged closely behind.

Quickly, Sal was placed in handcuffs. Mosely peered inside the opened crate, only to find the single tin container lying on top of the wood moss. He picked it up and gave it a slight shake. Sal's eyes were fixated on the tin box as Mosely holstered his weapon and proceeded to open it.

"Well look what we have here," commented Mosley as he peeked inside the box before opening his hand and pouring a portion of the contents into his palm.

What Sal witnessed was not what he expected to see. He was not the only one amazed at what lay in the hand of the detective. The assisting police officers were also struck with astonishment.

"Hello there," said Mosley as he stared at six uncut diamonds, each being at least five to six carats. Sal's eyes widened when the light struck the diamonds, projecting a radiant sparkle.

"What is this, Sal?" asked Mosley. Defiantly, Sal answered,

"How should I know? I just came in here to ask for directions."

"This look like a gas station to you, Sal?" asked one of the officers. Sal looked around and replied, "Yes, it does," directing his reply to the officer.

"You want to check the oil and wash my windshield, boy, I'll wait."

The officer didn't appreciate Sal's defiant attitude and looked at Mosley for permission to retaliate against him. Detective Mosley instructed the officer to place Sal in the back seat of his vehicle.

The officer grabbed Sal by his arm and led him to the detective's car. As they walked, Sal made another attempt to secure his freedom,

"Did you see those diamonds?" Sal asked the officer. "You know, there had to be at least a hundred-fifty-thousand-dollars in diamonds there. How would you like to bring home one of those rocks to your wife? It can be nice and easy. No one will get hurt and all you have to do is take me out of these cuffs." The officer opened the door to the back seat of the detective's car, allowing Sal to climb in.

"All I have to do is take the cuffs off?" asked the officer. "And you will give me two of those rocks?" Sal paused just for a moment to think about the offer.

"Yeah, okay, two rocks," agreed Sal. The officer smiled at Sal, then responded,

"Get in the car, dickhead." The officer placed his hand on top of Sal's head gently pushing down until Sal's head reached the height of the roof of the vehicle. The officer forcefully jammed the side of Sal's head into the roof of the car before Sal was completely inside.

"You mother fucker!" shouted Sal.

"Sorry, sir," replied the officer as he closed the door, securing Sal inside.

Detective Mosely instructed the returning officer to call and get a forensic team in to dust for prints and get some pictures. He also instructed the other officers to get a statement from the attendant and inform airport management of the incident.

The detective and one of the officers returned to Mosley's vehicle. The officer climbed into the back seat, as added security in transporting Sal to the station. Mosley started the engine, then looked at Sal in his rearview mirror.

"Are you comfortable, Sal?" he asked.

"Fuck you," responded Sal.

"Alright then, let's get back to the station. I'm sure there will be a lot more people who will want to ask you a bunch more questions."

The trip to the police station was nearly over. There was little to no conversation among the men the entire trip. Not until Mosley decided to get Sal to think about something that would not only anger him, but would also worry him.

"You know, Sal, I wish all the tips I get would pay off like this one did." Sal was very interested in what the detective had to say,

"You were tipped off?" he asked.

"Did I say that?" quipped Mosley. "Oh, sorry, but yes, I was tipped off." Sal quickly realized the detective was toying with him, hoping he would get angry and start saying things he shouldn't.

"Someone must really dislike you, Sal, to let you get pinched like that. It shows me there isn't much love there…what do you think? Am I right?"

"Fuck off, cop, talk to my lawyer."

The more Sal began to think about what the detective had suggested, the more he began to think that there may be some truth to what he was saying. He didn't have to think very long about who would do such a thing. There was only one name he had in mind… Michel Santoro.

Chapter 15

Thomas Califano was about to enjoy a pastrami on rye at his desk in the back of the Bay Street Grocery, when the phone rang. He had just taken a large bite of his sandwich. He motioned to one of his men who was sitting nearby to answer the call.

"Ciao."

"Is Thomas in?"

"Who's calling?"

"It's Sal." Thomas's man held the receiver to his chest and said,

"It's Salvatore."

Thomas had just taken another large bite of his sandwich and motioned for his man to set the receiver on the desk. After washing the sandwich down with a couple of swallows of beer, Thomas picked up the receiver.

"Salvatore, how did it go?"

"I'll tell you how it went…I got pinched. Some rat fuck dropped a dime on me. I'm at the police station now. I need you to get Lenny down here to bail me out."

"I'll give him a call, just sit tight and keep your mouth shut," instructed Thomas.

"You and I need to talk Thomas; I think I know who gave me up."

"I'll see you in a couple hours," replied Thomas. He ended the call and immediately dialed the number of the 'family' attorney, Leonard Klein.

The phone at the law office of Leonard Klein continued to ring without anyone picking up. Thomas Califano was for the most part, a patient man, except when a telephone rings endlessly without being answered. Thomas glanced at the clock on the wall. It was too early for the law office to be closed.

He's probably fucking his secretary again, thought Thomas. Suddenly he heard the receiver frantically being picked up.

"Klein Law Office, may I help you?" Thomas detected the shortness of breath coming from Klein's secretary as she spoke.

"Sherry, Thomas Califano; get off Leonard's lap and put him on the phone."

Sherry covered the receiver with her hand as she continued to ride her boss as he lay back in his leather desk chair with his underwear and trousers down around his ankles. He breathlessly asked, "Who is it?" in between passionate moans. Sherry answered, "It's Thomas Califano."

"Oh, fuck me!" mumbled Leonard.

"I am, baby, I am," whispered Sherry.

"I'm not talking to you!" groaned Leonard. The quickened rhythmic thrusts of Sherry's hips brought Leonard to an explosive orgasm. His audible sounds of pleasure could still be faintly heard through the phone by Thomas.

"Jesus Christ, Lenny! Put your fucking pants on!" shouted Thomas. Sherry clearly heard what Thomas had said.

"I think he's mad," whispered Sherry as she placed the receiver on the desk and climbed off the attorney's lap. Leonard leaned forward and grabbed the clothing covering his ankles and pulled them up as he stood. He fastened his trousers quickly, then picked up the receiver and said,

"Thomas! What a pleasant surprise!"

"Cut the shit Lenny. I need you to go downtown."

"What's going on?"

"Sal got pinched during a heist at the airport."

"What was he stealing?"

"About a hundred-twenty-thousand dollars' worth of uncut diamonds."

"You guys don't do anything small," mumbled Leonard as he scribbled some quick notes down.

"What was that?" asked Thomas.

"Nothing, Thomas, nothing. Did he shoot anyone?"

"I don't think so; I don't know."

"Alright, Thomas, let me get cleaned up a little and I'll head down there."

Thomas chuckled and said, "Good idea, any of those convicts get a whiff of your secretary, they'll be wanting to get a piece of you."

"Yeah right," responded Leonard, knowing what Thomas just said was true.

***

After a long drive from Florida, Michel Santoro parked the car on a street named Abercorne. The sudden quiet of a motionless car woke Giovanni and Angela from a late afternoon nap.

"Where are we?" Giovanni asked.

"We are in Savannah Georgia, son."

"What's in Savannah Georgia?" asked young Angela.

"Food," answered Bonnie as she pointed to a small diner across the street from where they parked. Angela was suddenly all smiles.

"Are you hungry?" asked Bonnie.

"Yes, ma'am," answered Angela and Giovanni.

"Well, let's get something to eat, and watch out for the cars," instructed Bonnie.

The Santoro family crossed the street and entered the diner. As they stepped inside, a woman tending the cash register called out, "Welcome! Seat yourself, please!"

At first glance, Michel saw that most of the tables were occupied, which was a positive sign that the food at this establishment must be good. Michel spotted a table for four being wiped off by a busboy.

"Bonnie, over there, toward the back," Michel said as he pointed to the back of the dining area. Shortly after they were seated, the waitress arrived with menus and glasses of water.

"How are ya'll this evening?" she asked.

"Fine, thank you," responded Bonnie.

"Tonight's special is an open-faced turkey sandwich with gravy, mashed potatoes, and green beans for two dollars." Michel and Bonnie appeared to like the sound of the special, but Angela and Giovanni caught a glimpse of a waitress delivering a plate with a tall hamburger surrounded by golden French fries and accompanied with a chocolate milkshake.

"I want that," said Giovanni as he pointed at what the passing waitress was carrying.

"Me too!" agreed Angela. Michel smiled at the relative ease with which they were able to decide as to what they wanted.

"I believe my wife and I will have the special with lemonade, and two burgers, with fries and two chocolate milkshakes." The waitress finished writing the order on her pad and retrieved the menus.

"Alright, we'll have that for you in just a few minutes."

The noise inside the crowded diner allowed Bonnie to speak to Michel softly and discreetly, in front of their children.

"I just realized where we are," whispered Bonnie. "You're here to see Denny, aren't you?" Michel lifted his glass of water and took a sip. He looked at Bonnie and nodded.

"He lives just around the corner on Gordon Street," confirmed Michel.

"When were you planning on seeing him?"

"While you and the kids have dessert." Bonnie just smiled acknowledging her husband's statement.

The speedy service of the diner was a pleasant surprise. The waitress served everyone their meal and said, "Make sure to save room for dessert!" Bonnie smiled and replied, "I'm sure they will."

The family's main course for dinner was nearing the end. Giovanni broke the silence that fell upon the Santoro's, when he asked his father,

"Is Savannah where we are going to live, Pop?" Michel took his last sip of lemonade and glanced out the large window of the diner that faced the street before answering.

"No, son, it's not what I had in mind."

"So, what did you have in mind? Why are we here?" asked Giovanni. Michel and Bonnie glanced quickly at one another. Bonnie was more than anxious to hear her husband's answers to the questions, as was young Angela.

"Well, son, I thought a small town would be nice to settle in. As far as why we are here, I need to see a friend of mine." Giovanni began to sense his father was purposely being ambiguous and concluded it was because it had to do with his profession.

As far back as he could remember, his father never discussed his business in front of him and saw no reason he would start now. The best thing for Giovanni to do was what he had done his entire life—keep his thoughts and comments to himself and just observe. That formula kept peace in the family and his father's wrath at bay.

The waitress returned to remove a few of the empty plates, but most importantly to see if anyone had saved room for dessert. Without hesitation, Giovanni and Angela ordered vanilla ice cream with chocolate syrup.

The waitress artfully described a warm piece of apple pie and a fresh cup of coffee to Bonnie and Michel. It took no further enticement from the waitress to convince Bonnie that a warm slice of apple pie and a cup of coffee was precisely the best way to top off the inexpensive meal.

Michel respectfully passed on the dessert.

"You should have some dessert with us, honey," suggested Bonnie after the waitress retreated to the kitchen to round-up the sweet treats. Michel leaned closer to Bonnie and spoke softly, but low enough for his wife to hear what he had to say.

"I can't," replied Michel. "I have some business to attend to, he's right around the corner." Michel retrieved his cash from his trouser pocket and laid a twenty-dollar bill in front of Bonnie. "Give this to the waitress when she brings the check. If I'm not back before you're ready to leave, just wait for me in the car. Okay?" Bonnie nodded then squeezed her husband's hand and said,

"Be careful." Michel stood from the table and looked directly at Giovanni as he put on his hat.

"Take care of your mother and sister while I'm away."

"How long will that be, Pop?" asked Giovanni.

"Not long," he replied. "I'll be back in a few minutes. Michel left the table shortly before the waitress arrived with the desserts.

"He didn't stick you with the check, did he?" chuckled the waitress. Bonnie and Giovanni laughed at the comment. Angela totally ignored the remark. Her eyes were fixated on the chocolate covered ice cream.

"No, no, nothing like that. He had to see a friend who lives just around the corner from here," explained Bonnie.

"Alright then, you folks enjoy the dessert," remarked the waitress as she placed the check on the table next to Bonnie and walked away.

Michel left the diner and immediately crossed the street to walk through one of many small parks scattered throughout the historical section of downtown Savannah. He crossed the street once more onto Gordon Street, then proceeded to the end of the block. There, he stood at the red painted gate of the house belonging to his friend, Denny 'The Blade' Burke.

Michel met Burke when Thomas Califano brought Burke by the Bay Street Grocery to meet Michel, shortly after he and Thomas set up shop in the back room of the grocery almost fifteen years ago.

At first, Michel didn't care for Burke. On several occasions Burke would surprise Michel when he came into the store, hiding around dark corners, behind doors, and occasionally in the meat cooler. Being surprised didn't bother Michel at all, he thought it helped sharpen his reflexes. What bothered him the most was when Burke ended their 'Cat and Mouse' game holding Michel at bay with a six-inch retractable blade under his chin, pressed against his throat.

Over the years, Denny Burke earned his keep with the 'Family' as an enforcer. The only difference was Burke never owned a gun and completed all his assignments with a knife. It was said he kept his knives so sharp; his victims never knew they had been cut until they felt their warm blood pouring down the front of their shirts. However, 'The Blade' ran into trouble when he killed a banker in Tampa ten years earlier. At the time, Burke didn't know the banker's brother-in-law was the Deputy DA for Tampa. The incident forced Burke into an early retirement.

He moved quietly to Savannah, where he soon came to be known as Mr. Eugene Simon, an eighth-grade schoolteacher at Oglethorpe Grade School.

In a short time, he had become a very popular teacher among students and parents in the Savannah school system.

As Michel pressed the doorbell at the front gate, he hoped Denny would remember who he was. If he was lucky, he would be able to tell Burke who he was before the retired enforcer slit his throat. There was no response to the doorbell. Rather than ring it again, Michel checked the latch on the gate, it was unlocked. He proceeded into the courtyard and closed the gate behind him. There didn't appear to be any lights on inside, and it didn't stop Michel from knocking on the door. Again, there were no sounds coming from inside.

"Shit!" mumbled Michel. He knocked once more. After waiting for about two minutes, Michel concluded that there was no one home. As he started to turn and step away from the door, a hand was forcefully placed on Michel's forehead, followed by the sharp sting from the pointed end of a knife breaking the skin under his chin.

"No one's home," whispered the deep voice in Michel's ear.

"Good, then no one will hear me when I break in," responded Michel.

"No one will see you leave alive either."

"Looks like we have a good old fashioned 'Mexican Standoff'" quipped Michel.

"Standoff? How so? You have nothing pointed at me?"

"Well then, pay no attention to this," remarked Michel as he lightly tapped the barrel end of his .45 against the man's groin. The man removed the hand he had on Michel's forehead but kept the point of the knife under Michel's chin. and said,

"I thought they put all you guinea bastards away?" the man asked.

"They would have, but all you mick assholes took up all the cells," claimed Michel. The two men laughed as Michel turned around to see the familiar face of his friend. Denny retracted his knife and Michel holstered his handgun. They embraced and patted each other on the shoulders.

"Let's go inside and sit," suggested Denny as he opened the door.

Denny invited Michel to make himself comfortable while he poured each of them a shot of bourbon.

"How did you find me Michel?" inquired Denny.

"It wasn't easy, just had to ask the right people."

"What brings you to Savannah? Vacation?" asked Denny. Michel swiftly tossed down the shot of whiskey before he spoke.

"I set up Sal Carducci to take the fall for a jewel heist." Michel watched Denny's reaction to the news closely. He knew Denny was an old school mobster. Something like this ever happened in the Irish mob; there would be no discussion or debate. They would send someone like Denny to make sure the person who turned on the 'Family' would be dealt with extreme prejudice. Michel prepared himself by opening his jacket and making access to his weapon easier, just in case Denny decided to start throwing daggers at him.

Denny stood up quickly, causing Michel to flinch ever so slightly.

"Relax, Michel," said Denny as he took Michel's glass from him to refill it. "I never liked that prick anyway. Couldn't have happened to a better person." Denny handed the refilled glass back to Michel. Denny held his glass up to toast,

"To Sal, may he rot in prison." The two men tapped their glasses together and drank to the demise of their colleague. "So why are you here in Savannah, Michel?"

"I was hoping you might still have connections to get me and my family new identifications."

"It's been years since I've had to do anything like that, but I think we can do something for you and your family."

"We? You have someone on the payroll?" asked Michel. Denny gave him a sheepish smile, "Payroll? No, just on standby."

"Now what would the Savannah school board say if they knew one of their teachers was a gangster?"

"They would probably be coming to me with their hands out wanting something to keep their mouths shut. Besides, I'm not just, "one of their teachers" I'm their star educator, they love me and would find it hard to believe such nonsense."

Michel couldn't help but laugh, "You certainly have them fooled; good for you," congratulated Michel.

"Give me until later tomorrow, if you can. Here, give me all the important information for everyone." Denny handed Michel a notepad and a pen. "Where is your family anyway?"

"They're probably sitting in the car around the corner. We had dinner at Murry's."

"Why don't you bring them here? I have plenty of room," suggested Denny.

"Thanks, but no. If they decide to look for me here, I don't want my family to be caught up in anything messy." Denny nodded, understanding Michel's point of view. "I'll drive up Abercorne, I'm sure there's a motel somewhere."

Michel stood from his comfortable chair after he finished writing down all the necessary information Denny needed and provided the latest pictures he had of himself and the family.

"I need to get back to my family," he said as he handed Denny the pad of paper. He put on his hat and started his walk toward the door.

"It's good to see you, Michel. Give me until 6 o'clock tomorrow evening, I should have what you'll need." Michel and Denny shook hands.

"Good to see you again, my friend," stated Michel. "By the way, why in the world did you choose to be a teacher?"

"Oh, that's easy, I love kids. It's adults I want to kill. It was very simple; I needed a profession working with people I didn't want to kill." Michel stood for just a moment looking at Denny to see if his comment would be followed by laughter…it wasn't. He was dead serious.

Michel remembered there were times in the past when he thought Denny Burke was more of a psychotic killer than Salvatore Carducci.

"See you tomorrow, Denny, goodnight," bade Michel as he walked out the door.

As Michel approached the family car, still parked across the street from the diner, he noticed everyone looked very relaxed and very bored.

"Sorry I took so long," apologized Michel. Bonnie patted him on the forearm assuring him it was alright.

"Did you see your friend, Pop?" asked Giovanni.

"I did, son. Let's see if we can find a decent motel for the night, what do say?"

The responses throughout the car were a resounding 'yes'!

Chapter 16

After a long grueling afternoon of processing, interrogation, and badgering from police officers, Salvatore Carducci was released on bail around 9:00 p.m. that evening. Attorney Lenny Klein led the way through the hallways of the station with Sal Carducci quietly in tow. As soon as they passed through the exit doors, Sal could no longer hold anything back.

"I'm going to kill that fuckin' rat son-of-a-bitch, you mark my words, Lenny!"

"You need to settle down, Sal," encouraged Lenny. You're lucky you didn't have the diamonds on you. They can't prove you were in the process of stealing them. For all they know, the kid was stealing them. So, all they have on you is an assault charge, and if the DA wants to be a bastard about it, he could roll the dice and try to get an attempted murder charge out of it."

"Do you think he'll try?" asked Sal.

"There's a chance, Sal. You must remember something; you've been on the DA offices' naughty list for nearly a decade. You've been able to skate doing any serious time, thanks to yours truly. However, they caught you holding your .45 against a kid's head. I can't get you off for that, but I can plead down your sentence."

"What do you think you could get me?" asked Sal. Lenny thought a moment as he unlocked his car door.

"If Thomas can get some money to the judge, I could get you five years, and be out in two." The two men climbed into Lenny's car and closed their doors.

"Not good enough, Counselor," remarked Sal. "Tell you what, take me by the store, I want to see what Thomas thinks about all of this."

Leonard Klein pulled to the curb in front of Bay Street Grocery. There were a few cars parked nearby, but the one Sal was looking for was Thomas Califano's, which was spotted on the side of the building near the rear entrance.

Sal and Lenny entered the grocery store. Thomas was sitting at the table playing a game of solitaire, patiently waiting for a word from Lenny. When Thomas saw the two men enter, he set his cards down on the table and walked over to the bar, poured Sal and Lenny a drink, then handed it to them. He returned to his chair, picked his cards up and continued to play. Without looking at either of the men, he asked, "How did it go?"

"I'll tell you how it went," snarled Sal.

"I'm not talking to you!" shouted Thomas. Sal shut up immediately as Lenny spoke.

"The theft charge has been dropped but they charged him for assault. If the DA presses the issue, they could possibly go after Sal for attempted murder. If they do, and if you can get to the judge, he could get five, be out in two." Thomas looked at Sal and asked, "What do you think?"

Sal's response was riddled with anger,

"Five years! Five fucking years! For what? What did I do? I think I should pay the DA a visit and put one in his fuckin' head!"

Thomas sat back in his chair, looked at Lenny and sarcastically stated, "The voice of reason."

A few of the other men sitting in the room chuckled at Thomas' remark, which didn't go unnoticed by Sal.

"What's so fuckin funny!"

"Alright, Sal, calm down. Let Lenny work on the DA, let's not get too far ahead of ourselves. This isn't the first time one of us has gotten pinched."

"Oh yeah, and about that, Thomas, I want…" Thomas raised his hand and motioned Sal to stop talking.

"Everybody, give us a minute," he ordered. Lenny tossed down the rest of his drink and said,

"I gotta go, Thomas, I'll keep you posted." Lenny walked over to Thomas and gave him a respectful kiss on the cheek.

"Thank you, Counselor," said Thomas.

The room had emptied. Sal went to the bar and brought back a bottle of bourbon. He poured each of them a drink and took a seat next to Thomas.

"Do you think Michel set you up?"

Sal nodded.

"I do Thomas, it was too easy for the cops to suddenly just show up. They were tipped off. Have you talked to him today?"

"No. I called his house earlier but there wasn't any answer. I would think he's probably on his way home by now. Orlando's not that far away."

"What if he did set me up, Thomas? What then?" Thomas began to run scenarios through his head, all of which didn't end well for Michel. Thomas was the only one who would make that decision if it came to that. "For right now, let's wait and see what tomorrow brings, then we'll go from there. Capito?" Sal nodded his head and replied, "Capito."

***

The following morning, Thomas Califano rose from a restless night's sleep. He was deeply troubled thinking about what his friend Michel may have done to one of his captains. This was a very serious situation, and he needed to get to the bottom of it as soon as possible. No matter how much he wanted to believe Michel did nothing wrong, there had to be a reasonable explanation of how the police were tipped off about the diamond heist. It came down to two possible people, the young attendant at the airport or Michel.

Thomas wanted to eliminate any suspicion of Michel as soon as possible. He poured himself a cup of coffee, took a few sips, then dialed Michel's home number. There was no answer. Thomas looked at the wall clock and saw it was almost 7:30 a.m.

Plenty of time had passed for Michel to have returned from Orlando. Once again, Thomas wanted to believe something else was keeping Michel from not returning home. Car accident, staying with friends, something seriously wrong with Bonnie, he thought to himself. He refused to think one of his closest friends was a rat. It was becoming to be a distinct possibility the latter were true.

Thomas decided to give his friend until noon to either call or answer his phone. Until then, he would not entertain a single thought of what he would have to do if Michel were guilty.

***

The Santoro family did the best they could to act like tourists strolling the streets of Savannah and taking in the historical sites. It wasn't enough to keep Michel's mind occupied even though the other members of the family thought he was enjoying himself. All he could think about was getting out of Savannah as soon as possible and beginning a new life, far away from what he left behind in Tampa. He couldn't decide where exactly he wanted to take his family. All he knew was that it had to be a small town in 'Nowhere USA'. He was hoping Denny would have a few suggestions.

***

Thomas agonizingly watched the hands on the wall clock strike twelve noon. He didn't hear from Michel and proceeded to make the call to his friend's house. With every ring, Thomas' anger grew. The call was never answered. He hung up the phone as his heart sank deep into his stomach. He had concluded Michel had betrayed him and the 'Family'. He was now faced with the decision as to what to do about it. He didn't have to have a sit down with anyone or get permission. He was a 'Boss'; it was his call. In order to keep the peace in the Family, but more importantly, administer justice for his Capo, Thomas had to give the order for Michel to be "taken care of." But he was not ready or willing to give such an order, at least not yet.

***

It was 5:55 p.m. when the Santoro family sat on the park bench just a block away from Denny Burke's home. They were enjoying the ice cream cones they had purchased from a street vender. Michel finished his quickly. He was to be at Burke's home in five minutes. He wiped his hands and mouth with a napkin and tossed it into a nearby trashcan.

"You going to be alright here?" he asked Bonnie. She nodded and replied,

"We'll be fine, hurry back."

"Can I go with you, Pop?" asked Giovanni. Bonnie stopped eating her cone and quickly chimed in,

"Absolutely not."

Giovanni did not let his mother's objection keep him from asking his father again,

"Can I go, Pop? Please?" Bonnie's stare began to burn into the side of Michel's head. He knew better than to look at her, because he knew he would see the disapproving look on her face.

"I don't see what it will hurt, sure, son, c'mon, let's go." Giovanni sprung from the bench and stood next to his father.

"Can I go too, Daddy?" asked Angela. This time Michel looked at his wife, but this time, the look on her face was an emphatic "No".

"Sorry, not this time, honey. Maybe next time, okay?" Even though she was disappointed, Angela replied,

"Okay, Daddy, next time." Michel gave Bonnie a kiss on the cheek and said, "We'll be back shortly."

"Be careful," she muttered.

Michel and Giovanni entered through the front gate and knocked on Burke's door.

"There's only one thing I need you to do once we are inside, speak only when spoken to…understand?" instructed Michel.

"Yes, sir," said Giovanni with his voice crackling a little bit. Michel sensed that his son may have been a little nervous.

"Relax, son, you have nothing to fear here."

"Yes, sir."

Denny Burke opened the door and immediately noticed Michel was not alone. His instincts told him it was his friend's son, or Michel had started recruiting his help at a younger age.

"Michel, please, come in." The two stepped inside as Burke closed the door behind them. "So, who do we have here?" he asked.

"This is my son, Giovanni; this is Mr. Burke." Giovanni extended his hand.

"What's with this Mr. Burke bullshit, call me Denny."

"You can call me John," said Giovanni. The two shook hands and suddenly the nervousness Giovanni was experiencing had left. Burke had a way of making strangers in his home feel welcomed.

"Your timing is impeccable, Michel; I had just put everything you need together and it's all right here." Burke picked up a manila envelope from the coffee table and handed it to Michel.

"May I?" asked Michel, indicating he wanted to look at what he was paying for.

"Of course! Please do. Here, have a seat. Burke ushered Michel to sit at a small table in the corner. Michel reached into the deep envelope and removed a stack of papers then placed them on the table. On top were two driver's licenses, one each for Bonnie and Michel and a paper with the new names of the Santoro family. Michel read each one to himself then handed the paper to Giovanni, it read…

Surname: Davis

Father: Carl

Mother: Rita

Son: Steven

Daughter: Angela

"How come Angela has the same name?" asked Giovanni. This was something Michel had anticipated,

"Remember what I told you before we came here?" sternly looking at Giovanni.

"Sorry, Pop, yes I do," answered Giovanni as he lowered his head in embarrassment.

"To answer your question, your sister may be too young to handle a completely different name. To make it easier for her, she will just need to remember her last name," explained Michel. "Do you understand?" Giovanni nodded silently. "You can speak son."

"Yes, I understand sir."

Michel reviewed the rest of the documents, finding all of them in order. He placed all of them back into the envelope. He stood from the table and reached into his front pocket and pulled out a folded stack of cash.

"What do I owe you Denny?" he asked.

"Your life," answered Burke with a straight face. Michel knew his friend was joking and couldn't help glance at his son to see his reaction to Burke's answer. Giovanni's eyes opened widely, and his mouth opened in disbelief. Both Denny and Michel burst out laughing at the expense of the young Santoro. Once Giovanni realized he was the target of the dark humor and joined in the laughter despite being red faced with embarrassment.

"But seriously Michel, I need $500 for everything," declared Burke. Michel peeled off five one-hundred-dollar bills and handed them to Burke.

"I have one more thing I need to ask you, Denny. Do you have knowledge of any small town that we may be able to settle in? Let's say somewhere between here and Atlanta?" Burke walked over to the coffee table and picked up a folded roadmap.

"I had a feeling you might be wanting something of the sort." He handed it to Michel.

"I marked the route for you, I think it will be perfect."

Michel looked at the outside of the folded map. It read…Sandersville, Georgia. "It's not far, three hours or so."

"Thank you, Denny," responded Michel. "I think we need to get going, my friend," said Michel. "We left Bonnie and Angela in the park."

"Who?" asked Denny. Michel paused a moment then replied, "Rita and Angela, I meant to say."

Burke escorted them to the door and shook each of their hands.

"Excuse me, Giovanni, I'd like to have a word with your father." Giovanni looked at his father for assurance that he would be alright.

"It's okay, son, wait for me out by the street, I'll be there shortly."

"Okay, Pop, nice meeting you, Denny."

"Nice meeting you, Giovanni, try to keep your old man in line," said Burke. Giovanni smiled and replied,

"Yes sir, I will."

Although Giovanni had left and was on the outside of the gate, Burke lowered his voice and said, "I almost forgot to tell you, word around the campfire is, they are looking for you in Tampa.

"Is that right?" said Michel trying to act surprised. "They won't find me there now, will they?"

"It won't be long before they come here and start snooping around," stated Burke.

"I know, sorry for bringing this to your door, Denny."

"Don't worry about it, it's the least I can do. Besides, I didn't like Sal very much either."

"You take care of yourself and your family, Michel. One day you can come back and tell me all about Sandersville." Burke patted Michel on the back and sent him on his way.

Michel and Giovanni returned to find Bonnie and Angela patiently waiting on the bench. Bonnie greeted Michel with a kiss and asked,

"Is everything alright?"

Michel nodded and said, "Why don't we stay here one more night and leave first thing in the morning?"

"I think that is an excellent idea, honey. Can we stay where we did last night?"

"Absolutely," confirmed Michel. "Besides, we have a lot to talk about before we go to sleep tonight." The comment peaked Bonnie's interest as she playfully snuggled up to her husband and asked, "You going to tell me all your dirty little secrets Mr. Santoro?"

Michel smiled and replied, "By morning, they will be your secrets too."

Chapter 17

The word was out about Sal's arrest. It had been left unsaid, but Thomas Califano expected to see more men at the Bay Street Grocery this morning. He wasn't disappointed when he entered the store.

Thomas entered through the front door and walked directly toward the back room, passing a few of his men drinking coffee and talking to the store owner, Georgy Kharkov.

"Finish your coffee boys, we have a meeting in five minutes," instructed Thomas. It took less then fifteen seconds, for the men to finish their morning brew and follow Thomas to the back room.

As Thomas entered the back office, one of his soldiers called out, "Alright, ladies, put the fuckin' cigarettes out and gather round."

Thomas made his way through the gathering of men to his desk and took his seat. A fresh cup of coffee was placed in front of him. He took a sip while he looked around the room to see who was in attendance.

"Let me start by thanking everyone who made it here this morning. In case you're wondering, Salvatore is fine. I gave him the day off, that's why you don't see him here this morning. We may have a problem. As all of you probably know by now, Sal got pinched yesterday and it appears the cops were tipped off. It's still too soon to say who the rat was, but all indications are pointing to Michel Santoro. Unfortunately, I can't talk to Michel about it, because no one knows where he is. In the meantime, I need all of you to find out what you can of his whereabouts. After this meeting, I intend to see what I can find at his house. Any questions?"

"What do we do if we find him?" asked one of the gang members.

"I don't want anyone to hurt him, I just want to ask him a few questions. Call me if you find him. Thanks for coming, now go to work."

After the room cleared, Thomas rose from his chair and called one of his soldiers over to have a word,

"Franky, has anyone been by Michel's house yet?"

"No, I don't think so." Thomas nodded and placed his hand on Franky's shoulder.

"I want you to stay by the phone until I get back. I'm going to go to Michel's house and have a look around."

"Alright boss, no problem," agreed Franky.

During the entire drive to Michel's house, Thomas ran scenario after scenario of what he should say and do when he saw Michel again. He was so preoccupied with how everything appeared for his old friend, that he ran two stop signs, and nearly rear-ended another vehicle. To say he was upset would be an understatement.

Thomas parked on the street about half a block away from Michel's house and turned off the engine. He wanted to see if there was any activity whatsoever at the Santoro residence, and to wait for the street to be relatively clear of cars and pedestrians. After about ten minutes, Thomas left his vehicle and casually walked to the front door of Michel's house. He noticed the drapes were closed in all the windows and there were two days' worth of newspapers lying on top of the steps. He didn't feel it was necessary to knock. He opened the screen door, and within a matter of seconds he had picked the lock on the door handle and opened the door. Because of the lack of sunlight coming through the windows, it took Thomas' eyes a few seconds to adjust to the darkness.

Everything appeared to be in order as he slowly walked through the house. There was no indication that Michel and his family abandoned their home. There were clothes still hanging in the closets, food was still in the refrigerator, and cherished family photos remained hanging on the wall.

For a moment, Thomas felt at ease. He wanted to believe Michel was still somewhere between Orlando and Tampa. He made his way back to the living room and sat on the couch. At this point, he didn't know what to think. His only hope was that Michel, and his family were safe.

Feeling satisfied from what he saw, Thomas stood and began to make his way toward the front door. He had his hand on the doorknob, then suddenly stopped. There was one thing he hadn't checked—Michel's stash of weapons he had strategically placed throughout the house. It was something Thomas encouraged him to do. In fact, Thomas assisted in the placement of the weapons.

Thomas turned slowly, looking back toward the interior of the house. The first place he looked was in the coat closet near the front door.

There should be a .45 on the shelf, he thought to himself. He felt underneath small items of clothing and found no weapon. He went to Michel's bedroom and looked in both nightstands, and the closet, there were no weapons. He continued his search in both bathrooms and the kitchen, there were no weapons to be found. The last place he needed to check was the garage. Thomas searched every possible hiding place in the garage and found a box of .22 caliber bullets. To his disappointment, there were no weapons. He made his way back into the kitchen and sat at the table. It was becoming clearer to him each passing minute; Michel was on the run.

***

The Santoro family were about an hour from the Sandersville city limits. They decided to stop at a gas station that advertised iced cold drinks. The Georgia heat and humidity along with a near empty gas tank prompted Michel to stop and take a break from driving.

As he pulled into the station, he noticed it had a telephone booth on the outside of the building. The family exited the vehicle and headed inside the building. An attendant met Michel at the back of the car and asked,

"Fill it up sir?"

"Yes, and could you get the windshield please?" Michel asked.

"Yes sir."

"Does the phone work?" asked Michel pointing to the booth.

"Yes sir, at least it did yesterday," replied the attendant. Michel made his way to the booth while digging for the correct change in his pocket to make a call.

He inserted the correct amount and dialed the number to the store in hopes he would find Thomas there.

Thomas' soldier, Franky, who he assigned to standby the phone while he was out, was extremely bored until suddenly, the phone rang.

"Yeah," was all he said when answering. Michel was not familiar with the voice of the person who answered and hesitated before saying anything.

"I need to talk to Thomas," responded Michel.

"Who is this?" asked Franky.

"Never mind who the fuck this is, put Thomas on the phone!"

Franky never had a problem taking and following orders, but taking orders from a stranger over the phone was something that did not sit well with him.

"He's not here, asshole," Franky replied gruffly. Revealing his identity was not in Michel's plans, but his options were limited if he wanted to speak to Thomas.

"This is Michel, I need to speak to Thomas," he demanded. Franky immediately sat up in his chair.

"Michel, Thomas is looking for you, where are you?"

"Never mind that, where is he?"

"He said he was going to your house." Franky glanced at the clock, then continued, "He should be there by now." Michel ended the call then dialed the operator and placed a call to his house.

Thomas stood from the table and returned the chair to its proper position. As he turned to exit the house from the kitchen door, the phone rang. Thomas stopped and decided to answer it.

"Hello," he greeted then remained silent, all the while hoping this call would help him find his friend, Michel.

"Thomas?" The voice sounded familiar, but he wasn't quite sure, prompting him not to respond right away.

"Thomas, it's Michel." With mixed emotions, Thomas responded, "Mikey, are you alright?"

"I'm fine."

"And the family?"

"Everyone's fine, Thomas."

"Where are you Mikey? We need to talk, today!" he demanded.

"Unless I go in and get a pocket full of change, which I have no intention of doing, I will make this call short and sweet."

"Alright, go ahead, I'm listening," responded Thomas.

"I'm assuming you are at my house because you want to talk to me about Sal, and to see if I've left town."

"You're correct on both accounts, Mikey," remarked Thomas.

"Yes, I arranged for Sal to get pinched," confessed Michel. "I wasn't going to let that piece of shit bleed me dry from something I created and worked hard for. Then, to appoint him to be my boss was a slap in the face, Thomas. I didn't expect that from you, especially when you knew

I was the better pick for the position." The more Michel talked about it, the angrier he became.

"I'm sorry Mikey, I…"

"Don't call me that, Thomas, not anymore!" ordered Michel. "I wanted to let you know I have left Tampa and I am now declaring my retirement. I want nothing more to do with you or the 'Family'."

"So, you think you can just walk away and live happily ever after?" asked Thomas. "You will have to pay for what you did," he added. Michel wasn't quite sure what Thomas meant by "pay".

"How much?"

"How much what?"

"How much do I have to pay?" Michel heard Thomas snicker.

"At this point, I have no idea," admitted Thomas. "There will be a sit down to discuss what happened of course, but as far as your punishment, it's too early to say. It will all depend on what happens to Sal."

"You going to give me a pass, Thomas?" Michel asked his long-time friend. The dead silence on Thomas' end of the line was all Michel needed to hear. "I thought so," said Michel, then promptly hung up the phone. Thomas put the phone down and whispered,

"God be with you, Mikey."

Michel turned to open the door to the booth and found Giovanni patently waiting on the other side.

"What is it, son?"

"I was hoping you would let me make a quick call before we get back on the road," suggested Giovanni.

"Who do you want to call?"

"I just wanted to call Rebecca and say hi."

"I don't know son; we should be getting on our way." Giovanni's head lowered in disappointment, but Michel recalled the days when he was young and how he missed talking to Bonnie when he was away.

"Alright, here's some change." Michel gave his son what change he had left then asked, "You know how to make a long-distance call?" Giovanni shook his head. "Here, let me show you." Michel took the change from his son and placed it on the small corner shelf located just underneath the pay phone. Michel walked Giovanni through the process then started to close the door to the booth and said,

"You have two minutes once Rebecca answers, you'll have to put more money in to talk longer, but what you have left won't buy you much more time." The phone at Rebecca's house began to ring and Giovanni quickly grabbed the handle to the booth door and started to close it, barely allowing his father to get his foot out of the way. To Giovanni's delight, Rebecca answered the phone.

"Rebecca, this is John."

She had been caught off guard. She preferred him to use his real name, Giovanni. She was not fond of the name 'John.' Her silence indicated she was not sure who she was speaking to.

"It's Giovanni."

As Michel walked to the car, he realized he had forgotten to remind his son not to reveal where they were. He stopped and turned around to face the phone booth. He then decided to have faith in his son and hoped he would use discretion when he talked to Rebecca and continued his journey back to the car.

"Where are you?" asked Rebecca.

"We are in Georgia," replied Giovanni. "Listen, I don't have much time to talk. I just wanted to tell you that I miss you, and to let you know, I will be back for you. Please tell Dante hello for me."

"I will Giovanni, I miss you too." Not having any experience of a timed phone call, Giovanni had said all he wanted to say believing the call would end abruptly at any moment, when in fact, he still had another minute.

"I love you Rebecca, I hope you remember that." To Giovanni's surprise, Rebecca responded by saying, "I love you too." With the sound of those words, Giovanni's heart leapt with joy. He knew no matter how far away he was, he would one day return and claim Rebecca as his wife.

"I have to go; I will call again soon! Bye!"

"Goodbye, Giovanni," responded Rebecca. The call ended. Giovanni scraped up the change that remained on the shelf and put it in his pocket. He returned to the car smiling from ear to ear. Bonnie and Michel couldn't help but notice the gleam in their son's eyes.

"I take it the call went well?" asked Bonnie.

"And then some," assured Giovanni.

***

Thomas returned to the store. When he entered the backroom meeting area, there were still a couple of soldiers besides Franky still hanging around in the event Thomas needed them for anything. Franky rose from the chair usually reserved for Thomas, but Thomas motioned for him to remain seated. Those in the room kept silent and waited for their boss to start talking about Michel. He didn't and he wouldn't, at least not to them. His next discussion about Michel would be with someone further up on the food chain.

"Any calls Franky?" Thomas asked.

"Michel called, Boss, he…"

"Anyone else?" Thomas asked, cutting Franky off in mid-sentence.

"Yeah, Don Barzetti, he wants to meet with you tomorrow at the Palms Hotel in Fort Myers at noon tomorrow." Thomas walked over behind the bar and poured himself a shot of whiskey. He tossed it down hitting the back of his throat and mumbled,

"Now it begins."

Chapter 18

The Santoro's, now known as the Davis family, entered the Sandersville city limits. At first glance, there didn't seem to be anything special about the town. It appeared to be just like many other small towns in the southeastern United States.

There were several family-owned businesses and a few chain stores like Piggly Wiggly. Since there was very little vehicle traffic and the occasional farmers horse-drawn wagon, Michel was able to drive through town very slowly to see what it had to offer.

Bonnie and Giovanni were the first to spot a café.

"Honey, why don't we stop here and have some dinner?" suggested Bonnie.

"Yeah, Pop, I'm starving," urged Giovanni.

"I'm a bit hungry myself," added Michel. He pulled over and parked diagonally against the curb. "Angie, you hungry, honey?" he asked as he turned to look into the back seat.

"She's sound asleep, Pop," commented Giovanni. Michel reached back and placed his hand on her knee and lightly nudged her leg. Her eyes opened immediately as her gaze was directed at her brother, thinking he was the one who interrupted her peaceful slumber.

"Leave me alone, John," she grumbled. Michel quickly made sure his daughter knew who woke her.

"It was me, honey, we're here. Are you hungry?" Angela sat up and looked out her window and saw the café.

"Yes, Daddy, I'm hungry, and I have to go to the bathroom!"

"We best get on with it then," commented Michel.

***

Since school had let out for the summer, and being part of this year's graduating class, Rebecca Stone decided to celebrate the anticipated freedom with her girlfriends at the nearby Malt Shoppe.

She was casually walking on the sidewalk about two blocks away from reaching her house, when Dante spotted her. He had been getting a little driving practice without his parents' consent to use the car. He tapped the horn as he pulled up next to the curb where Rebecca was walking. At first, she had no idea who was in the car, until Dante shouted, "Headed my way, beautiful?"

She bent down to see who was at the wheel. A smile streaked across her face as she responded, "Not with a creep like you!"

The two began to laugh.

"Give you a ride home?" asked Dante. Rebecca walked over to the car and peered inside through the open window on the passenger's side and said, "You're a little late, my house is right there." Pointing to the house just three houses away.

"Thought I would ask," replied Dante.

"What are you doing driving? You don't even have your learner's permit, do you?"

"No, that's why I need to get the car home before my dad gets home. By the way, have you seen or heard from Giovanni?" he asked.

"Oh yeah, I talked to him yesterday, he told me to tell you hi."

"So, he's doing alright?"

"I guess so," responded Rebecca. "He said they were in Georgia."

"Is that where he moved to?"

"I don't know, he didn't say." Dante looked straight ahead through his windshield and wondered why Giovanni didn't call him.

"Alright, I need to get this car home. The next time you talk to him, tell him I think he's an asshole for not calling me." Rebecca chuckled, then said, "Okay, I will. Talk to you later."

"Bye, Becky!" shouted Dante. Then, as all teenagers do when they are not driving with their parents, he floored the accelerator and squealed the tires as he sped away.

***

"Will there be anything else for anyone?" asked the waitress when she returned to pick up payment for the family's dinner.

"No, that will be all thank you," replied Michel. The waitress smiled and picked up the money along with the bill. She saw there was a twenty-dollar bill and a five.

"I'll be back with your change."

"No, that's fine," informed Michel. The waitress was surprised to receive such a generous tip.

"Well thank you very much!" exclaimed the waitress.

"Before you go, could you refer us to a nearby motel? We just got into town and aren't very familiar with the area."

"Why, sure, hon," responded the waitress. "If you keep driving north through town, you'll see the Starlight Inn on the right just outside of town."

"The Starlight, sounds pleasant," remarked Bonnie.

"It should be my brother owns it. He runs a tight ship over there. You won't find any hanky-panky or rough housing around there. He was a platoon Sergeant in the war and doesn't take crap from anyone. Tell him Mary sent you."

"That sounds wonderful, Mary, thank you very much," said Michel.

"Are ya'll here to stay?"

Michel hesitated before answering. He wanted to introduce his family but suddenly realized he didn't remember everyone's new name. However, he did remember their new last name.

"We are the Davis family and I'm sure we will be seeing you often, Mary."

"I'm sure you will," responded Mary. Everyone stood from the table and casually made their way to the exit door.

As all of them walked to the car, Giovanni began to reflect on what he had just observed. His father lied to a total stranger and didn't miss a beat. His conversation with the waitress was convincing, and delivered in a way that there was no reason for anyone to suspect anything.

He asked himself, is this what I will have to do the rest of my life, lie to everybody? Without any further deliberation, he reached a decision right then… No way in hell am I going to live a lie my entire life.

The seed of determination had been planted. Giovanni would not be living this way for very long. He would be turning eighteen years old in a couple of months, and when he did, he would be leaving his family to begin his own life. Hopefully, with Rebecca.

***

Dante Carducci's father, Sal, finally returned home after being away for nearly two days. Sal had informed his wife of his short stay at the police precinct after being arrested for assault.

The two of them never disclosed information concerning Sal's wrongdoings to Dante. Keeping secrets was becoming more difficult as Dante grew older, especially when Sal was missing without any word.

Sal entered his home through the front door causing Dante to emerge from the kitchen, where he was pouring himself a tall glass of sweet, iced tea.

"Hey Dad! Where have you been?" asked Dante. Sal made his way to his favorite lounge chair in the living room and sat down, ignoring his son's question. Curious for an answer to his question, Dante joined his father in the living room and sat next to him in his mother's recliner. Once again, he asked, "Where have you been Dad?"

Sal knew his son would be relentless in finding out where he had been if he felt he was being lied to. His answer must be very convincing to avoid his son's interrogation.

"I've been in jail, son," was Sal's answer. Dante knew very little of his father's business. What he did know was that his father was not your normal nine-to-five working stiff and was sure at times he probably bent the rules of law.

To be arrested was not what Dante wanted to hear about his father. It was nothing to be proud of. Fearful to hear what he was arrested for, Dante struggled to ask his father that very question,

"What were you arrested for, Dad?"

"You might read things in the paper, or maybe even see a story about me on the news, but the fact of the matter is, I was arrested for fighting," responded Sal. Dante looked closely at his father's face and saw no evidence of him being in a fist fight.

"You must have gotten the best of him Dad, I don't see a scratch on you."

"Yes, I did, son, he never connected once." Within a matter of seconds, Dante went from a concerned son that assumed his father had done something so terrible he had to go to jail, to someone who was proud to see that his father knew how to take care of himself.

"Will there be a trial?" asked Dante.

"Trial? C'mon son, they don't have trials for fighting. The worst possible thing they will do to me, is put me in jail a couple of weeks, then life will be back to normal."

Dante wanted to believe what his father had told him was the truth, but there was a small sliver of doubt that crept into his heart. He decided to let it go for the time being but planned to investigate on his own to find the truth.

"Well, glad to have you home, Dad." Dante left his father and went upstairs to his room while Sal remained in his lounge chair contemplating when and how he would make his move on the person he believed put him in this situation, Michel Santoro. Suddenly, Sal's wife, Linda, came rushing into the room smiling from ear to ear.

"Hi, honey! I'm so glad you're home," exclaimed Linda. She leapt onto his lap and gave him a hug and kiss.

"Are you hungry?" she asked.

"No, I'm fine. I just want to relax for a little while and think." Linda slid off Sal's lap and held one of his hands between both of hers.

"So, tell me, how bad is it?" she asked, not really wanting to hear anything that would make her cry. Sal took a deep breath and said, "Well, Thomas has the Jew on it…"

"The Jew?"

"Yeah, the Jew; the lawyer, Lenny Klein."

Linda hated it when Sal would snap at her because she didn't remember the names of his associates. She committed very few to memory. She believed the less she knew, the safer she would be. She acted like she recalled the name to avoid aggravating her husband any further.

"Of course, the Jew, sorry, I remember now," even though she didn't. "So, when will you hear anything?" inquired Linda.

"If everything goes smoothly, all of this should be behind us in a couple of days."

Linda patted the back of her husband's hand and gave him a comforting smile.

"I'm going up to take a bath, and from the smell of you, you need to join me," coaxed Linda. The thought of climbing in a hot bath with his wife appealed to Sal. He didn't have to give it much thought and when he lifted his arm to smell his armpit, there was no further persuading necessary. He stood from his lounge chair and said,

"Lead the way."

Chapter 19

ichel and Bonnie rose early from a good night's sleep. Michel showered and proceeded to shave. While doing so, he realized his family needed to start using their new names. There wasn't a better time than the present to have everyone begin using their new aliases, so he started with his wife, Bonnie.

"Rita! Would you please get me another hand towel?" As he suspected, there was no response. "Rita!" Suddenly, the bathroom door opened with Bonnie poking her head inside.

"Who are you talking to?" she asked.

"I'm talking to you, Rita," answered Michel. Bonnie stood there for a moment, then realized what her husband was doing.

"Oh, that's right, I'm Rita," she mumbled. "What was it you wanted?"

"Nothing. But I do need you to work with the children today and get them used to using their new names," instructed Michel. Bonnie nodded in agreement then remarked, "I guess I'll start when I go to wake them up. What are your plans today?" she asked her husband. Michel finished shaving and combed his hair.

"I was going to take a walk-through town to see if I can find work and a place for us to live. I was thinking you and the kids could stay here and enjoy the swimming pool they have in the courtyard." Bonnie's eyes widened as she replied, "Yes! I saw that when we came in last night. It looked nice. There was a little coffee shop just a short walk toward town from here. Why don't I wake the kids and we can all take a walk to have breakfast?" Michel finished getting ready and gave his wife a kiss on the forehead as he passed through the bathroom doorway and went directly for his suitcase. He pulled out a fresh change of clothes and started to get dressed.

"Sorry, honey; I'll let you take the kids for breakfast, I have to get into town." Michel finished dressing, which by the way was in casual attire. The last thing he wanted to look like in this small town was a gangster. He walked to the nightstand, picked up his .38 caliber revolver and tucked it inside the front of his waistband, covered by his untucked shirt. He then grabbed his watch and put it on, then walked up to Bonnie and wrapped his arms around her, giving her a passionate hug.

"Have fun today, and take it easy," he said. Bonnie returned the warm embrace and said, "Those are instructions I will not have a problem following my dear."

"I'll be back as soon as I can," assured Michel. He gave Bonnie a kiss then left.

Bonnie went next door to where the children were staying. She heard no activity coming from the kid's room and assumed they were still sleeping. She knocked on their door and waited for one of them to open it. No one came to the door, so she knocked again. There was still no answer. There were no housekeepers around to let her into the room, so she decided to take another approach. She went back to her room, picked up the telephone and dialed the kids room number. Once it began to ring, she set the receiver down and walked next door a second time.

The ringing telephone could be clearly heard by Bonnie as she patiently waited to hear one of her kids answer the phone. It kept ringing. Bonnie was no longer annoyed that her children didn't answer the phone, she began to imagine something terrible had happened to her babies.

She started to imagine they had been killed by those who were looking for her husband. Panic began to set in. She needed to get into their room but didn't want to bring any attention to the family. She started to look around for the housekeeper but saw no evidence they had begun to clean the rooms. Her last option was to go to the check-in desk and ask the attendant to let her in.

Bonnie politely asked the attendant at the front desk to give her a key to the kid's room, so she could wake them and get them ready for the day. A little trick Bonnie learned from her husband when asking anyone for a favor, was to entice them with cash. When she placed a crisp new twenty-dollar bill in front of the attendant, there were no questions and Bonnie was given a key to the kids' room. She returned to their room, slipped the key into the lock, and opened the door.

The door swung open allowing enough light into the room for her to see her children still snuggled in their beds. The telephone was still ringing. Bonnie couldn't believe her kids were still sleeping, despite all the noise.

"Steven! Angela! Wake up!" shouted Bonnie. Giovanni stirred and responded,

"There's no Steven here, lady, you got the wrong room!"

"Giovanni! Angela! Get your butts out of bed," ordered Bonnie. The two quickly sat up and looked at their mother. Bonnie entered the room and immediately walked directly over to the phone which was located on the nightstand between their two beds. She picked up the receiver and set it back down, ending the call.

"Did you two not hear the phone ringing?" Giovanni and Angela looked at one another and shook their heads.

"Unbelievable," mumbled Bonnie. Bonnie turned her back to the kids and made her way to the entrance door, Giovanni began to slide back down under the covers. "Don't you even think about going back to sleep, Giovanni; you two have an hour to get ready for breakfast." Bonnie walked back to the check-in desk to return the key, then returned to her room and started to get ready herself.

***

Michel drove himself into downtown Sandersville and parked his car along the main road running through the small town. He walked slowly on the sidewalk taking in what this small Georgia town had to offer. It appeared Sandersville was big enough to have everything his family would need, and small enough for no one to know it was there. The most important thing he needed right away was a job, but he was not seeing any 'Help Wanted' signs.

However, there was one sign that piqued his interest, a 'For Sale' sign in the window of a hardware store. He tried to open the front door of the store, only to find the door locked and a 'Closed' sign hanging on the inside of the door. Michel peered inside through the glass and noticed the store was still completely stocked. He stepped back to see if there were any telephone numbers posted anywhere but couldn't see any.

One thing he did notice, was an elderly black man dressed in denim overalls sitting in the shade at the far end of the front of the building, whittling a piece of wood. Michel approached the man and said,

"Morning, Pops," greeted Michel. The old man looked up at Michel and replied, "Good morning to you young fella, how are you today?"

Michel sat down next to the man on the concrete window ledge of the hardware store.

"I'm fine, thanks. Tell me, how long have you lived here in Sandersville?" The old man stopped witling for a moment to calculate how many years it had been.

"Oh, I would say better than fifty years when me and Ma settled here. It sure has grown since then that's for sure." Michel realized he hadn't introduced himself. He held out his hand to the old man and said,

"My name is Mic...,"

He suddenly stopped speaking and realized he was about to use his real name. "Carl Davis." The old man placed his knife in his left hand and firmly shook Michel's hand.

"Nice to meet you, Carl. You sure that's your name? You looked like you forgot it."

The long-time resident of the small town didn't miss much when it came to strangers. Michel knew he needed to be extra cautious when speaking to this gentleman. He could sense his attention to detail. It didn't matter how old he was, this guy was sharp.

"I'm Grady Booker," said the old man. Michel immediately recognized this man's name was the same as what was on the hardware store sign.

"Is this your store Grady?" asked Michel.

"Can't get much by you can I, young fella?" chuckled Grady.

"That's why my wife urges me to run for President," joked Michel. The two men laughed.

It had been quite some time that Michel had a good laugh. Meeting Grady was what he needed. It would make the transition to a new town much easier.

"Why are you selling the store?" inquired Michel.

"It's time," answered Grady. "When my two boys died in the war, Ma sort of lost her will to live. The store made for a great distraction, it kept her mind off the boys and kept her busy, until last winter when she got pneumonia. It was too much for her and she died. So, there was no one to inherit it, so, I decided to sell it move back to the state I was born in, Alabama."

"I'm sorry to hear that about your family, Grady."

"Thank you, Carl, it'll be alright." Unexpectedly, Grady was struck with an idea, "Why don't you buy my store Carl?" Michel shook his head and begun to laugh,

"I couldn't run a hardware store, I wouldn't know the first thing about it," he confessed.

"You know what the business end of a shovel is, young fella?" asked Grady. Michel looked at Grady waiting for the question to be followed up with a joke. The joke never materialized. He could see on the old man's face he was dead serious, so he answered.

"Of course, I do Grady."

"Then you can run a hardware store, my friend." Michel considered the suggestion, but his priority was to find a place to live.

"Let me think about it Grady, I need to find a place to live for me and my family first before I go buy a store."

"How big is your family?"

"There are four of us, wife and two kids."

"Perfect," responded Grady. "Above the store is a furnished three bedroom, two bath apartment." Michel eyes lit up like a Christmas tree. It was beginning to look as if he would be able to kill two birds with one stone.

"I'm interested Grady, what are you asking for everything, apartment, store and inventory?" The old man continued to whittle as he worked up a dollar amount in his head. He then looked Michel in the eye and held out his hand as if he were ready to seal the deal with a handshake,

"I'll take $75,000 for everything." Michel responded in kind by extending his hand as well as he countered the offer,

"$57,000 as is, sight unseen." Grady's hand remained extended, but he dismissed Michel's counteroffer with a shake of his head and replied,

"$60,000, and I'll teach you how to run the cash register." Michel kept his hand extended as well and asked,

"Will I be using that cash register very often?"

"This store has been here for forty years, young fella, that should answer that question." Michel knew the old fox had him cornered. It didn't matter, he enjoyed the negotiation.

"Alright old timer, it's a deal. Cash alright?" Michel asked.

"Sure, it is, Carl, as long as it's not "funny money". Michel was taken aback momentarily by the comment but proceeded by shaking Grady's hand to seal the deal.

"You've seen a lot of this "funny money" around here much Grady?"

"Oh, you know how it is these days, those gangster types come up here from Florida passing their fake money around, doing nothing but hurting us hard working folks. Those kinds of people don't last long around here. We run their criminal asses out of town when we catch 'em. Nope, we don't put up with that shit here in Sandersville."

"I'm glad to hear that. I was hoping this was a law-abiding town," Michel said. "But you know how it is, those gangsters don't care who they hurt. It's hard to get away from them sometimes," he added.

"Damn straight," agreed Grady. Michel stood up and brushed the seat of his trousers off.

"Give me an hour Grady, and I'll be back with your money," said Michel.

"Why don't you make it two hours. I'll need to get the title and have Richard get all the papers together."

"Who is Richard?" asked Michel. Grady smiled and started to snicker.

"Well, today Richard will be my attorney, in the meantime, he is the chief editor of our newspaper, and on weekends he's known to be the town drunk."

"Sounds like Richard is a busy man."

"He is, he is," responded Grady nodding his head. As long as he stays busy, he's a good man, unfortunately, he's not too busy on the weekends."

"Sounds good, Grady, I'll see you in a couple hours," confirmed Michel. He returned to his car and couldn't wait to share the good news with the rest of the family.

***

Thomas Califano arrived at the Palms Hotel in Fort Myers one hour before his meeting with Don Vincenzo Barzetti.

The Mafia Don always conducted his meetings in posh hotels away from his hometown of Miami. He would always obtain a luxury suite on short notice, so that the Feds would not have time to bug the room or plant an agent inside the hotel. He would never use his real name to book the room and always paid the hotel managers well to look the other way. Those he was scheduled to meet with would wait in the hotel lounge until they were summoned. He was extremely intolerant of anyone who waited for him in the lounge to drink alcohol.

He demanded sobriety in his meetings. Those who tried to bend the rule were immediately dismissed from the hotel and dealt with later. Depending on who it was, the most defiant ones were never heard from again after their meeting with the Don.

Thomas sipped his tonic water, glancing at his watch every few minutes. It wasn't until five minutes before noon, a soldier of Barzetti's came down to the lounge to escort him up to the meeting room.

Upon arriving at the suite, another one of Barzetti's soldiers searched Thomas for weapons. Thomas knew better and left his pistol in the car. The soldier found no weapons and lightly tapped on the suite door. It swung open and Thomas was escorted to the main living area of the suite where Don Barzetti was waiting.

"Thomas!" shouted Barzetti as he rose from his chair and walked over to greet one of his most trusted underbosses. The two men greeted one another by kissing each other on both cheeks and shaking hands. Barzetti ushered Thomas to a chair next to where he was sitting and offered Thomas something to drink. Thomas graciously declined.

"There seems to be discourse among some of your family members in Tampa, what's going on Thomas?" asked Barzetti. Thomas attempted to play it off as if it were nothing important.

"It's not that serious, Don Barzetti. Just a couple of my guys not getting along, that's all," explained Thomas.

"Thomas, Thomas, my old friend, you were the last one I ever expected to come to a meeting with the intentions of trying to blow smoke up my ass."

"No, Don Barzetti, I…"

"Shut the fuck up, Thomas," ordered Barzetti. The Don had never spoken to Thomas in that manner. It was a bit unnerving. Thomas squirmed in his chair and began to look around behind him to see where the Don's soldiers were standing. None of them had moved. They were standing in the same area they had been when he entered the room. "I heard the whole story. It looks like your golden boy Michel has a problem with your new Capo, Carducci. Is that right?"

"Yes, Don Barzetti, that's correct."

"So, where is Michel Santoro now?" asked the Don.

"I don't know, Don Barzetti," Thomas reluctantly admitted. Barzetti appeared to be agitated with Thomas' answer.

"You don't know," repeated the Don. "What else don't you know Thomas? I bet you don't know there has been a new Prosecuting District Attorney appointed for Tampa, who is looking to make a name for himself by locking all of us up, did you?"

"No, Don Barzetti, I didn't."

"You apparently don't know shit do you Thomas?" Barzetti stood from his chair and started to slowly pace around the room. "Here's what's going to happen when you get back to Tampa, Thomas. You're going to prepare for Salvatore to be gone for a few years. I've done what I could with the judges in Tampa to make sure he doesn't get more than five years. Your new life's mission is to find your boy Michel. Not only are you to find him, but you are also to retire him and his entire family. I'm sick and tired of these traitors that become members of our family, then turn into backstabbing cowards who have no honor or loyalty. All of them are to die! Do you understand me, Thomas?!"

Thomas couldn't look at the Don when he answered,

"Yes, I understand."

Thomas' heart sickened as he thought about the order he had just been given. Having your oldest friend and his family eliminated was going to be one of the hardest things Thomas ever had to do. As far as he was concerned, he hoped Michel would take him to the grave as well.

Chapter 20

Two weeks later

It was move-in day for Michel and his family. The apartment and hardware store sales went through smoothly since Michel paid for everything with cash.

Michel and Bonnie were relieved to see how Giovanni's and Angela's attitudes toward relocating had improved. Angela was easy. Her young spirit was always up for a new adventure, and Giovanni's was lifted when Michel explained that he would need his son's help running the store. Little did Michel know in one month; his son would be leaving his family to start a new one with Rebecca back in Tampa.

The move was quick and easy since the Santoro family had only their luggage. Michel took advantage of the minimal time it took to move in and spent it working with the previous owner, Grady, on how to run the daily business of the hardware store. By the end of the day, Michel was confident he wouldn't have any major issues running the business. To celebrate, he picked up some fried chicken with all the sides and a bottle of champagne.

***

The receptionist at the law office of Leonard Kline, Salvatore Carducci's attorney, forwarded the incoming call from Tampa Bay's new District Attorney to Kline's desk.

"Leonard Kline, how may I help you?" greeted the attorney.

"Mr. Kline, Russell Harris, District Attorney. Do you have a few minutes to discuss your client's case, Salvatore Carducci?"

"Yes, of course, Mr. Harris."

"Great," responded the DA. "I'd like to get directly to the point."

"By all means," agreed Kline.

"Your client is not a good guy. He has been on this state's watch list for quite some time, and it looks like his luck has just run out."

"What list would that be exactly, Mr. Harris?"

"The state's organized crime list."

"I'm sorry, I'm unfamiliar with that list," explained Kline.

"You shouldn't be Kline; half of your clients are on it."

"I thought you said you would get straight to the point, Harris. I'm still waiting for it. You must like hearing yourself talk. All I've heard so far is about a list of bad people; maybe you need to forward it to Santa Claus; he might need it in a couple of months."

"Very funny, Kline," remarked Harris. "Let's see how funny this is. If Carducci takes this to a jury trial, he will lose, and because of his record, we will put him away for so long that he'll come out an old man who talks to his shadow. Or he takes the plea deal, gets five, and will probably serve two."

The plea deal piqued Kline's interest.

"What's in the deal?" he asked, intriguingly.

"We want Carducci to testify that he is a member of the Barzetti crime family. We want to know the members' names in the Tampa Bay area. We want to know who killed Senator Meeks and his attorney, Donald Patterson."

"Mr. Harris, I'd like to inform you that my client is not high on the family food chain. It's doubtful he knows anything about it," explained Kline.

"You know Carducci just made Capo a few weeks ago," stated Harris.

"No, I didn't know that," replied Kline, even though he was knowledgeable of the event.

"Go ahead and play dumbass counselor, we are going to take Carducci down. He will have to decide who's going down with him." Kline was not intimidated by the bullish DA; he cherished the challenge from the 'new blood' the Governor had brought in on the case.

"I'll discuss your offer with my client and get back to you as soon as possible, Mr. Harris."

"You do that, Kline," replied Harris, abruptly ending the call.

Kline reconnected the phone line and called Sal Carducci's home. Sal had been ordered to stay at home until things had blown over. Keeping him off the street was the best thing Thomas could do for his Captain.

"Hello," answered Sal.

"Salvatore, Lenny here."

"Hey, Lenny, what's the good word?"

"It looks like we will have our work cut out for us, Sal. The new DA sounds like a real bastard. He has his sights set on us here in Tampa and will use you to launch his career."

"What the fuck is that supposed to mean, Kline?"

"It means he's going to take you down and anyone else who tries to stand in his way."

"A real fuckin' cowboy, hey counselor?" responded Carducci.

"It looks that way, Sal. He put a plea offer on the table for us to consider."

"Oh, what was that?"

"He wants you to give up the names of those in the Barzetti family operating in Tampa." Sal was ready to respond but waited to hear the DA's exclusive offer from Kline first. "For that information, you will get five years and be out in two."

Leonard Kline could hear Sal laughing at the DA's offer through the phone.

"Glad to see you find the offer amusing, Sal," remarked Kline.

"Amusing? No counselor, not amusing, more like ridiculous. You can tell that piece of shit I'm not giving anyone up, not now, not ever."

Kline already knew what Sal's answer would be. He had already started putting a defense together for his client long before he spoke with the DA. The only thing he had left was to negotiate the sentence down to a minimum stretch behind bars.

"Your boss has instructed me to keep this case out of the courtroom, Sal. This means you will have to accept what they give you."

"You better work some magic, counselor; I'm not going to spend any more time in prison than I have to."

"Alright, Sal, let me see what I can do. I'll be in touch." The attorney ended the call and was suddenly lost in thought about what to do next.

Kline knew trying to convince Sal to take the deal would be futile. He also knew the DA had him in an awkward position regarding how much time Sal would have to serve. His case for his client had little to stand on since Sal was caught threatening the airport attendant at gunpoint with over a hundred thousand dollars of uncut diamonds lying on the floor between them. His only option was to have Thomas Califano, Sal's boss, order him to take the fall and do his time. Kline placed the call.

Thomas was standing over a road map he had spread out on his table in the back room of the store. He was almost certain Michel was staying somewhere in the southeastern portion of the United States. Where exactly was anyone's guess. A call came into Thomas' backroom meeting place. It rang twice. No one, not even Thomas, appeared to try to answer it. Thomas continued staring at the map. Franky, one of the soldiers remained seated reading the newspaper; another was making himself coffee. After the sixth ring, Thomas's gaze moved from the map to his soldier, Franky.

"Franky! Answer that; it's giving me a fuckin' headache," ordered Thomas.

Franky's size didn't allow him to move very quickly. By the time he reached the phone, the number of rings was nearing twelve or thirteen.

"Sometime this week, Franky!" vocally encouraged Thomas.

"Hello?" said Franky. He listened for a moment, looked at Thomas, then held out the receiver directing it toward Thomas, "It's Leonard Kline for you." Thomas looked up at Franky and said,

"Bring it here," as he held out his hand. It took several seconds before Franky looked like he was about to walk across the room. "On second thought," said Thomas, "I'll come to you." Swiftly, Thomas made it over to the waiting Franky and took the receiver from him, then whispered, "Lose some fuckin' weight, would ya?" Franky nodded, then slowly returned to his chair and newspaper.

"Lenny, what's up?" Thomas asked.

"We are going to have a problem with this new DA. I just got off the phone with him. He called to make me an offer."

"What was the offer?" inquired Thomas.

"He wants Sal to give up the names of the family members working in the Tampa area and the name of who killed Senator Meeks and his attorney Patterson. For that, he will get five years and serve two."

"And if he doesn't?" asked Thomas.

"If he doesn't, it will go to trial. I must confess, Thomas, I don't have much of a case. They will win, and Sal will go away for a long time because of his record."

"Is that it, Lenny?"

"That's it, Thomas."

Thomas began to run all his options and scenarios through his mind. He wasn't fond of any of them. All he knew was that one of his men would have to spend time behind bars without incriminating anyone else or hurting the family. The path forward suddenly came to him.

"Listen closely, Lenny. Here's what I want you to do…" The phone cord on Thomas' phone was rather lengthy so he could pace the room during an important conversation. He took advantage of it and walked to a secluded corner of the room to finish the call. After a few minutes, he ended the call and returned to the map on the table.

"Everything alright, boss?" asked Franky. Thomas smiled and said,

"Everything's fine, just fine."

Chapter 21

In hopes of catching District Attorney Russell Harris in his office, Leonard Klein made the short two-block walk to the Tampa Courthouse.

Showing up without an appointment or invitation was common for the smartly dressed and confident Leonard Klein.

"Good morning, young lady," Klein greeted the young woman at the reception desk.

"Good morning," replied the smiling young woman. "How may I help you?"

"I'm here to see Russel Harris if he has a moment."

"Do you have an appointment Mr...."

"Klein, Leonard Klein, and no, I do not have an appointment. If I had, I would have mentioned it. However, I do have some crucial information for Mr. Harris. So, if you wouldn't mind, give him a buzz, tell him I'm here, and I promise you, he will be glad that you made him aware of my presence." The receptionist wasn't impressed with Klein's approach. Lenny reached that conclusion quickly when she rolled her eyes. Despite the voice of reason telling her to send this fish oil salesman packing, the young receptionist rang Harris's phone.

"Yes?"

"A Mr. Klein is here to see you." Harris paused a moment to recall the name. When he realized who she was referring to, he immediately said,

"Yes, yes, of course, please send him in. Thank you." The receptionist was taken by surprise by Harris' response. Klein could see it on her face.

"Told you he would be happy to see me," remarked Lenny.

"Please, go right in," instructed the receptionist.

"Thank you, dear."

Just as Klein reached Harris's door, it swung open with the DA standing there with an extended hand.

"Mr. Klein, this is a surprise!" Harris exclaimed. The two shook hands as Harris welcomed him inside.

"Lenny, call me Lenny." The DA invited Klein to have a seat in front of his desk. Lenny briefly scanned the room and commented,

"Nice office. Is this Oak?" he asked as he ran his fingers lightly over the edge of the DA's desk.

"No," answered Harris. "It's Teak."

"Ah, I have Rosewood myself." In the attorney world, you must take any victory over the opposing attorney, no matter how small. Klein had just claimed victory over whose desk was more expensive.

"What brings you here this morning Mr. Klein?" asked Harris.

"Lenny, please call me Lenny."

"Of course, Lenny." Obliged Harris.

"We have considered your offer and would like to counter your offer with one of our own."

"I'm sorry, Mr...." Harris stopped mid-sentence to keep from using the formal address,

"Lenny, I don't believe you are in any position to make any kind of offer," stated Harris.

"Oh, I believe you are mistaken, Russ; let me explain it before you quit listening. We may know who killed Senator Meeks and the attorney Patterson." Kline could see he had Harris's undivided attention. "We could give you the name in exchange for the lighter sentence of two years for Salvatore Carducci. I know this isn't everything you were shooting for, but hey, you're just starting. Going after the one who murdered a senator is big news. You'll be in every paper across the country. That's what you want, isn't it, Russ?"

Harris leaned back in his high-backed leather chair, staring into the eyes of Klein, contemplating the offer.

"Alright," said Harris, what's the name?" Klein chuckled,

"Not so fast there, Russ, this is going to make you famous; agree to the two years first, then you get the name," stated Klein.

"Alright, two years for assault; he'll be out in six months." Klein sprung from his chair and extended his hand to Harris to close the deal. The men shook hands in agreement.

"The name," demanded Harris. Klein picked up a blank sheet of paper and a pen from Harris' desk and wrote the name down without speaking it. He handed the paper to Harris, who quickly looked at it. It read, Michel Santoro. Harris grinned with satisfaction and looked up at Klein.

"This is Thomas Califano's golden boy, isn't it?" Suddenly, Lenny Klein snatched the piece of paper with Michel's name on it from DA Harris's hand, lit it on fire with his cigarette lighter, and then tossed it into an empty wastebasket nearby.

"What the fuck are you doing?" the angry DA asked.

"Evidence Russ. Can't let you keep it," explained Klein sporting a Cheshire cat grin.

"Do you know where I can find Mr. Santoro?" asked Harris. Klein picked up his briefcase that was on the floor next to his chair and replied,

"No, I don't; no one knows where he is right now." The DA suddenly felt he was being tricked into a one-sided agreement, which began to show by the expression on his face.

"I tell you what, Harris, based on what knowledge I have of Michel Santoro's whereabouts, I would focus on looking for him somewhere in the southeast, say Georgia, Alabama, maybe Louisiana," suggested Klein. Harris's facial expression changed dramatically as if he knew something he wasn't letting Klein know. From the start, it reignited the flames of mistrust Klein had for the DA. Klein made his way to the office door. He placed his hand on the doorknob and turned to look at the DA, then said,

"Happy hunting."

Within seconds of Klein leaving the DA's office, Harris called the local FBI office, informing them of the possible whereabouts of the alleged shooter in the Meeks/Patterson murders. In less than an hour, an all-points bulletin with a photo was sent out to Georgia, Alabama, Louisiana, and Florida.

***

It was nearing lunchtime. Giovanni finished sweeping the floor of the hardware store while his father completed the sale of a new water hose for a resident of Sandersville.

"I know it's not noon yet, Pop, but can I run over to the grocery to get some meat for sandwiches?" Michel glanced at the wall clock; it read 11:47.

"I don't see why not; besides, I'm a little hungry." Giovanni quickly removed his work apron and returned the broom to its rightful location.

"What kind should I get?" asked Giovanni. Michel reached into his pant pocket, pulled out a small, folded stack of cash, and gave his son a ten-dollar bill.

"Get something we all like, just as long it's not bologna."

"Okay, Pop, I'll be back shortly,"

The grocery was a short distance down the street from the hardware store. As he walked and passed several other merchants in the small town of Sandersville, he politely waved at the store owners who liked him and his family. The entire town didn't take long to know who the Davis family were.

As Giovanni approached the front entrance door of the grocery, something caught his attention out of the corner of his eye…a phone booth. He stopped short of entering the grocery store and slowly made his way over to the phone booth. The hunger for a sandwich was quickly replaced with thoughts of calling Rebecca. He stepped inside the booth, lifted the receiver from its cradle, and brought it to his ear. The urge to make the call was abruptly reduced when he reached into his pant pocket for his change and discovered he only had twenty-five cents. He hung the phone up and decided to use some of the money his father gave him for the sandwich meat.

His journey to the grocery store now had a different purpose. He needed to get the sandwich meat as soon as possible, so he could call Rebecca before his father started to miss him.

The purchase took only a few minutes as Giovanni exited the grocery with a pound of sliced turkey and change for the phone call.

Rebecca answered the phone after three rings.

"Rebecca, hi, it's Giovanni," he excitedly greeted.

"Giovanni! Hi, how are you?"

"I'm fine. No, I'm not fine," he replied. "I miss you, Rebecca; I want to come home. I don't want to be here!"

"Where are you? Are you still in Georgia?"

"Yes, we are in a small town."

"What's the name of the town? Maybe I can come to see you." Hearing those words coming from Rebecca tore Giovanni's heart. It made him miss her even more and encouraged him to return to Florida when he turned eighteen.

"It's called Sandersville." Rebecca wrote down the town's name on a pad of paper her parents kept by the phone for messages. "I'm going to look for it on a map, and if it isn't too far away, maybe my parents will let me come see you."

"That would be great!" said Giovanni. "Listen, write down my address; you can write me that way," he suggested. Rebecca picked up the pencil once again and said,

"Okay, what is it?"

"It's 219 Center Street, Sandersville, Georgia. Rebecca, I have to go, my father will be wondering where I am, but I wanted to say one more thing, I love you, and I swear, I will come back for you."

"I love you too, Giovanni; I'm looking forward to seeing you again; goodbye for now."

Giovanni hung up the receiver and seriously started planning when and how he would return to Florida for Rebecca.

The hardware store became rather busy shortly after Giovanni left for the grocery. Michel didn't realize how long his son had been gone. At least not until Giovanni walked in through the hardware store's front door. It was then he glanced at the wall clock.

"Did they have to slaughter the cow before slicing it for sandwiches?"

"It was a turkey, Pop, not a cow; here's your change." He had a fist full of bills and coins. Michel was too hungry to bother with it and told him to keep it, which delighted Giovanni because now he didn't have to explain how the missing money went for a phone call to Rebecca. "I'll run upstairs and make us some sandwiches, Pop," he said as he headed for the stairway leading up to their apartment.

After their telephone conversation, Rebecca became lost in her thoughts about Giovanni. One of her favorite places to relax and think was on the bench swing located on the front porch. She tore the small sheet of paper from the notepad with Giovanni's address on it, walked out onto the porch, and sat on the swing. As she gently swung back and forth, she started to work on her approach in asking her parents if they would allow her to travel to Georgia to visit Giovanni.

She daydreamed about the moment she saw Giovanni and his reaction. Her heart told her it would be the right thing to do; she couldn't deny she was in love with Giovanni and would do almost anything to see him, even if it came to the point of lying to her parents. She whispered to herself, "God, please make it so."

"Are you praying?" asked the curious, boisterous Dante as he stood on the porch steps. Rebecca was so wrapped up in thought she didn't notice Dante walking up the driveway or the sidewalk leading to the porch. To Dante's delight, he caused Rebecca to jump when he revealed his presence.

"Sorry about that, Rebecca," he said. "I didn't mean to interrupt your prayer."

"Dante, what are you doing here?" she inquired.

"Hello to you too, Rebecca," he quipped.

"I'm sorry, Dante, I just got off the phone with John. He left me with a lot to think about." Dante's eyes widened when hearing his close friend's name.

"John? How is he."

"He's doing fine; he said to say hi to you when I saw you." Although Giovanni said no such thing to Rebecca, she believed Dante still needed to hear that his dear friend was thinking of him. He was happy his friend kept in touch, even though it wasn't directly with him.

"So, when is the wondering gypsy returning?" asked Dante. Rebecca shrugged her shoulders and replied,

"He didn't say, I don't think his family plans to return."

"Did he say that?"

"No, but what he did say led me to believe they weren't."

"Well, what did he say?"

"He said he was coming back for me, and it sounded like he meant alone. I told him that I would ask my parents if I could go and see him."

"Have you asked them yet?" Rebecca shook her head.

"I'm trying to build up the courage to ask." Rebecca could see the wheels of thought and planning turning in Dante's head. Suddenly, an idea came to him.

"What if both of us went to see him, my folks would let me take my mom's car, we could surprise him, and your parents would most likely let you go with me since I'm going to be a police officer." Rebecca wasn't quite sure if she heard Dante's last statement correctly due to the fact, she was envisioning leaping into Giovanni's open arms.

"Excuse me, what did you just say?" she asked with a sense of surprise. Dante's smile grew even bigger,

"I've applied for a sheriff deputy position; I'm going to be a cop." Rebecca jumped up from the swing and gave Dante a sincere congratulatory hug.

"Oh my god Dante! That is fantastic!" Dante was slightly embarrassed but proud of what he intended to do for his career.

"What do your parents think about it?"

"I don't know; I haven't told them yet. My mom will like the idea, my dad, not so much."

"Why wouldn't your father like it?" asked Rebecca. Dante never discussed what he knew about his father's occupation with anyone except Giovanni. He couldn't come up with a believable excuse for his father not approving of the career choice he was making, so he tried to act like it didn't matter what his father thought; he was going to go through with it anyway.

"I don't know; I think he wanted me to be a banker of some shit like that; he'll just have to get over it; I'm going to be a cop." Rebecca left it at that and returned their conversation about going to see Giovanni.

"So, when do you go into the academy?" asked Rebecca. "We need to see John before that so you can surprise him with the news."

"Not until the end of next month, so if we are going to see him, we must do it soon."

"Before we get too far ahead of ourselves, where is John living?" Rebecca picked up a small sheet of paper from off the bench swing and handed it to Dante.

"This is where he's at; I haven't had a chance to look at a map to see exactly where it's at; all I know is it's Georgia. Dante read the address and committed it to memory.

"Do you have a map?" asked Dante. "We can look now and see where our wondering friend is holding up." Little did Dante know; it was exactly what his friend and his family were doing.

"I think we do; I'll be right back." Rebecca sprinted into the house and located a map tucked away in a kitchen drawer with several miscellaneous items.

"Got it!" she exclaimed as she returned to the porch. The two sat on the porch swing and unfolded the map. They used the map index and found Sandersville, Georgia.

"Why in the world would they be in Sandersville? There's nothing there or even close by!" commented Dante. Rebecca was confused as well.

"I haven't any idea; I'm sure there has to be a good reason," stated Rebecca. "How many miles is it to Sandersville from here?" Using the mile scale, Dante roughly measured the distance,

"I would say it's over 300 miles."

"That's not bad," said Rebecca; I'll ask my parents tonight; I hope they say yes."

"I'll tell you what; I'll stop by tomorrow, and you can tell me what they said. If they say no, we'll go anyway," Dante said, smiling. Rebecca nudged her friend and said,

"You're so bad."

Chapter 22

The day for Salvatore Carducci to stand before a judge and receive the expected light sentence for assault had arrived. Leonard Klein entered the near-empty courtroom with his client by his side. DA Harris was already present and sitting at his assigned table with one of his interns. Klein and Carducci took their designated seats and patiently waited for the judge to enter.

Not only was Klein relaxed and worry-free because of the deal that was struck with the DA, but he was also informed that the judge who was to hear the plea from the defendant and issue a sentence was also in the pocket of Don Vincenzo Barzetti. To Attorney Klein, being in the courtroom with his client was a mere formality. Klein was so confident; he didn't even open his briefcase to retrieve his client's file.

Several minutes had passed beyond the scheduled time, and Sal Carducci was annoyed by the delay.

"Where the fuck is the judge?" he whispered to Klein. His attorney motioned for Sal to take it easy and relax. But that was the last thing one could expect from him. The man was not known for being the epitome of patient. He wanted everything to be over with in a flash. He had better things to do and places to be.

"Patience, Sal. We will have a judge on our side; it's worth the wait."

Klein purposely didn't tell Sal the judge appointed to the case was on the Barzetti payroll. He always wanted his clients to think he was the greatest attorney ever, especially when the sentences were very light.

"All rise!" announced the bailiff, "This court is now in session. The honorable Judge Winston Lang is presiding."

"Be seated," instructed the judge. Leonard Klein suddenly felt sick; Judge Lang was not the judge they were supposed to have. He quickly opened his briefcase and pulled out his client's file. The first paper he came to was the formal notice the court gave him for the date and time he was to be present. What stood out on the paper was the name of the presiding judge in bold type, Judge Harold Pickens.

"This isn't right," mumbled Klein, who was overheard by Sal, who responded,

"What isn't right, counselor?" Before Klein could explain it to his client, the judge spoke,

"If my presence here this morning has confused anyone, I am sitting in for Judge Harold Pickens. Judge Pickens had a family emergency to attend to. Klein was caught completely off guard and wanted to approach the bench. As soon as he pushed his chair back so he could stand, the DA beat him to the punch,

"Your Honor, permission to approach the bench."

"Granted," replied the judge. DA Harris spoke very little when he was at the bench. The conversation lasted less than a minute. It was Klein's turn next,

"Your honor, permission to approach the bench."

"Granted, make it quick, counselor." Klein practically sprinted to the bench.

"Your honor, with all respect, I was not expecting you to be sitting here today. Furthermore, I wanted to inform you, in case you haven't had time to review the case, DA Harris and I have reached a plea deal. This was only supposed to be a formality; the case is practically closed.

"First of all, counselor, I'll be the one who decides if the case is closed or not. Secondly, I'm sorry I ruined all your plans. A good attorney adapts to any situation, no matter who's sitting on the bench. I'm not giving you an extension; we are all here now, so let's get on with it.

Klein returned to his table, not feeling as confident as he was when he entered the courtroom. He felt something bad was about to happen.

"Will the defendant rise," ordered the judge. Klein stood with his client, preparing himself to be blindsided.

"Mr. Klein, I understand you and the district attorney have agreed on a plea deal?"

"Yes, your honor," answered Klein.

"And what do you plead,"

"Guilty, your honor," replied Sal.

"Very well, Let the record show the defendant has pleaded guilty to assault with a deadly weapon."

"What?" shouted Klein. "Deadly weapon? Your honor, a deadly weapon was not part of the original charge! We would not have pled guilty to that!"

"Well, you just did, counselor." Sal turned to his attorney, looking incredibly angry,

"What the fuck is going on, Lenny?" he asked.

"I will impose your sentence now," announced the judge. Klein's stomach nervously tightened.

"Mr. Carducci, after giving your case considerable thought, not to mention the laundry list of your past offenses, I believe this court has been much too lenient with you. Therefore, I sentence you to three to five years in the state penitentiary. Bailiff, take Mr. Carducci into custody, please. This court is adjourned." The gavel came down; it was over.

The bailiff immediately approached Sal and instructed him to put his hands behind his back. Sal complied as he began to shout at his attorney,

"What the fuck is this shit, Lenny?! This isn't right!" Klein placed his hand on Sal's shoulder and said,

"It's going to be okay, Sal. I'll get this straightened out." Consoling his client did not affect Sal's disposition.

"You goddamn right, you'll straighten this out, counselor; you better do it soon, or you'll get a visit!" The bailiff led Sal away as he continued to protest,

"You have until the end of the day, counselor! Do you hear me? The end of the day!"

Once Sal was removed from the courtroom, Klein quickly left, found the nearest pay phone, and called Thomas.

***

Thomas Califano had just finished reading his morning newspaper and was enjoying his last cup of coffee in the back room of the store when the phone rang. He let it ring four times before answering.

"Yeah," was his greeting.

"Thomas, this is Lenny."

"Good morning, counselor; how did it go with Sal?"

"Not well, Thomas; the DA and the judge pulled a fast one. They charged Sal with assault with a deadly weapon and gave him three to five years." The news angered Thomas.

"What the fuck are we going to do about it, Lenny?"

"I'm going to file an appeal."

"Appeal, what will that do?" Thomas asked.

"Another judge will take up the appeal."

"Then what?"

"Then we wait?" explained Klein.

"How long with that take?" asked Thomas.

"It depends."

"Depends on what?" Thomas asked, raising his voice.

"Depending on what judge we get, it could take a couple of months." The attorney's answer infuriated the Underboss,

"That's not good enough, Lenny!" he shouted. "Who was the judge?"

"Winston Lang." Thomas knew exactly who Lang was.

"Lang! That piece of shit is as corrupt as they come; who's the DA?"

"Russell Harris."

"I don't know him," said Thomas. "He has Lang in his pocket. Alright, Lenny, do what you must; file whatever you must file. I'll let Sal know we are working on it."

"Alright, Thomas, I'll be in touch." The call ended with Thomas considering who he would bring up to cover for Sal. He already knew Sal was going to prison. The judge and district attorney were too much in the spotlight right now. Any move made on either would bring too much attention to the 'Family.' It was to become a waiting game for possibly five years.

***

Dante was in the kitchen helping his mother prepare their celebratory dinner after his father returned home from his court appearance. Leonard Klein reassured him and his mother that Sal would have dinner with them that evening. Dante had also planned to tell his parents he had applied for the sheriff deputy position the day before.

The telephone rang just as Dante was in the middle of draining the boiled potatoes of water. His mother was nearby with free hands, so she answered it with a silly, playful voice, assuming it was one of her son's many girlfriends.

"Hello?"

"Mrs. Carducci, this is your husband's attorney, Leonard Klein; how are you today?"

"I'm fine, Mr. Klein, thank you. I'm sorry my husband isn't here now; I…."

"That's quite alright, Mrs. Carducci; I know where your husband is."

"Oh, then how can I help you, Mr. Klein?"

"I'm calling to inform you that Sal was sentenced to prison today." At first, the information did not register with Linda Carducci.

"You must be joking; you told my husband everything would be alright, and today was just a formality."

"That's correct, ma'am, it was supposed to be a formality, but the DA, who I had made a deal, reneged on it. His dishonesty blindsided me. Let me reassure you that this is not over. I will be filing an appeal tomorrow morning."

"How long will that process take?"

"It could take up to two years, Mrs. Carducci." Attorney Klein could hear nothing from Linda Carducci. He began to think she had either hung the phone up or had passed out. "Hello? Mrs. Carducci, are you there?" There was nothing but silence until Klein heard faint sobbing from Mrs. Carducci. She couldn't suppress her sorrow any longer and started to cry aloud. Dante listened to his mother's weeping and rushed over to her.

"Mom, what's wrong?" he asked. Dante could hear Leonard Klein calling out his mother's name through the receiver she held at her side. Dante slowly and gently pried the receiver from his mother's grasp, then brought it to his ear. He could still hear the attorney calling out her name.

"Hello?" said Dante causing Klein to stop speaking momentarily.

"Yes, hello, responded Klein. "Who am I speaking to?"

"This is Dante Carducci."

"Dante? Great, are you Sal's son?" Before he answered, he escorted his mom to the kitchen table and encouraged her to have a seat.

"Yes, I am," he responded.

"Dante! Yes, of course. Will your mother be, okay?" inquired Klein.

"That depends on what it was you told her."

"I hate being the bearer of bad news, but I informed your mother that Sal was sentenced to prison for three to five years. I ensured your mother I would be filing an appeal tomorrow morning."

"Prison?" a puzzled Dante asked.

"That doesn't make sense, Mr. Klein; my father said he was arrested for fighting."

"I don't know who told you that Dante, your father, was arrested and charged with assault with a deadly weapon." Just the sound of the offense scared Dante. He immediately assumed his father would be in prison for decades. He did all he could to keep from breaking down and crying with his mother, not to mention feeling the urge to vomit. "I want to assure you, Dante; I will get your father out as soon as possible. If you or your mother have any questions, please call my office anytime." Dante's thoughts wildly raced through his head. After being told, his father was sentenced to prison; he didn't hear anything the attorney said. All he knew then was that his father would not be coming home anytime soon. "I'll be working on your father's appeal, Dante. Let me know if your family needs anything; bye for now." Klein ended the call. Dante stood there, lost in thought, holding the receiver to his ear, not realizing the attorney was no longer on the line. He didn't come out of his trance until his mother approached him and removed the receiver from his hand as he did for her.

The two held each other to calm their fears.

"Don't worry about anything, Mom; we'll be alright." Linda smiled, knowing her young man was worried about her.

"I don't know what we will do for money, son. Your father and I have some savings, but it won't last." Suddenly, Dante was struck with a solution to their problem. The only problem was that he would have to confess he had snooped in their room when they were out of town.

"I may have the solution to our money problems, Mom." His mother released him from her embrace and asked,

"What might that be, son?"

"A while back, when you and Dad were out of town, I snooped around in your room." Linda blushed, assuming her son came across her lingerie and sex toys. She quickly composed an explanation for having the items in her head. "I found a place in the floor of your room where Dad had stashed things." Dante could see by the look on his mother's face that she was unaware of the hiding spot. "Dad had a lot of money in there; I think it would be enough to get us through this." Although Linda was surprised that her son had violated their privacy, she was more eager to see her husband's secret hiding spot.

"Show me," responded Linda.

Once they had reached his parents' bedroom, Dante walked directly to the loose floor panels and removed them.

"Would you hand me a flashlight, Mom, if you have one here?" Linda walked over to the bedside nightstand, removed a small flashlight from the bottom drawer, then handed it to her son. Within a few seconds, Dante pulled up a large cloth sack full of money, opened it, then poured its contents onto the floor. There were thousands of dollars tightly rolled up and secured by a rubber band.

"Oh, my god," remarked Linda. "How much do you think is there, Dante?" After performing a quick calculation, he answered,

"I would guess at least a hundred thousand or more, Mom. As I said, we'll be fine for a while. Linda felt uneasy staring at the thousands of dollars lying on her bedroom floor. Especially not knowing how her husband obtained such a fortune.

"Quick put all of that back," she ordered. She knelt on the floor to help her son return the money to the cloth sack. Just as Dante was about to close the sack and return it to its hiding spot, Linda snatched it from Dante, opened it, pulled out two rolls of cash, then handed the sack back to her son. Dante looked at his mother with a surprised look on his face. Linda, somewhat embarrassed, replied, "For household expenses."

Chapter 23

(One Month Later)

The Santoro family, now known as the Davis family, were settling in the Sandersville Georgia community quickly. Their new hardware store provided a steady income to support the family and served as a welcomed distraction for each member of the family, especially Michel. At first, they all struggled with the new names they adopted but in a short period of time, all of them learned to use their new names in public and in mixed company. The family use their real names with each other, only when they were secured in their apartment. There were no exceptions.

Bonnie met a few women her age who were also raising a family. Daughter Angela enjoyed accompanying her mother when the women would travel to Macon Georgia for a day long shopping excursion. One of the other mothers would bring along her daughter who was near Angela's age. The two girls hit it off nicely and soon became good friends when they discovered they would be attending the same school. On Saturdays, Angela hung around the hardware store to learn a little bit about the family business. She enjoyed running the cash register and handling money. Michel would boast, saying that it was a trait she got from him and not her mother. Joking that Bonnie loved to handle money albeit only when she was spending it.

Besides working with his father during the week at the hardware store, Giovanni found a nondenominational church to attend. He volunteered his time on the weekends to assist the pastor in the forming and running of the youth Bible study group that met on Sunday evenings. Giovanni's dedication and working with the pastor, opened his heart to God. He had become a role model for some of the younger parishioners of the church to look up to. He strongly believed he was doing the work that God intended him to do. He had become quite a popular young man around town. However, his deepest love remained in Florida. He would just have to wait for his eighteenth birthday, which was only a few days away to be with Rebecca. Giovanni would secretly phone Rebecca from a pay-phone booth at least once a week. Their conversations were mostly about what they wanted to do after they were married. They had agreed upon finding a church to where they could start their own youth fellowship ministry, but their main goal was to be together.

As for Michel, he threw himself into his business. The days passed by so quickly, it was hard to believe his family had been in Sandersville just over one month. He had not been in contact with anyone he was associated with in Tampa, but he never let his guard down. He was constantly surveying large groups of people to see if he recognized anyone. No matter where he was, he was always aware of his surroundings and always carried a weapon, be it a knife or a pistol, Michel did not have the luxury to trust anyone, anywhere. He knew that one day, they would find him. His only hope was that his family was nowhere around when they came to kill him.

***

The day that Giovanni had been anxiously waiting for had finally arrived. Today was Giovanni Santoro's eighteenth birthday. He had rehearsed the speech he had planned to give his parents concerning his leaving several times. All he needed now was the most appropriate time to tell them. It was his morning opening the hardware store. His father offered him the day off, but Giovanni wouldn't hear of it.

"I'm a man now Pop," he said. "Today is just like any other day, I don't need to celebrate like I'm ten."

The unusually crisp morning air forced Giovanni to wear a light jacket as he swept the sidewalk in front of the family's hardware store.

Like clockwork, the elderly morning walkers were making their way toward Giovanni as he was finishing his daily chore of providing a clean entrance to the store. The walkers believed Giovanni was doing it for them so that they would be safe and not slip on anything as they passed by.

"Good morning, Steven," greeted one of the elderly women who had taken a liking to Giovanni. He always responded with a smile, despite the growing frustration of having to keep his identity a secret.

"Good morning, Mrs. Yates. How are you this morning?" replied Giovanni.

"I'm freezing!" she exclaimed. "It's too early to be this cold."

"I agree, much too early," responded Giovanni.

"You have a blessed day now Steven, I'll see you Sunday at church."

"And you as well Mrs. Yates, see you then."

Giovanni headed back inside the store and flipped the 'Sorry we're Closed' sign hanging on the door to 'Yes, we are Open'. He walked to the back of the store and turned on the ceiling lights to make the opening official. The only thing left to do was to get the cash from the safe and put it in the cash register. The safe was in the floor behind the counter near the register. The entire time Giovanni was behind the counter handling the money, his back was to the front door. He had no idea two people had quietly entered the store except for feeling a sudden rush of cool air. The two customers slowly made their way to the counter without a sound, but Giovanni sensed they were nearby. He assumed it was a couple of older men who couldn't move fast even if they wanted to, therefore none of their steps were heard.

"Good morning! I'll be with you in just a second," Giovanni announced. There wasn't any reply from the customers, so Giovanni assumed the older customers were nearly deaf as well.

As Giovanni was placing the dollar bills into the register, a voice behind him said,

"Since you have that register open, why don't you just pass all that money to me." Startled, Giovanni froze with fear.

"Don't turn around, just put the money on the counter," instructed the would-be thief. Giovanni did as he was told.

"The coins too!" demanded the thief. The order to hand over the coins as well struck Giovanni in a strange way. He had never heard about any robber wanting the coins. They were heavy and made a lot of noise. He had to make sure he heard the thief correctly and asked,

"You want the coins too?"

"Absolutely, we need the change for the candy and soda machines, ain't that right Rebecca?"

Hearing the name Rebecca prompted Giovanni to snap his head around quickly. To his surprise stood his best friend Dante and the love of his life, Rebecca. The two pranksters burst out laughing.

"You assholes!" shouted Giovanni laughing as well. Rebecca scurried around the counter and leapt into Giovanni's arms. The two kissed each other deeply then held their embrace. Neither one wanted to let go until Dante tapped Rebecca on the shoulder and said,

"My turn!" Rebecca hesitantly surrendered her place in Giovanni's arms to Dante.

"How the hell are you, John?" boisterously asked Dante as the two embraced.

"D, so good to see you!"

"No kisses from me and watch those hands!" joked Dante. They patted one another on the back and shoulders as they separated. Rebecca didn't waste the opportunity to place herself back into Giovanni's arms.

"Why didn't you tell me you were coming?" asked Giovanni.

"We wanted to surprise you on your birthday, and Dante has some very exciting news," responded Rebecca. Giovanni turned and looked at

Dante and noticed he was wearing a 'Cat who ate the canary' expression on his face. This sparked an immediate response from Giovanni,

"You got busted trying to pick up a hooker." Dante shook his head slightly but maintained his mischievous smile. "You got caught robbing kids for their lunch money."

"No smart ass," replied Dante as all of them began to laugh. "I'm going to be a cop!" he exclaimed. Giovanni waited for his best friend to begin laughing, he didn't.

"Alright, enough with the jokes, tell me what the news is," insisted Giovanni.

"I just told you,"replied Dante whose facial expression turned to one of seriousness and truth. Giovanni looked at Rebecca and received the same look.

"You're serious, aren't you?" Dante nodded. "Well, that is fantastic buddy, congratulations." Giovanni extended his hand. The two shook and Giovanni gave his friend another hug, slapping him on the back. "You'll be a great cop, make us proud. When do you start your training?"

"This coming Monday is orientation, and the training will start on Wednesday."

"That's great, I'm happy for you D." The joy and excitement shared by Dante's friend Giovanni suddenly came to a halt. He realized the son of a known mobster was hired by the sheriff's office. He had to know how his friend managed to pull that off. Giovanni put his arm around Dante once more and led him away from Rebecca so that she would not be able to hear what he was saying to his oldest friend.

"How did you get hired if your dad is a gangster?" whispered Giovanni.

"Benefits of having your father in the mob, he had a fake I.D. made for me a year ago with a different last name and address." He eagerly pulled the new I.D. from his wallet and showed it to Giovanni.

It read Dante Rossi on the flawless counterfeit identification card. "Why did you need a fake I.D. a year ago?" he asked.

"I didn't," responded Dante. "For when that day comes, is what he said when he gave it to me. I didn't understand exactly what he meant by that, but now I do."

"Okay you two, enough with the guy talk," chided Rebecca. Giovanni slapped his friend on the back once more and said,

"Sounds good." The two made their way back to Rebecca and Giovanni kissed her cheek. He whispered, "Sorry about that, just guy stuff." The explanation was enough for her as she returned to Giovanni's arms.

"So, what are you doing here on your birthday," Dante asked. "Didn't your dad give you the day off?" Suddenly, Giovanni realized what a terrible mistake it was for Rebecca and Dante to be there. He had betrayed his father's trust by telling his friends where they were. The look of extreme anxiety and dread covered Giovanni's face. He released Rebecca's hand from his grasp. The smile that Giovanni had that extended from ear to ear was gone. Dante was the first to notice,

"What's wrong John?" he asked. Giovanni's anxiety was now replaced with fear. He grabbed both of their arms and quickly ushered them toward the store entrance.

"You have to go!" he nervously exclaimed.

"Go? Why do we have to go?" asked the confused Rebecca.

"I'll explain later, but you need to leave now!"

"What the hell's wrong, John? What's going on?" pressed Dante for an explanation. Rebecca and Dante freed their arms from the frantic Giovanni just before reaching the entrance door.

"I can't explain right now, you can't…"

"Well, hello there!" Giovanni's stomach began to nervously churn. His father had unexpectedly come down from the apartment above the store to wish his son a happy birthday. Dante and Rebecca, still unaware of why their friend wanted them to leave, greeted Mr. Santoro with warm smiles,

"Hello Mr. Santoro, surprised to see us?" asked Dante. Michel returned the smiles with one of his own and said,

"You have no idea." Michel walked up to the two visitors and extended his hand to Dante and said,

"I know this guy; Dante how are you?"

"Fine sir." The two shook hands then Michel focused his attention on the girl who was holding his son's hand.

"Pop, this is Rebecca Stone." Rebecca let go of Giovanni's hand to shake his father's hand.

"So, you are the infamous Rebecca who my son sneaks off to call," Michel said smiling. He quickly glanced over to Giovanni, only to find him in a state of curiosity as to how he knew about the phone calls.

"Are you two leaving already?" he asked. The unexpected guests looked at one another then at Giovanni. They weren't sure what to say since Giovanni tried to get them out of the store quickly, with no explanation.

"No," answered Giovanni unconvincingly. "They were going to walk around town and wait for me so I could have lunch with them."

"Oh, I see," replied Michel. He reached in the front pocket of his trousers and pulled out a neatly folded stack of cash and peeled off a crisp ten-dollar-bill. "Why don't you take your friends to lunch, on me."

"But it's not lunchtime yet Pop, I was going to work today," said Giovanni.

"Nonsense, son, today's your birthday, and your friends are in town. Go have some fun."

Giovanni could see that his father was trying to smooth over the situation, when in fact, he was doing his best to calm the anger he had toward his son and heal the wound of betrayal Giovanni had inflicted.

Giovanni took the ten dollars from his father and shoved it into his pocket. He could see the hurt in his father's eyes when he took the money from him. He felt terrible. So much, that he didn't even want to spend the day with his visiting friends.

"Thanks Pop, I'll be back for dinner."

"Would you two like to stay for dinner?" asked Michel.

"No thank you sir," responded Dante. "We need to be back home tonight. Rebecca's parents and my mom don't know we are here. Besides, my mom doesn't allow me to drive out of state, but I wanted to have one last disobedient fling before I get into the academy.

"Academy? Military?" asked Michel.

"No sir, I've been hired by the Tampa Sheriff Department, I begin training on Wednesday."

"That's great Dante, you'll do well, I'm sure of it." The picture that ran through Michel's head at that very moment was one of Dante arresting his own father. He had all he could do to keep from smiling.

Michel had to ask one more question, even though he knew what the answer would be even if Dante didn't tell the truth.

"So, your dad knows you're here?" Dante had hoped he wouldn't have to tell the Santoro family about his father. But, since Michel had worked with his father at times, he thought he would want to know.

"My dad is in prison, Mr. Santoro."

"Prison! What on earth for?"

"He got into a bar fight and really hurt a guy; they gave him time for it."

"That's unfortunate. Do me a favor, the next time you see him, tell him I said hello."

"Yes sir, absolutely."

"I guess we'll be going now Pop," stated Giovanni. He made a motion toward the exit door with his friends following close behind.

"You kids have a great time!" bade Michel. Rebecca and Dante turned and waved goodbye.

The smile that was on Michel's face vanished as soon as they left the store. His jaw clenched tightly as his heart rate increased. He stepped into the restroom that was in the store and closed the door. He leaned over the sink and rested his hands on each side of it. He struggled to calm himself while thoughts of how to rectify the situation with Dante and Rebecca now knowing where they lived. He kept reaching the same conclusion, Dante and Rebecca couldn't return to Florida alive. He turned the water on and splashed some water on his face then looked into the mirror and asked himself,

"What kind of monster are you?"

Chapter 24

It was 5:00 p.m. On a typical weekday, the streets of Sandersville roll up to the point that by 5:30 p.m. it looked like a ghost town. Everywhere except the local bar which was located at the end of town near the railroad viaduct.

Bonnie made her way down the stairs from the apartment to help her husband close the store and take care of the money they had earned that day. Michel closed the store and was locking the door when Bonnie arrived.

"How'd we do today honey?" she called out.

"Not too bad, I think we cleared over two hundred dollars," was Michel's estimate. "Before you start doing what you have to do, I need to speak to you about something." Bonnie walked over to her husband with undivided attention.

"What is it?" Michel finished locking the entrance door and looked both ways down the street to see if there was any sign of Giovanni and his friends. He placed his hands on Bonnie's shoulders and said,

"We have a problem." Bonnie knew immediately it was serious just by the look in her husband's eyes. "Dante Carducci and Giovanni's girlfriend Rebecca are here." Bonnie gasped because she knew the implications of this unfortunate event.

"How did they find us?"

"Giovanni has been calling Rebecca."

"You're not going to…"

"No, but don't think the thought hadn't crossed my mind," Michel said abruptly.

"Thank God," said Bonnie as she breathed a sigh of relief. "What are you going to do?"

"There's not much I can do. They will be headed back soon. They came up to see Giovanni without their parent's consent, there's no telling who they told what they were doing."

Bonnie could see her husband was at a loss as to what to do. She stepped closer to him and wrapped her arms around him and rested her head on his chest, while Michel softly and slowly caressed her back.

"Any ideas," Michel asked. Bonnie took a moment then answered,

"Pay them off." Michel stopped caressing his wife's back.

"Do you think it will work?"

"If it doesn't, we'll know soon enough," replied Bonnie. Michel kissed Bonnie and said,

"I'm sorry to put you through all of this." Bonnie gave him a kiss of reassurance and jokingly responded,

"That's what I get for marrying a gangster." Michel playfully slapped her on the ass.

"I'll let you finish what you have to do, and I'll see you upstairs."

"I'll only be a couple minutes hon, then I'll be up," commented Bonnie. Michel ascended the stairs to the apartment and went directly to the cash he had hidden in the floor of their bedroom. He retrieved two-thousand-dollars and replaced the plank he took from the floor. He made his way back to the kitchen and placed the two stacks of money on the kitchen table. Bonnie had finished what she needed to do for the store and met Michel in the kitchen.

"Damn honey, how much are you giving them?" she said after seeing the stacks of cash.

"Hopefully it will be enough to keep them quiet," he said.

"If it doesn't, I'll kill them myself," she jested.

Michel and Bonnie could hear footsteps coming up the exterior stairway leading to the apartment. Michel quickly snatched the money from the table and stuffed it into his back pocket. The door swung open, and in walked the reunited trio.

"Mom, Pop, they wanted to come up and say goodbye before they left," informed Giovanni.

"Hello Dante," greeted Bonnie. She approached him and gave him a warm hug. "This must be Rebecca," She gave her a warm hug as well. "This is such a surprise to see you two!" exclaimed Bonnie.

"We've been planning this for a while, so we decided what better day to surprise Giovanni than on his birthday," stated Rebecca.

"That's so sweet of you two, but you shouldn't have done something like this without your parent's permission." The two were embarrassed by the friendly scolding.

"I've always said, better to beg for forgiveness than to ask for permission," quipped Dante. Bonnie and Michel responded with a slight grin.

"Well, I guess we should be going if we are going to get home tonight," said Dante.

Giovanni's gaze never left Rebecca. Michel saw this and got Bonnie's attention. He looked at his son, then back at Bonnie, slightly jerking his head indicating he wanted her to take Giovanni out of the room.

"Goodbye Mr. and Mrs. Santoro," bade the two as they began to make their way toward the door with Giovanni closely behind.

"Giovanni?" called out Bonnie, stopping her son in his tracks. "Would you please help me with something in the storage room downstair? Your father will see them out." Michel patted Dante on the back and said,

"I'll walk them to their car, don't want anything to happen to them on the mean streets of Sandersville." Dante and Rebecca found Michel's comment humorous, but Giovanni thought the gesture to walk them all the way to their car was a little strange but said nothing. He quit trying to understand his father's sense of reasoning ever since they left Tampa. He had become unpredictable and difficult to read.

"I'll talk to ya'll later! Drive safely!" bade Giovanni as his friends and father left the apartment.

"So, what do you need help with mom?" asked Giovanni.

"Nothing son, your father needed to have a minute with Dante and Rebecca."

"What about?" Bonnie couldn't believe her son didn't grasp the magnitude of their location being revealed. She looked at him in disbelief and stated,

"I don't recall dropping you on your head when you were a child, maybe your father did and didn't tell me."

"What's that supposed to mean mom?"

"Never mind, I'm sorry," she said. Giovanni was not getting the answers he was looking for and decided to say what was on his mind.

"What's pop doing with them, is he going to hurt them?" Bonnie decided it was time to talk to Giovanni like an adult, in hopes he would understand the situation a bit more clearly.

"Your father is going to give each of them a large amount of money and make them promise not to mention to anyone that they have seen us, do you understand?" Giovanni nodded.

"What if they do tell someone? What happens then?" he asked, dreading to hear the answer.

"It will bring the wrath of your father down on anyone who attempts to find us, and those who told them." Giovanni's face turned pale. He understood exactly what his mother was saying.

"Pop would hurt Rebecca and Dante?" Bonnie did not verbally answer her son's question. She did it with a look into the eyes of her son, who read what she didn't say. Giovanni said nothing more and went directly to his bedroom and closed the door.

***

The two teens made it to Dante's car, awkwardly escorted by Giovanni's father. Once again, they bade Michel goodbye and proceeded to open the doors to the vehicle.

"Before you two leave, I would like to have a word with you," stated Michel. Dante closed his door, as did Rebecca, who then circled around the back of the car joining Michel and Dante. "I know the sudden departure of our family from Tampa has many people curious as to why we left. Me and my family were in danger if we had stayed. I'm sorry Giovanni was unable to give you two more notice, but we had to make the decision quickly and quietly. You with me so far?" asked Michel. The two silently nodded their heads. "I can't express enough just how important it is that no one knows we are here. I am prepared to do whatever it takes to keep this secret; therefore, I'm giving each of you one-thousand dollars to forget you ever saw us. But most importantly, never to tell anyone where we are." Michel reached into his back pocket and removed two stacks of cash and handed one to each of them. It was the most money either one of them had ever held in their hand, and the wide-eyed opened mouthed reaction confirmed that. Dante was the first to speak,

"This is a lot of money Mr. Santoro." Rebecca was in shock and agreed by nodding her head.

"Our privacy and the desire to be left alone is worth it," Michel responded. "There is just one more thing, I implore you never to come back here. If you do, I cannot guarantee your safety." The comment compelled both to take their eyes off the money they were holding and focused their attention on the expression on Michel's face. He wasn't smiling. He was dead serious and hoped they understood that he was not playing. Rebecca was too frightened to speak. Dante was as well, but managed to get out two words,

"Yes sir." Dante opened the driver's door giving Rebecca immediate access into the car and away from Michel. She slid across the seat allowing Dante to slide in right behind her. Dante started the car and put it in gear. Both kept their eyes facing forward and never looked in Michel's direction again.

***

Michel returned to the apartment by way of the outside stairway that led to the kitchen. He found Bonnie and Angie preparing one of Giovanni's favorite Italian meals for his birthday, Minestrone. For dessert, she made him a layered white cake with chocolate frosting.

"Dinner will be ready in a few minutes, I just have to re-heat the Minestrone," informed Bonnie.

"Where's Giovanni? Michel asked.

"He's in his room, I told him what you were going to give Dante and Rebecca. It upset him."

Bonnie, Angela, and Michel were unaware that Giovanni had retrieved his large suitcase from under his bed and started to pack. He was now eighteen years old. He had had enough of keeping the family secret. He was embarrassed, disgusted, and hurt to hear that his father had paid his friends off. He was determined to set out on his own. If that meant never seeing his family again, then sobeit. He had plans to marry Rebecca, and the two of them living their lives serving God.

He quickly packed his clothes and left behind the unessential's. He closed the suitcase and slid it back under his bed. He pulled down a shoebox he had hidden on the shelf in his closet. The shoebox contained money he had saved while working for his father and running errands for a few of the elderly residents in Sandersville. His savings amounted to One-hundred-sixty-four dollars. It was plenty for a bus ticket. He had already acquired a bus schedule and learned that the next scheduled bus passing through Sandersville would be at 4:30 a.m. the following morning.

Bonnie knocked on her son's bedroom door, startling him.

"Dinners ready honey."

"I'll be right there!" shouted Giovanni. He quickly scanned his room, making sure everything looked in place and walked briskly to the kitchen to start his birthday celebration with the family he would soon be leaving behind.

***

Giovanni managed to get a little sleep that night. He couldn't set his alarm clock in fear it would be heard by his parents. He relied on his internal alarm clock to wake him in time to catch the 4:30 a.m. bus, which meant he was waking up every fifteen minutes.

It was now 3:45 a.m. It was time to go. He slid his suitcase from under the bed, slipped on a lightweight jacket and made his way to the bedroom door, suitcase in hand. He looked back one last time at his room. It didn't surprise him that he felt nothing. He was more than ready to leave. Opening his bedroom door quietly, he poked his head out and looked down the hallway at his parents' and sister's rooms. Their doors were closed. Taking one step slowly and quietly at a time, he managed to make his way through the kitchen and out the door. Once at the bottom of the stairs, he stepped out onto the sidewalk and looked up and down the street to ensure they were empty. He took a deep breath and mumbled,

"Time to go."

Chapter 25

Linda Carducci hadn't discovered her son Dante, had left with her car until later the previous day. He did ask for permission and informed his mother where he was going and who with. As expected, she prohibited him from doing so. He went anyway, knowing he would be punished when he returned.

Linda heard Dante come in at a very early morning hour but decided to address his disobedience at breakfast. It was 8:00 a.m. and Dante showed no sign of waking and joining his mother for breakfast. The longer she waited for him, the angrier she became. At this point it didn't matter how much sleep he didn't get; she was going to wake him up.

"Dante, time to get up!" she barked as she knocked on his door. There were no responses to her call. She tried again,

"Dante, get up! We need to talk!"

"About what?" replied Dante who was standing behind his mother outside of his room. Linda practically jumped out of her skin.

"Goddamn it son, you're going to give me a heart attack!"

"Sorry mom, I was in the bathroom, what's the problem?" Linda needed a moment to collect herself.

"Breakfast is waiting, I will see you downstairs." Dante went into his room and changed out of his pajamas chuckling the entire time. He wasn't looking forward to the scolding he knew he was going to get, but in the end, it would be worth it.

Dante and his mother ate breakfast with minimal conversation. Once the breakfast dishes were cleared and cleaned with Dante's help, Linda asked him to take a seat at the table. This seemed like the perfect opportunity to tell his mother about his new job and upcoming training.

"Before we get started mom, I want to tell you something." Linda agreed,

"Go ahead." Dante cleared his throat and before he could compile his presentation in his head, he blurted out,

"I'm going to be a cop." Linda heard him clearly, but couldn't believe her ears,

"What did you just say?"

"I've been hired by the Tampa Sheriff department to be trained as a deputy sheriff, pretty cool huh?" he said smiling.

"That's what I thought you said. When did you do all of this?"

"I applied a couple of weeks ago. They called me and told me I would begin training this coming week." Linda took in everything her son was telling her. Like Michel, the image that flooded her mind was one of Dante arresting his father. Unlike Michel, she didn't think the scenario was amusing. Linda struggled to find the right words on how she felt about the news.

"I think that is wonderful son." Although her true feelings were one of fear that this would drive an inflexible wedge between her son and his father. Linda didn't want to think about the news any longer. To dwell on it at this point would only create increased anxiety. There would be plenty of time before it came to fruition. It was time to change the subject.

"Why did you disobey me yesterday? I thought I was very clear about you taking the car."

"You were mom, but…"

"I'm not finished," scolded Linda. "Dante, you are too young to be driving across the country."

"Mom, it was just Georgia, only three hundred miles away, there was hardly any traffic. I knew what I was doing. Hell mom, I'm going to be a deputy sheriff, don't you think they will be wanting me to drive all over the place? Not only that, but sometimes at a very fast speed!"

"Nevertheless, the point I'm trying to make is this, I know you are going into law enforcement, which is a very honorable profession, but as long as you are living here, you will live by our rules, do you understand?"

Dante was hoping his mother would not be playing 'My house, my rules' card but she did. For the time being, it was something he would have to abide by. As soon as he would be able to, he would buy himself his own house and live by his own rules.

"I understand mom, I'm sorry." Linda believed in her son's sincerity and realized her 'child' was now a man, punishing him like a child would serve no purpose. She decided to end the conversation on this topic. "Now, you and I have an appointment to visit your father this afternoon."

"We're going to see Dad at the prison?"

"That's right. By no means do I want you to tell him about your new job. News like that could get your father in serious trouble."

"Okay mom, no problem," assured Dante.

***

The drive to the penitentiary had gone well. However, the closer they came to their destination, the more difficult it became for Linda to keep her composure. She had to pull over and let Dante complete the drive. Linda was eagerly looking forward to seeing her husband, although it would be heartbreaking. Dante on the other hand controlled his emotions and assured his mother that things would be alright, and he would be there for her.

The two made their way through visitor security and were directed to the large visitation area where the visitors were allowed to sit at a table and visit with the prisoners. This accommodation helped Linda's disposition immensely. She was able to pull herself together before seeing her husband. Her main objective on this visit was to assure her husband she and Dante would be alright while he was away.

After about a fifteen-minute wait, Sal entered the room and approached the table where his family sat. Linda sprung from her chair and threw her arms around her husband, prompting the guard who oversaw the visiting room to rush over and remind the two that touching was prohibited.

"Hi Dad," greeted Dante as he held back his tears.

"Hello son," responded Sal. The Carducci family made themselves comfortable and sat down. At first, no one spoke. All three sat and etched the visual images of their loved one into their brain.

"How are you holding up?" asked Linda. Sal shrugged his shoulders and responded,

"I'm okay, how are you two doing?" Dante nodded while forcing a smile.

"We're fine, we're doing fine," replied Linda. Even though the rule of physical contact was prohibited, Linda slid her hand slowly across the table and took her husband's hand into hers.

"Mom, you're not supposed to do that!" exclaimed Dante with a whisper.

"It's alright son, most of the 'Hacks' let you get away with holding hands," explained Sal.

"Have you heard anything from the attorney?" asked Linda.

"No, nothing that is going to change anything. It looks like the wheels of justice have come to a grinding halt. Before I forget, how are you doing for money? Thomas told me he would look after you while I'm gone. Has he been by?"

"No, I haven't seen or heard from Thomas, besides, Dante showed me your little hiding place in the floor of our bedroom." Sal's head snapped in the direction of Dante.

"With what we found in there, we should be fine until you get out, providing we watch our spending," added Linda. Sal became a bit angry with Dante for snooping but couldn't express his disappointment with him.

"What were you looking for Dante?" Dante shook his head slightly and said,

"Honestly Dad, I don't remember, I saw the loose plank in the floor and lifted it out. That's when I found it."

Sal became silent, as did Linda and Dante. Linda could see there was something on her husband's mind, but he was holding back.

"What is it, Sal?" she asked. He looked at her then over at his son.

"I'm going to assume you found more than just money, didn't you Dante?" he asked. Dante nodded. It was at that moment Sal decided to educate his son on what really happened, and who he worked for.

"I know you've been told I was arrested and put in here for fighting."

"Sal?" Linda tried to interrupt her husband to keep him from revealing the truth to their son. Sal ignored her attempt.

"I'm not here for fighting, I'm in here for pointing a gun at a guy during an attempted diamond heist at the airport."

"What?" asked Dante even though he heard every word.

"That's right son, your old man is a gangster. I'm a member of the Barzetti crime family. I've been a member before you were born, it's how I make a living." Surprisingly enough, Dante was not shocked by what his father was telling him. Somehow, he had suspected it for months, just not on the level his father was confessing to.

"Sal?" Once again, Linda tried to keep her husband from revealing anything more.

"There you have it son, that's who I am."

"If you have been doing this for that long, what happened? Why did you get caught?" questioned Dante.

"Because someone set me up and ratted me out to the police, that's why. Now, this next piece of information will absolutely floor you."

"Don't you think that's enough for one day Dad?"

"Shit no, this is the fun part. The person who turned on me is your best friend's father, Michel Santoro."

Dante will never forget how he felt at that very moment. Although he strongly believed his lifelong friend had no knowledge of his father's betrayal, he couldn't help but feel he had been betrayed as well. He suddenly felt angry at everyone and everything. He wanted nothing more than to confront Giovanni to see if he knew anything about this. Deep inside he didn't want anything to happen to his friend, but on the other hand, someone had to pay.

Sal could see the hurt on his son's face and wanted to ease his pain.

"No need to worry son, everything will work itself out. Like the saying goes, there's no honor among thieves." Apparently not, thought Dante.

The guard overseeing the visiting area casually approached the Carducci's table and said,

"Time." Linda looked at her husband for clarification to what the guard meant.

"He's telling me my time is up for this visit," explained Sal. Dante was ready to leave right now. He stood up from his chair and slid it back to the table.

"I'm going to wait in the car mom, it was good to see you Dad, take care, I'll see you again soon." Sal nodded and replied,

"I love you Dante," Dante managed a slight smile and mumbled,

"Love you too." He headed for the exit door and Linda stood from her chair.

"He had some news of his own, but after what you told him, he may change his mind," said Linda. Sal stood and faced his wife and asked,

"What was the news?"

"He's been hired by the Tampa Sheriff Department. He starts his training this week." The look on Sal's face went from confidence and strength to one of confusion and concern.

"You got to be shitting me." Linda shook her head.

"It's true. I'm not sure what he'll do now after what you've told him, but I would like him to see it through." Once again, Sal couldn't believe what he was hearing,

"You got to be shitting me! Have both of you lost your fucking minds?"

"Let him be honey, who knows, it may work out to your advantage," rationalized Linda. She looked at the guard and saw he was focused on her and her movements. It didn't matter, she wrapped her arms around her husband and gave him a kiss on his cheek.

"Sal!" called out the guard as he moved toward them. Linda ended her goodbye hug and held her hands out to her side for the guard to see.

"I'll see you next week," she said, and began to head for the exit.

Sal made a casual walk back to his cell all the while thinking, My son the cop. This is gonna be interesting.

***

The telephone rang as Rebecca entered the living room to watch television.

"Hello." she greeted."

"Rebecca, it's Giovanni."

"Giovanni, hi! Where are you? It's very noisy."

"I'm at the bus station in Tampa." Rebecca's heart leapt for joy knowing he was nearby, even though he was still several miles away. "I was hoping you could come and get me if it isn't too much trouble."

"Sure, Giovanni. I think I could ask my father even though he wasn't too pleased with me going to Georgia with Dante." Suddenly, Rebecca remembered she had just come into a relatively large sum of money for a teenager, courtesy of Giovanni's father. "Wait, I have a better idea, I will take a cab and come to get you. What's the address?"

"Rebecca, a cab will be very expensive, where are you going to get that kind of money?"

"Don't worry about that; give me the address."

"It's 610 Polk Street." Rebecca wrote down the address and said,

"Give me about an hour, okay?"

"Wait Rebecca, I know this may be a bit forward, but do you think your parents could put me up for a few days at your house?" Rebecca chuckled,

"I'll put you up Giovanni, we'll get you a room."

"I can't afford a room!" he exclaimed.

"No, but I can," she replied enthusiastically. "I'll see you in an hour!"

Chapter 26

Dante had just returned home from a grueling ten-hour day of police training. His mother Linda heard him come in while she was in the kitchen preparing their dinner.

"Dante! I have a phone message for you. Rebecca wants you to call her right away." Dante walked into the kitchen and gave his mother a kiss on the cheek as she peeled potatoes.

"Hi mom, did she say she was at home?"

"No, she had me take the number. It's on the piece of paper over on the table." Dante quickly swiped a piece of raw carrot from the colander that sat in the sink and walked over to the table and picked up the message. He didn't recognize the number his mother had jotted down.

"I'll go and give her a call in the living room."

Dante sat in his father's favorite recliner next to the telephone and began dialing. After just one ring, Rebecca answered the phone,

"Hello?"

"Hi Rebecca, Dante, I didn't recognize the number, where are you?"

"Just outside of Tampa."

"What are you doing there,"

"I had to pick someone up at the bus station."

"Are you okay?" he asked.

"I'm fine. I have someone hear who wants to speak to you." There was a slight pause. Dante could hear the phone being passed to the mystery caller.

"Hey D, guess who." A nervous sensation ran through Dante's entire body. He was speechless. He had rehearsed in his head many times as to what he would say to Giovanni when he next spoke with him. For reasons unknown, the words were no longer there.

"D, you still there?"

"Tell me you didn't know what your father did to my dad." The comment had taken Giovanni by surprise. He had no idea what his best friend was talking about.

"Dante, what are you talking about?" Dante calmed himself down enough to reply.

"Your old man set my father up. Now he's in prison," snarled Dante.

"What in the world are you talking about," asked Giovanni once again."

"My father was caught trying to steal some diamonds. Your piece of shit old man told the police what he was going to do, and they caught him. As far as I'm concerned, I don't want to see you or your fucking family again." Dante wanted to slam the phone down at that point but wanted to hear what his one-time friend had to say.

It all started to make sense to Giovanni as to why his family secretly left Tampa, not to mention the entire family having to change their names.

"Dante, you must believe me, I didn't know any of this. My father never told me anything about this. Granted, I thought leaving Tampa the way we did was a bit mysterious and confusing, but I never knew it was because of what he did to your father."

"You should have asked him!" shouted Dante.

"It wasn't my place to question my father. We trust the decisions he makes for the family, but you must believe me, I knew nothing about this."

"Ignorance is no excuse. Goodbye, Giovanni Santoro, I hope your old man burns in hell." Dante slammed the phone down ending his lifelong friendship with Giovanni.

"What is going on?" asked Dante's mother who could hear her son's angry voice and the slamming of the phone receiver, just before she entered the living room. Dante jumped up from the recliner and darted past his mother on the way to his bedroom.

"What happened?" she asked as her son made his way swiftly up the staircase.

"I don't want to talk about it right now mom!" he shouted, then slammed his bedroom door. He walked over to his bedroom window that faced in the direction of where Giovanni used to live. Memories of him and Giovanni walking and riding their bicycles down the streets helped ease the pain of losing his best friend who he missed already.

Giovanni hung the phone up and suddenly realized his life was about to change. He wanted no part of what his father had done. He never wanted to return to Sandersville Georgia. He was ready to start a new chapter in his life with Rebecca and now was as good a time as any to start it.

Rebecca had returned from the bathroom and sat next to Giovanni on the full-size bed in the motel room. She noticed Giovanni seemed to be troubled about something. She put her arms around him and asked,

"What's wrong? Is Dante alright?" He nodded and replied,

"He's fine. I don't believe I will see him again though."

"What happened?" pressed Rebecca.

"I have just learned that my father set up Dante's father to be arrested for stealing diamonds. That's why he's in prison. He didn't get sent there for fighting like Dante told us. Which explains why my family left Tampa. My father is on the run from his gangster friends. Rebecca's eyes widened,

"Your father is a gangster?" Rebecca asked cautiously.

"I believe so, which brings me to a decision that I need to make right now."

"What would that be Giovanni?" He reached for her hand and held between his and asked,

"Will you marry me?" Rebecca's complexion suddenly turned pale. Her heart began to beat faster, and she began to feel sick to her stomach. She stood from the bed and began to pace around the room.

"Oh my god, oh my god," she called out as the speed of her pacing quickened. "This can't be happening!" she cried. Giovanni sprung from the bed and wrapped his arms around her to calm her down.

"It's going to be alright, I have it all figured out." Rebecca gently pushed him away shaking her head.

"How can you have it all figured out John? Where are we going to live? What are we going to do for money? What will our parents say?" Giovanni slowly approached her and wrapped his arms around her again.

"It will all work out. The first thing we must do is tell our parents. I'll be first." He released Rebecca and went straight to the telephone as Rebecca stood by and watched silently. He dialed the operator and placed the long-distance call to Sandersville Georgia. He sat on the bed and motioned for her to come and sit beside him. She approached slowly and sat close to him. She took his arm and placed it around her across her shoulders.

***

The Santoro family were unnerved about the disappearance of their son. Michel did not open the hardware store that morning. He and Bonnie sat close by the telephone in hopes they would hear from

Giovanni. Michel had his hunches as to wear his son was but had no solid proof. Suddenly the telephone rang causing both to practically jump out of their skin. Michel quickly answered it,

"Hello."

"Pop, it's Giovanni."

"Giovanni, where are you? Are you alight?" Tears of joy began to run down Bonnie's cheeks.

"I'm alright pop, I'm in Tampa." The news calmed Michel's heart, but within seconds his anger toward his sons' unannounced disappearance rose to the surface,

"Goddamn it son, your mom and I have been worried sick! What the fuck is wrong with you!?" he shouted.

"I'm sorry pop, I know I should have left a note or something, but I wasn't thinking."

"No shit you weren't thinking. What are you doing in Tampa?" Giovanni looked deep into Rebecca's eyes one last time before delivering the news.

"Rebecca and I are getting married." Rebecca rested her head on Giovanni's shoulder and inched closer to him. There was no response from his father. There was dead silence.

"Pop?"

"Tell your mother what you just told me," responded Michel. He handed Bonnie the receiver.

"Honey are you alright?" she asked.

"Hi mom, I'm fine."

"What did your father want you to tell me?"

"Rebecca and I are getting married." Suddenly Bonnie became lightheaded. Michel could see she was about to faint. He grabbed her by the arm and guided her to her seat at the kitchen table.

"Mom! Mom!" Michel took the receiver away from his wife who had it tightly clenched against her chest.

"Your mom is as shocked as I am, perhaps a little more. I think you should come home so we can all talk about this.

"I can't do that pop."

"Why not?"

"I found out why we moved to Georgia, you helped put Dante's father in prison. Because of you, I've lost my best friend, and you have probably put our entire family's lives in danger." Michel could hear his son's voice begin to crack. He could tell that his son was extremely upset."

"Giovanni, it's not that way at all."

"No pop, it is that way!" Giovanni gathered himself and said,

"I love all of you. I pray God keeps all of you safe. You won't see me for a while, goodbye pop." Giovanni ended the call then handed the receiver to Rebecca, indicating it was her turn to make her call.

Rebecca's parents were also surprised and extremely disappointed in their daughter's decision to run off and marry someone who she had known for less than a year. Despite her parents' efforts to change her mind Rebecca assured them that she and Giovanni would not live very far away. After the tears and sorrow of losing their daughter to someone in marriage, Rebecca's parents gave her their blessing and her father promised to help them get started financially. Rebecca ended the call and immediately jumped onto Giovanni's lap, showering him with hugs and kisses.

Chapter 27

(Four years later)

Salvatore Carducci was being escorted to the exit gate for released prisoners by a security guard. The walk for Sal seemed endless, especially when he caught a glimpse of his wife Linda, standing on the opposite side of the prison gate.

"Open up!" called out the guard. As the gate slid open, the smiles of relief and joy streaked across Sal's and Linda's faces. "So long dick head, see you again soon!" shouted the guard. Sal and Linda embraced one another and showered each other with kisses.

"What would you like to do first?" asked Linda as she seductively placed her husband's hand on her backside. Sal had been away for four years, but he certainly remembered what his wife's ass felt like. Only this time, Linda added a pleasant surprise, she wasn't wearing any underwear under her lightweight linen dress.

"Mrs. Carducci, you naughty girl," commented Sal with great satisfaction and anticipation.

"I have a room already reserved just five miles up the road. Room service will be waiting for your food order when we get there," informed Linda.

"Fuck the food," said Sal. Linda coyly looked at her husband and replied,

"You could, but I would be better." Sal slapped Linda on her ass and said,

"Let's get out of here."

***

Giovanni Santoro was putting the finishing touches to the Bible lesson he was presenting to his class at the youth detention center for boys this coming Sunday, when Rebecca, placed a tall glass of sweet, iced tea in front of him.

"You looked like you could use a break," she said as she slowly worked her way onto her husband's lap.

"Thank you honey, how is the little man this morning?" he asked as he gently caressed Rebecca's stomach.

"Your little girl is doing just fine, thank you very much."

"How are you feeling? You look a little tired," asked Giovanni.

"I don't feel too bad, although I was up late last night with heartburn."

"Must have been the sausage and peppers we had for dinner," suggested Giovanni.

"You may be right, our little girl might not like Italian food."

"I sure wish my mom gave me a little more insight on how I was going to be feeling when I was pregnant, oh well, it's too late now," stated Rebecca.

"That's why God made women so strong, I don't think us men could handle it," Giovanni said.

"I will certainly agree with that my husband," remarked Rebecca. "I'll leave you alone so you can finish." Rebecca kissed Giovanni on the cheek and slid off his lap. "I think I'll go lie down for a little while." Giovanni took his wife's hand and said,

"I'll be quiet, love you."

"Love you too," replied Rebecca, "I'm not going to let you do this to me again!" Giovanni smiled and realized he had married a wonderful woman.

***

Dante walked out of his precinct Captain's office smiling from ear to ear. He couldn't wait to get home and share the news of his promotion with his girlfriend Kate. After being with the sheriff department for only four years, Dante was one of the department's best deputies. His achievements had not gone unnoticed, and his hard work landed him a detective position in homicide.

The new position would allow Dante access to information on criminals throughout the country, which he intended to use to alert the Georgia authorities of the whereabouts of the mafioso, Michel Santoro. Dante kept Santoro's whereabouts to himself for four years. He feared that if he told his father or any of his associates in Tampa, they would have sent someone to kill Michel and perhaps his family as well. Although Dante ended his friendship with Giovanni a few years ago, he still didn't want to see any harm come to the entire Santoro family.

As Dante drove home, he realized that today was the day his father was being released from prison. He and his mother decided that he would stop by his parent's house tomorrow, so that they could have some time alone. Dante was eager to see his father as a free man, without any barriers or guards watching their every move. The one thing he wasn't looking forward to was his father berating him for becoming a police officer. His father never spoke of his career decision in law enforcement while he was in prison. The wrong set of ears overhearing such a conversation would have put all of them in danger.

Salvatore Carducci was a patient man when it came to a vendetta. The opportunity for revenge may only come once, and Sal had spent the last four years planning the day of reckoning.

***

One day later, Michel's daughter Angela walked into the family's hardware store and greeted her father with a kiss on the cheek and a handful of mail that she retrieved from the family's mailbox.

"How was school today asked Michel."

"It was fine," responded Angela. "How was your day?" she asked.

"It was fine," answered Michel, mocking his daughter's vague and simplistic response. Both had a laugh once Angela caught on to what her father was doing.

"Thanks for the mail!" shouted Michel as his daughter ascended the staircase leading to their apartment above the store.

"You're welcome!" shouted Angela. Michel placed the small stack of mail on the register counter and began to look at each envelope before opening any of them. A letter addressed to him caught his eye as he glanced at each envelope. There was no name on the return address, in fact, there was no address. All it read was Savannah.

Michel had a hunch as to who sent the letter, but he wouldn't be certain until he opened it. The envelope contained a single sheet of paper with a single sentence, it read…

The hound has joined the hunt, he's out.

Michel knew immediately that Denny 'The Blade' had sent the letter, but more importantly, who the 'Hound' was. It was Salvatore Carducci.

Michel sighed and started to think about what he and his family needed to do to prepare for the day Sal showed up in Sandersville, Georgia. The thought of his son Giovanni, who had left to marry and follow his own dreams of teaching the youth and young adults in the community, the value of having Christ in their lives, filled his thoughts every day. He knew where Giovanni and Rebecca lived through the postmarked letters they would send on rare occasions. Michel and Bonnie could only hope their son was safe and stayed clear of any contact with the Carducci family.

There was one thing that confused Michel, if he were a hunted man, why haven't there been any attempts on his life for the last four years. Evidently, Dante hadn't told his father the Santoro family was in

Georgia, which means he may have a bit more time to decide what he needed to do. Nevertheless, he decided to always carry a pistol with him if Salvatore Carducci was coming for him.

***

The door to the backroom of the grocery that led to Thomas Califano's office violently swung open, causing everyone in the room, including Thomas, to reach for the guns they were carrying.

"Relax shit heads, your troubles are over, I'm back!" announced Sal. Once those in the room realized it was Sal, they released the grasp they had on their guns.

"Salvatore!" several shouted as they moved to greet their Capo. Thomas came from behind his table and greeted his Captain with a hug and a kiss on the cheek.

"So good to see you Sal," said Thomas. "Doesn't look like prison did anything to your appetite," Thomas commented as he patted Sal's stomach.

"Thanks to you Thomas, and all the nice food you had sent. It would have been an insult if I hadn't eaten every bit of it."

"It was the least I could do Sal, come sit," invited Thomas who directed Sal to take a seat at his table. "Franky, bring us a bottle, would you?" ordered Thomas.

The two men talked for nearly an hour about Sal's recent stretch in prison and Thomas' history of how he avoided any lengthy stays in such a place. After drinking half of the bottle of booze between the two, Sal asked Thomas if he could have a private talk. Thomas obliged,

"Franky!" called out Thomas, "Clear the room for us, we have business to discuss."

Franky did as ordered, then asked,

"You want me to leave boss?"

"No, you stay. Just give us room." Franky nodded then walked over behind the bar, picked up a newspaper and began to read. Sal began the conversation.

"First off, do you know where Michel is," he asked.

"No." replied Thomas. "Look, Sal," continued Thomas, "It's been a while, why don't you give Mikey a pass." Without Sal speaking one word, Thomas could see the anger brewing in his Captain.

"If you don't sanction this Thomas, the Barzetti crime family will be the laughingstock with the rest of the families. The Don won't stand for that. Hell, he would probably have all of us wacked."

Thomas knew Sal was right. Somehow, he brought himself to realize that giving the order to have his old friend killed was not personal, but business. Thomas reluctantly nodded and gave the go ahead to Sal.

"I don't want anything to happen to the rest of the family, is that understood?" said Thomas. Sal stood from the table smiling and mumbled,

"Sure."

"We believe he may have stopped to see Denny Burke."

"The Blade?" asked Sal. Thomas nodded.

"I hate that fuckin' guy, he's like a fuckin' ghost. You never hear or see him until it's too late."

"He is talented, I'll give him that," agreed Thomas. "We think Michel may have seen him to get changes of identification for the family."

"Then I'll go see him first," said Sal. "Is he still in Savannah?"

"Yes, I'll get you the address."

"What's he been doing in Savannah all these years? asked Sal.

"He's a grade schoolteacher."

"No shit?"

"No shit," replied Thomas. "I'll have Franky go with you."

"I don't need Franky, Thomas."

"Yes, you will, I know you've been away for a few years, but you are not dealing with some punk in prison who wants to fuck you in the ass while you take a shower. Don't forget, you are dealing with 'The Blade'." Sal agreed.

"One last thing Thomas, is that piece of shit attorney Klein still representing us?" Thomas frowned and shook his head.

"No, we let Klein go."

"You fired him?" asked Sal.

"No, we let him go out of his sixth-floor office window. We found out he was taking bribes from the governor's hand-picked DA, Harris."

"Damn, I wish I could have been there, you guys have all the fun."

"Well, keep your ass out of prison, I'm sure we will have more fun times," chuckled Thomas. "Are you headed to Savannah?" he asked.

"I will be there in the morning," answered Sal. "Franky! go pack an overnight bag, I'll meet you here at 6:00," he instructed as he left the room.

Chapter 28

Sal made his way home from his meeting with Thomas. As he pulled into his driveway, he noticed an unfamiliar car parked on the street in front of his house. Before he got out of his car, he checked to see if there was a round in the chamber of his .45 caliber pistol. Discovering that there wasn't, he immediately racked a round into place and put the pistol back into his shoulder holster.

He climbed out of his car and cautiously walked up the front steps to the porch. He quickly peered into the front bay window to try to catch a glimpse of who may be in the house besides his wife Linda. He saw no one. He stood at the front door and placed his left hand on the doorknob, keeping his right hand free to pull out his weapon if he needed to. He turned the knob slowly to minimize any noise. He stepped in and quietly closed the door behind him. He could hear Linda speaking to someone in the kitchen. What she was saying wasn't clear. Sal heard nothing from the person she was speaking with. It was at that point, Sal assumed she was on the telephone. He suddenly felt at ease and proceeded to the kitchen. He turned the corner into the kitchen and saw Linda standing, facing him. There wasn't a telephone receiver in her hand, and the expression on her face was one of nervous anticipation.

Something didn't feel right to Sal. He started to raise his right arm and moved his right hand toward his chest with the intention of taking his gun from his shoulder holster.

"I wouldn't do that if I were you," whispered someone behind him. Sal slowly moved his right arm back down to his side.

"You're slipping old man," the person whispered. Sal detected familiarity in the voice and began to snicker.

"You little shit!" He quickly turned and saw his son Dante with an ear-to-ear grin on his face.

"Hi Dad! Welcome home!" Father and son embraced each other, displaying love and happiness to see one another again.

Sal relaxed the embrace he had on his son and stepped back, but remained at arm's length. He looked at how Dante was dressed, expecting to see an officer's uniform.

"Not working today?" asked Sal.

"Actually, I am," responded Dante. "I haven't had the chance to tell you, but I've been promoted to detective."

"Is that right, what division?" inquired Sal, hoping that it wasn't going to be a division to where their paths would cross.

"Homicide," proudly stated Dante. Sal nodded, understanding that perhaps one day his son maybe be called upon to investigate the aftermath of his father's handywork. Until then, Sal decided to keep his son's position with the police department between himself and his family. As far as he was concerned, no one needed to know.

"So, you have time to stay and have dinner with me and your mother?" Sal asked. Dante looked at his mother to get an idea of when dinner would be ready.

"Dinner should be ready in about thirty minutes," informed Linda. Dante smiled and looked at his father who stood anxiously awaiting his answer.

"Sure, I can stay, Dad. Just let me call and check in." Dante's decision to stay pleased his father very much. Sal hugged his son again and patted him on the back and said,

"That's wonderful son let's go into the living room and sit," suggested Sal as he placed his hand on Dante's shoulder, guiding him toward the living room.

As the two sat talking about the small things in their lives, Dante could sense that his father was trying to avoid discussing the situation that put him behind bars for the past four years. As soon as Sal quit chatting about things that didn't really mean anything, he sprung the question Dante was waiting for,

"Have you heard from your friend Giovanni Santoro lately?" Dante shook his head,

"No, I haven't, ever since the Santoro's left, I never heard from him again." Dante could see his father watching him closely. Looking for any sign of deception. He saw and heard nothing.

"Correct me if I'm wrong son, don't you have access to information concerning the whereabouts of criminals in the United States?"

"Not necessarily, if there is an APB issued…"

"APB, what's that?" asked Sal.

"All Points Bulletin. If that is issued, we get information on the subject's last known location and any other information to help us locate and apprehend them safely." Sal nodded, signaling he understood what his son was saying.

"So, you will let your old man know if you get one of these APBs about Michel Santoro, wouldn't you?" Dante sat quietly for a moment before answering,

"Perhaps, but it would depend on what you would do with that information Dad."

"What would I do? Is that your question? I would kill him of course," responded Sal with an intense look on his face."

"Dinners ready!" called out Linda. Sal stood from his chair and said,

"Let's go eat, I'm hungry."

***

Early the following morning, Sal stopped by the grocery to pick up Franky. When Sal arrived, he spotted Franky standing on the sidewalk in front of the store. Franky knew better than to leave Sal waiting.

"Good boy Franky," Sal mumbled to himself. Because of Franky's large frame, he found it difficult to climb in and out of some vehicles, Sal's was one of them.

Even though it took Franky just a little over a minute to get into the front passenger seat, it seemed like an eternity to the impatient Sal Carducci.

"Morning Sal," greeted Franky. "Do you think we can stop for breakfast in a little while?" he asked.

"Jesus Christ Franky, you don't need breakfast. We'll stop for an early lunch," stated Sal.

"But Sal, if I don't have something to eat in the morning, my blood sugar gets low and then I don't feel good."

"Alright, alright, we'll stop once we get out of town for a coffee and donut, nothing more!" A smile graced the face of the bulky gangster.

"Thanks Sal, you're the best."

"Yea, yea, I'm a real sweetheart," responded Sal sarcastically.

To look at Franky, you would guess he might be a chef who loved to eat his own cooking. Or even a janitor or mechanic. The last thing you would guess would be an enforcer for the mob. His tenacity was legendary. He was a cold-hearted killer who would not stop coming at you until he was dead. Despite his appearance, there wasn't anyone Sal would feel more secure working with than Franky.

The time it took to drive to Savannah seemed to pass quickly, despite having to stop several times to satisfy the insatiable appetite of Sal's traveling partner Franky. To Sal's surprise, they reached Savannah at the time he had planned. The streetlights were beginning to come on. Soon, it would be dark enough for Sal and Franky to pay Denny Burke a visit. Sal was fortunate to find a perfect parking space across the street from Burke's house. They would be able to see anyone coming or going without attracting any attention to themselves. All they had to do now was wait.

"What time you got Franky?" asked Sal. The streetlight cast just enough light into the car for Franky to read his watch.

"It's 9:25." Sal surveyed the area one last time to ensure there were no potential witnesses nearby.

"Alright Franky, time to go to work. Remember we don't want to hurt him until he tells us where Michel is. Tie his ass to a chair, and don't forget to gag him. When you have him under control, come out and get me, I'll take it from there, you ready?" Franky had just finished attaching a silencer to the barrel of his .45 semi-auto pistol. He looked at Sal and nodded,

"Ready."

Franky climbed out of the car and lit a cigarette as he slowly walked to the street corner directly across from Denny Burke's house. He smoked his cigarette as he nonchalantly examined the front entrance of the house. It appeared to be very accessible.

The courtyard gate was left open. There were no lights illuminating the walkway to the front door. No lights were on inside that Franky could see. He took the last draw from his cigarette, dropped it on the sidewalk and put it out with the first step he took toward Burke's house.

The front door lock wasn't a challenge for Franky to pick, he gained access within seconds. Once inside, he pulled his .45 from his jacket and began to cautiously make his way through the house. He noticed a staircase next to the entrance of the kitchen, that he assumed led to the bedrooms upstairs. It was his hope he would find Burke fast asleep. Unfortunately, his extreme weight produced the occasional popping noise from the steps. His only hope was that Burke was a sound sleeper. His slow and sometimes noisy assent didn't appear to have alerted his target to his presence. Once he reached the top of the stairs, he was faced with three closed doors to choose from. He needed to make his first selection the correct one, because he may not get the opportunity to make a second. He chose the one to his left. With his weapon in his right hand, he moved his left to the doorknob and slowly turned it, feeling the door unlatch. As the door quietly swung open, Franky held his weapon out in front of him, aiming it at what appeared to be Burke sleeping on his side facing away from him. Franky moved cautiously around the bed to get to the other side that Burke was facing. Franky's eyes never left the slumbering Burke as he kept his .45 pointed at him. Halfway there, Franky passed an open doorway that led to the bathroom. With the speed and stealth of a ninja assassin, Denny Burke sliced through Franky's wrist with an extremely sharp and heavy meat cleaver, severing the hand in which he held his weapon. The severed hand fell to the floor still holding the pistol. In the same motion, Burke reeled around slicing Franky's throat before he could scream. Franky instinctively brought his left hand to his throat and looked into the eyes of his killer. Burke stepped back, allowing Franky to drop to his knees. He suddenly realized that if his victim fell straight forward, which most likely would have, he would fall directly onto his new Oriental rug he had purchased a week earlier. Burke quickly pushed Franky with his foot redirecting his fall away from the rug.

"That was close," he whispered in relief.

***

Sal was beginning to get impatient, but mostly concerned for Franky's wellbeing. What his partner needed to do shouldn't have taken this long. He debated on whether to go to Burke's house himself but decided to let things play out. It was beginning to get a little stuffy in the car, so Sal rolled his driver's side window down to get a little fresh air into the car. Sal looked around in hopes of seeing Franky, but to his disappointment, Franky was nowhere to be seen. Sal stared straight ahead out of the windshield, thinking about the day he would see Michel again. Suddenly, out of nowhere, something heavy and wet dropped in his lap, causing him to lurch backward in his seat. He immediately looked at what was in his lap. He had all he could do to keep from vomiting. It was Franky's severed hand still holding his pistol. Sal reacted violently tossing the hand on the seat next to him. As fast as someone whose clothes had been set on fire, Sal exited the car and pulled his pistol from his shoulder holster. He stood in the street pointing his gun in every direction, ready to kill whoever did this. There was no one to shoot. There wasn't a single soul anywhere.

Once Sal had calmed himself, he reached into his car and retrieved his partner's hand from the front seat. He picked it up by the barrel end of the gun while the hand kept its death grip securely on it. He walked to the back of the car, opened the trunk, and tossed it inside. He closed it hoping to never have to see it again and said,

"Let's go home Franky."

Chapter 29

A fierce pounding on the back door to Thomas Califanos' office at the grocery, startled everyone. Those who hadn't had their first taste of morning coffee were now wearing it down the front of their shirt. The unexpected noise even caused Thomas to jump. Fortunately, he had just set his cup of morning joe down to begin his daily routine of counting the money his soldiers had brought in the night before.

"Joey, go see who's trying to break down my door this early in the morning," ordered Thomas.

"Yea, whoever it is, put a bullet in his head, I just spilled coffee all over my new shirt!" shouted one of the men.

No one thought it was the police. If it were the police, they would have easily busted the door in, and would have entered the room from the back, as well as the front, all at the same time. Joey returned. Everyone's eyes focused on the doorway to see who followed Joey in. It was Sal. The blood from Franky's severed hand had dried on the lower half of the front of his shirt, and down the front of his trousers.

"What the fuck happened to you?" asked Thomas. "Are you hurt? Where's Franky?"

Sal made his way to the coffee pot, poured himself a cup, then made his way to a chair where Thomas was seated. Thomas could see that the blood on Sal was not his, and concluded he wasn't hurt.

"Where's Franky, Sal?" Sal removed his hat and placed it on the chair next to him and sighed.

"Franky's hand and his favorite .45 is in the trunk of my car," said Sal as he held up the car keys waiting for someone to take them from him.

"Joey," called out Thomas. Joey immediately came to the table and stood next to Thomas.

"Go get what's in the trunk of Sal's car, get rid of it, and don't bring it in here." Joey snatched the keys from Sal's hand and exited out the back door.

"I'll assume you weren't able to have a talk with Denny," stated Thomas.

"That fuckin' animal, he didn't have to do that to Franky. After I take care of Michel, Burke will be the next in line," declared Sal.

"Good luck with that, you said it yourself, Burke is like a ghost. You never see the son-of-a-bitch until it's too late. I would say Denny is no longer in Savannah." Sal knew everything Thomas said was the truth. What he didn't know was Thomas underestimated Burke. "The Blade" didn't go anywhere despite knowing he would be on Sal's hit list. Sal needed to focus on the matter at hand, finding Michel Santoro.

Sal left the grocery a short time later. As he drove home slowly to avoid getting pulled over, it gave him time to plan his next move. One thing that continued to trouble him was whether his son Dante told him the truth about knowing where the Santoro's lived. After a few more miles and deep contemplation, Sal came up with an idea that may turn his son against him, but he was willing to take that chance.

***

The following day, Sal made the drive to the Tampa Bay police department building, where his son Dante worked. He made a few phone calls the previous evening to his associates who knew everyone in that precinct's detective division.

He learned all he needed to know about one detective in particular, Dean Healey. Healey had been in the detective division for twenty years.

He had been decorated several times for his bravery and willingness to go the extra yard to produce positive results in cases that most detectives avoided. He was respected by all and admired by rookies in the division. One of those rookies was Dante.

Sal patiently waited and watched everyone who entered and exited the building. He had an 8" x 10" black and white photo of Detective Healey lying on the front seat next to him to reference if he saw anyone that resembled the detective. There was one distinctive feature of Detective Healey that would be easy to spot, he had a large nose that was always red, and if you stood close enough to him, you could also see several blue blood vessels adorning his protruding snout. It was a tell-tale sign that the detective had a profound relationship with alcohol, but it never interfered with his work.

Several hours had passed. Sal became increasingly impatient. He didn't plan to spend his entire day looking at the front door to a police station. There must be a better way than this. He thought to himself. He started his car and said,

"Fuck this." As soon he shifted the car into gear, he saw who he believed was Detective Dean Healey exiting the building. Sal's fatigue from sitting around for most of the day vanished. He watched Healy walk across the parking lot and climb into a car. Sal waited for Healey to leave the parking lot and within seconds was following him, maintaining a two-car gap.

Twenty minutes had passed. There was no indication Healey realized he was being followed. Sal recognized the area he had followed the detective to, then muttered,

"I bet it's your time for a liquid dinner, isn't it detective." Sal was correct, Healey turned into one of his favorite watering holes, The Hideaway. Sal snickered. The Hideaway was where Sal knocked out two gold teeth from a man who couldn't pay his debt for losing a pool game. Sal took his teeth to settle the bet.

Sal found himself once again, sitting and watching for the detective. An hour passed with no sign of the detective. Sal decided to stretch his legs and take a stroll around the outside of the Hideaway, hoping to get a glimpse of the detective and to see if he was drinking alone or had company. The windows of the bar were small and few. This design prompted the naming of the bar. The owner wanted to give his patrons the feeling they were 'hiding away' from the daily grind and enjoying a drink with friends.

Sal peered through a couple of the windows and eventually found the detective sitting at the bar having a drink with a woman who was more than likely, one of the regulars. He observed the bartender placing new drinks in front of them. Sal realized he would be there a bit longer and proceeded to walk back to his car. As he passed the detective's car in the parking lot, he was struck with what he considered a brilliant idea on how he was going to get the detective into his car and drive him to the vacant building he had in mind. Sal turned around and slowly walked back to the detective's car, surveying the area for any possible witnesses. He saw no one. He quickly walked to the front of Healey's car, which was parked nose in first, and opened the hood. He then unplugged every sparkplug cable and closed the hood easily so that he would not make any noise and draw attention to himself.

Proud of what he had accomplished, Sal felt much more confident in his plan to abduct the detective. He walked back to his car and proceeded to wait another hour and a half for Healey to emerge from the bar. The only problem left that he would have to deal with, would be if the female bar fly keeping Healey company left the bar with him.

Detective Healey finally came out from the Hideaway, and to Sal's delight, he was alone. Healey climbed into his car and tried to start it. It wouldn't turn over. He tried several times with no success. Sal got out of his car and slowly walked up to the back of Healey's disabled car. He observed the detective roll the driver's side window down to hear what the engine was doing. Sal approached and called out,

"Engine trouble?" A startled, Healey replied,

"I think so, it was running fine when I got here."

"Mind if I have a look? I'm a mechanic," stated Sal. A smile came to the detective's face, and said,

"Sure! Today must be my lucky day." Sal walked to the front of the car and muttered,

"You have no idea." After opening the hood, Sal reached in and pretended to make what adjustments he could without any tools. "Try that!" said Sal a few times with Healey having no success.

"What do you think?" called out the detective.

"I think you need to see this," suggested Sal. Healey exited the car and walked to the front to see what Sal wanted to show him. Healey looked at the engine and saw that all the sparkplug wires had been disconnected.

"What the hell is…" The detective felt a gun shoved into his side. He looked at Sal totally surprised. "What are you doing?" he asked.

"You'll see," replied Sal as he reached inside of Healey's coat and removed his weapon from his shoulder holster. "We are going to walk to my car, and you are going to get in the driver's seat. You try anything, I'll drop you where you stand." Sal pushed his pistol into the side of the detective once again and directed him on which way to go to get to his car. The detective began to raise his hands to show Sal he wasn't going to try anything.

"Put your fucking hands down, do that again I'll blow them off." Healey lowered them and continued to walk in the direction Sal ordered. Once they reached the car, Sal instructed Healey to stand next to the driver door while he stood directly behind him next to the rear passenger door.

"When I say now, I want you to open the door and get in, got it?" The detective nodded. "What did you say?" asked Sal.

"Got it," responded the detective. Sal glanced quickly at the area around them, then gave the command,

"Now." Both men simultaneously opened the doors and climbed inside. "Close the door," ordered Sal. Both closed their door. "This is what's going to happen," continued Sal. "I'm going to give you directions on where we are going. You do anything to draw attention to us, I'll put a bullet in the back of your head. You can walk away from all this alive if you do what I say, Capito?" Sal using the Italian for understand, prompted Healey to look back at Sal in the rear-view mirror.

"I thought you looked familiar," stated Healey. "You're Sal Carducci, aren't you?"

Sal's picture had shown up several times over the years in the detective division. Like most good detectives, they had committed the faces of the most dangerous to memory. Despite Healey's love of alcohol, he practically had a photographic memory when it came to identifying criminals.

"You're a regular Sherlock Holmes, aren't you?" quipped Sal. "Just keep your eyes on the road," he ordered.

"Where are we going?" asked Healey.

"Take the causeway over Old Tampa Bay to Bayshore Drive, I tell you where to go from there." The detective did as he was instructed. They reached Bayshore Drive without incident and Sal directed the detective to pull into where a recently closed warehouse stood. The lights on the outside of the warehouse still burned bright, which indicated the building still had power. It was what Sal had hoped for, he would need a telephone to make an important call once they were inside.

Sal had Healey pull up to a small flight of stairs that led to a small office near the shipping dock. The two exited the car and climbed the stairs, only to find the door was locked. Sal used his pistol to break the glass on the door near the lock. He ordered Healey to reach in and unlock the door. Once inside the two men walked into the shipping manager's office and turned on the lights. There was a desk, four file cabinets, and a couple of chairs including a chair on rollers next to the desk. Sal grabbed the back of one of the regular chairs and pushed it to the center of the room toward Healey.

"Sit down," ordered Sal. The detective complied. Sal spotted a handheld tape gun on top of one of the cabinets. He picked it up and went behind Healey. He pressed his pistol against the back of Healey's head and ordered him to put his hands behind his back. "Don't move," ordered Sal as he proceeded to wrap the detective's hands together with the tape. Once his hands were secured, he made several passes with the tape gun across Healey's chest and around his back, securing him to the chair. "Do I need to tape your legs to the chair too?" asked Sal.

"No, it will be alright," ensured the captive detective. Sal didn't agree and wrapped his legs to the legs of the chair anyway.

Once Sal was satisfied that the detective wasn't going anywhere, he discovered there wasn't a telephone on the desk. He looked out of the windows of the office and saw a high standing desk in between two bay doors. It apparently was a phone for the drivers to use.

"Don't go away, I'll be right back," he mockingly informed his prisoner. Because of the distance the phone was from the office, Healey could barely hear what Sal was saying, but it was apparent the telephone worked, and Sal looked content when he returned to the office. "Looks like we wait a little while."

"For what?" asked Healey.

"The man of the hour, I guarantee you won't be disappointed?" answered Sal.

Chapter 30

While Sal waited for the arrival of the mystery guest, he decided to take a stroll through the warehouse to see if there was anything of value left behind. During his search he found an excellent vantage point to observe anyone entering the warehouse parking lot.

He stacked a couple empty wooden crates to sit on then lit a cigarette. Occasionally, there were echoing noises throughout the warehouse that attracted his attention. He attributed them to rats and never gave them a second thought.

Shortly after finishing his cigarette, headlights from a slow approaching vehicle streaked across the exterior walls of the warehouse, indicating they had made a turn into the parking lot. Sal watched the vehicle slowly pull up next to his car and stop. He quickly ran back to the loading dock. As he turned the corner around some metal storage racks, he could see Detective Healy doing the best he could to inch his way out of the office while he was still taped to the chair. He made it just outside the office doorway when he saw Sal approaching.

"Where the hell do you think you're going?" asked Sal. Even though Healey's mouth wasn't taped, he didn't answer. Standing in front of the detective, Sal raised his right leg and forcefully planted his foot in the middle of Healey's chest, tipping him backward and falling to the concrete floor. He managed to keep his head from hitting the floor, but the impact forced the air out of his lungs. Sal stepped behind him and lifted the detective back to an upright position. He then grabbed the back of the chair and dragged his hostage back into the office. The strenuous physical exertion caused Sal to perspire. He wiped his brow with the sleeve of his shirt, clenched his fist and struck Healey on the right side of his mouth, splitting his upper lip. The detective moaned when he received the powerful blow then asked,

"What did you do that for?" asked Healey, still trying to catch his breath. Sal replied,

"You made me sweat." Sal still had a clenched fist and prepared to deliver another punch to the detective's face. Suddenly, someone began to pound on the metal entrance door of the loading dock, keeping Sal from abusing his prisoner any further. He wiped the perspiration from his forehead once more and made his way to the door to answer it. Healey lowered his head and closed his eyes preparing himself to take another beating from who he assumed was another mob enforcer.

"Come on in, look what I have," said Sal.

"What the fuck is this, Dad?" asked Dante. Healey raised his head and saw Dante standing in the doorway.

He had met Dante only once when he was being introduced to everyone in the detective division. Dante, however, knew of Detective Healey from other officers. All of them praised Healey for his distinguished record, and hoped to be as good as he was one day. The detective recognized Dante but couldn't remember his name. He only remembered that he was a rookie.

"You going to tell me this piece of shit is your father, rookie?" asked Healey with blood flowing from his swollen upper lip.

"Hey, no need to be calling anyone names," interjected Sal. Dante could see his father was enjoying himself. Dante was becoming angry and wasn't amused by his father's cruelty.

"Why Dad? Why is Detective Healey taped to that chair? Why have you brought him here? What has he done to you?" Sal stood silently and grinned with every question his son asked.

"Are you about through son?" Dante only stared at his father, and with every passing minute, loathed what his father had done.

"The reason the distinguished Detective Healey is honoring us with his presence, is very simple Dante, I know you know where Michel

Santoro is, or at least was at one time when I was in prison. I couldn't think of a better way to get the truth out of you than to torcher one of your most decorated detectives right in front of you. Dante wanted to test his father to see how far he would go.

"I told you Dad; I don't know where he is!" shouted Dante. Sal immediately punched Healey in the face once again, causing the blood already in his mouth to spray onto the wall next to him. Dante hated to watch this man being beaten, but if that's all his father was going to do, he believed the detective could handle it.

"Where is Michel Santoro, Dante?"

"I told you; I don't know! You have to believe me!" pleaded Dante. Again, Sal punished his victim with another forceful punch, only this time breaking his nose. The blood flowed like water out of a faucet down the front of Healey's shirt. The punch Sal delivered hurt his hand causing him to shake it to help relieve the pain.

"Alright, enough of this shit," Sal said as he pulled his pistol from his shoulder holster and pressed the gun against Healey's temple. Dante called out,

"Dad, no! Don't do that! I'll tell you!" Sal lowered his weapon, holding it to his side, pointed at the floor.

"Let's have it, where is he?" demanded Sal. Before Dante answered, he could picture his father bursting into the Santoro's home and killing everyone inside. It was an image he couldn't erase from his mind's eye.

"You have to promise one thing, do what you have to do to Michel, but leave the rest of the family alone." Sal thought about it for a moment and agreed,

"Alright, only Michel. Now where is he?" Dante glanced one more time at the detective and believed he would be doing the right thing.

"He's in Sandersville Georgia. He owns a hardware store called Grady's." Sal displayed a smile of contentment and said,

"Thank you, son." Sal quickly raised his pistol, pointed it at the side of Healey's head and pulled the trigger, blowing half of the detective's head onto the wall of the office. Instinctively, Dante began to reach for his weapon holstered on his hip, which drew his father's attention,

"What's on your mind boy?" asked Sal. "You going to shoot your old man?" Dante moved his hand away from his weapon. "Good boy," commented Sal.

"What the fuck is wrong with you!" Dante shouted. "You are a psychotic asshole!" Sal stood back and admired his work with satisfaction.

"Why did you have to do that?" asked Dante, searching for a logical explanation from his murderous father. Sal holstered his pistol and replied,

"I couldn't leave him here; the rats would have eaten him alive." Dante's anger toward his father boiled over. He turned and took two steps out of the office, stopped then spun around pointing his finger at his father,

"I'm finished with you! I don't want to see you ever again," he shouted. He spun back around and made a hasty exit out the door. Sal turned the office light out and casually walked out the door to his car. He climbed in and sat for a moment, replaying his son's angry departure in his head. He sighed and muttered.

"He still loves his old man,"

***

The following morning Sal met Thomas at the grocery.

"What the hell are you so happy about?" asked Thomas, who noticed Sal's cheerful disposition when he arrived.

"May I sit?" asked Sal as he stood in front of Thomas who was seated at his table. Thomas gestured and invited his Capo to sit.

"I found him," stated Sal. Thomas wasn't sure who Sal was referring to and responded with just a look of confusion.

"Michel, I found Michel."

"How did you do that?" asked Thomas.

"I have my way," answered Sal not wanting to disclose any details. "He's in Sandersville Georgia, I'm headed there as soon as I leave here."

"Who do you want to take with you?" asked Thomas. Sal shook his head and said,

"Nobody, I'll do this by myself."

"You sure? Michel will not be an easy hit," stated Thomas.

"I'll be fine," assured Sal.

"Have it your way, I'll want you to come here when you get back. By the way, you know anything about a detective they found executed in a warehouse by the bay?" Sal acted like he was giving the inquiry considerate thought before answering,

"No, sorry boss, can't help you."

"We frown on that sort of thing you know." Sal nodded his head in agreement,

"I know, I know." Sal had a feeling Dante had alerted the police of the murder. He was certain he did so anonymously. "Well, I better get going," announced Sal as he stood from the table.

"See you in a couple days, give Michel my best," said Thomas.

***

A day and a half later, Salvatore Carducci entered the city limits of Sandersville Georgia. Agonizing over the posted low speed limit, Sal was able to get a good idea of the layout of the city streets. They appeared to be in a simple square block configuration. Sal also took note of where the local police station was located and how many patrol officers were on the street at a given time. As he neared the end of the main street that ran directly through the middle of town, his eye caught the sign he was looking for, 'Grady's Hardware'. Sal pulled to the curb immediately, staying a half a block away from the front of the hardware store. He sat in his car for an hour smoking cigarettes and watching everyone who entered and left Grady's. To his satisfaction, foot traffic was minimal, which played well into his hand for leaving the town in a hurry and lowering the chances of anyone providing a description of him to the police.

To get a better look inside the store, Sal decided to walk past and peer inside. As soon as he opened the car door a man wearing a denim work apron exited the store carrying a bucket of soapy water, a squeegee, and a rag, and proceeded in washing the large window on the front of the store. It was Michel. Sal slowly and quietly closed the car door. Within a few moments, a women exited what Sal presumed was an upstairs apartment and descended the stairway that poured onto the sidewalk that ran in front of the store. The women approached Michel and kissed him on the cheek. She continued her walk past the hardware store and entered another store two blocks away. Initially, Sal did not recognize the woman, but assumed it was Bonnie. From what he saw, he believed the past four years of living the life of the wife of a business owner agreed with her. She looked well, and so did Michel.

Once again, the front door to the hardware store opened and a younger girl emerged. The girl brought some more rags out to Michel. The two chatted for a few minutes, then the girl went back inside. Sal vaguely remembered Michel and Bonnie had a younger daughter. He could only assume that the younger girl he was thinking of had grown to be a very attractive young woman.

The only one missing was Dante's friend, Giovanni. Sal understood that Giovanni was now the same age as Dante. Which meant, Giovanni may very well be living elsewhere and not with his parents. This could be very problematic having a young man avenging his father's death. However, Sal recalled Giovanni becoming an advocate for Christianity. Perhaps he became a preacher or something like that, Sal thought, if that's the case, I won't need to worry about him.

The time on Sal's watch read, 4:45 p.m. It was nearing closing time for most of the stores in Sandersville, Grady's Hardware was one of them. Sal watched the last person that had entered the hardware store leave. Bonnie had returned home a few hours earlier. Everyone was accounted for accept Giovanni. It was time for Sal to pay the Santoro family a visit. He removed his .45 caliber pistol from his holster and attached a silencer to the end of the barrel.

Sal entered Grady's Hardware. He saw who he believed was Michel's daughter, behind the cash register, making entries into a logbook. She didn't look up to see who came in, so Sal flipped the Open/Closed sign that hung in the glass window in front of the store to 'Closed' and locked the door without Angela noticing. She could hear Sal's footsteps getting closer to the counter. She stopped what she was doing and directed her attention to the customer that entered.

When Angela looked at Sal, she reacted as if he was just another customer. Sal suddenly realized she did not recognize him.

"Good afternoon, may I help you?" asked Angela.

"I hope so," replied Sal. "I was curious why such an attractive young lady as yourself, is working in a hardware store?" Angela began to blush. Compliments even from boys her age were rare, but coming from and older man was embarrassing.

"I'm helping my dad." She looked around before leaning closer to Sal and whispered,

"Believe me, I couldn't do this for the rest of my life."

"So, what do you want to do when you get older?" Sal made Angela feel at ease speaking with him and decided to engage in further conversation with the stranger.

"Well, since you asked, I would like to become a chef. I think that would be a job I could do for the rest of my life."

"That sounds like something you would be good at." Angela blushed again with embarrassment, and quickly changed the subject.

"Now, what can I help you with, Mr.....?"

"Carducci, Salvatore Carducci," replied Sal. Angela's eyes widened.

"You're not going to believe this; my brother had a friend with that last name. Are you related to Dante Carducci?" Sal smiled, and immediately pulled his .45 pistol from his shoulder holster under his jacket and pointed it directly into Angela's face and said,

"He's, my son." Angela stood motionless and terrified. "You scream, I'll blow your head off. Where is your father?" Angela was so frighted she could hardly speak. Sal made his way around the counter keeping his pistol pointed at Angela's head. He brought the pistol closer to Angela's face. "Where is he?" Sal asked again, only this time with suppressed rage in his voice.

"He...He's upstairs," nervously answered Angela who was on the verge of tears.

"Get him down here," ordered Sal.

"I can press that button," pointing to what looked like a button for a doorbell mounted on the inside edge of the counter. "He will come down if I do that."

"Then do it," demanded Sal.

Sal didn't know the Santoro family had created a secret alert when using the button. If one of them pressed the button quickly, three times, it meant they needed help with a customer, or they were so busy with customers they needed help. One long uninterrupted press was the danger signal.

Angela pressed the button, keeping her finger on it for at least five seconds. Sal quickly moved in behind her and used her as a human shield. The danger signal was heard by Michel and Bonnie. Michel quickly sprang into action retrieving his pistol from atop the refrigerator. Bonnie was terrified that her daughter was in danger and grabbed her husband's arm as he headed for the door at the top of the staircase which led to the store below. Michel looked at Bonnie and said,

"She'll be alright, you stay right here." Her husband's words were not enough to calm the fearful dread that was tearing at her soul.

Michel slowly made his descent down the staircase. As he neared the bottom, he tried to see what he was walking into. Sal, on the other hand, saw Michel's feet and lower portion of his legs taking one step at a time. When Michel's legs were completely exposed, Sal fired two shots, placing one bullet in each leg. Michel immediately lost the strength in his legs and tumbled down the remaining steps to the landing below.

"Daddy!" shouted Angela who was still being used as a shield for Sal. Michel's fall left him sitting up with his back against the wall on the staircase landing with gun in hand. He could see his daughter being held facing toward him but could not clearly see who stood behind her.

"Daddy?" called out Angela.

"I'll be alright sweetheart, so will you," assured Michel.

"I wouldn't be so sure about that Mikey." The blood in Michel's veins ran cold. The voice he had just heard was one he thought he would never hear again. Sal slowly moved from directly behind Angela exposing his head and giving Michel a clear shot. Unexpectedly, Michel suddenly raised his weapon and fired. The bullet grazed Sal's cheek a fraction of an inch below the scar he had from the last time Michel shot at him years earlier.

Enraged, Sal placed the barrel of his pistol against the side of Angela's head and pulled the trigger. Angela's body went limp as she fell forward to the floor, exposing Sal completely.

"No!" shouted Michel as he watched his daughter's execution.

In the doorway at the top of the stairs, Bonnie stood looking at her husband lying at the bottom of the stairs bleeding from both legs and listening to what was transpiring in the store below. When she heard her husband call out in anguish, she knew something terrible had happened to her daughter. Her heart felt a sudden emptiness. She fell to her knees and began to cry.

Michel reacquired his target but before he could squeeze off another round, Sal fired three times, striking Michel in the chest, killing him instantly. Sal approached Michel's lifeless body. As he stood admiring his marksmanship, he heard Bonnie crying. He stepped over Michel to begin his assent to the top of the stairs. As he did, he shot Michel in the top of his head.

Bonnie could hear someone slowly walking up the stairs. She was hoping it was her husband. The possibility helped her to lessen her mournful sobbing. Her eyes were fixed on the doorway at the top of the stairs. Whoever was approaching, stopped their climb to the top.

"Michel?" she called out. Sal's last step placed him at the top of the stairs and in the doorway. Bonnie immediately began to sob uncontrollably when she saw who it was,

"No, no, no, she pleaded knowing her daughter and husband were dead. Sal said nothing. He raised his pistol toward Bonnie and precisely placed a bullet into her forehead. Her head snapped backward as she fell to her side.

Sal stepped over Bonnie and walked through the kitchen. As he passed a bowl of fruit sitting in the middle of the kitchen table, he stopped and picked out a fresh red apple and took a bite. He made his way to the door at the side entrance to the apartment. He placed his pistol back in its holster and left, locking the door behind him.

Chapter 31

(Three Days Later)

Dante sat at his desk unable to think about anything else other than witnessing his father torturing and executing a fellow detective. The slain detective's body had been discovered the previous day, thanks to an anonymous phone call to the station. Heartache and talk of avenging the death of their colleague swept through the entire Tampa Police Department.

Dante knew that too much time had passed if he were to come forward with what he knew about the murder. He knew he would go to jail for being an accessory to a murder. He knew he would not live long in prison. Corrupt and murderous cops never did. Dante made the choice to remain silent. It was a decision that would haunt him every day.

"Here's something for your scrapbook rookie," said one of Dante's colleagues as he passed by and dropped a copy of a bulletin that had just been issued. It read…

Sandersville, Georgia

Hardware store owner and family found murdered.

The identity of victims unclear at this time. Investigating

Father's connection to organized crime.

A sickening feeling came over Dante, knowing exactly who these people were. He closed his eyes struggling to keep from crying. As far as he knew, his one-time best friend Giovanni was dead along with the rest of the Santoro family. He couldn't help but feel he could have saved them by killing his own father.

The tragic news was too much for Dante to bear. He grabbed his suitcoat from the back of his chair and quickly left the station. Once he was in his car, he could no longer restrain his emotions and broke down crying. He pictured the faces of the Santoro family as he wept. After a few minutes, he dried his eyes and started his car. Something inside told him he needed to confirm for himself if Giovanni was alive or dead. To not draw any attention to himself, he had a better idea. Rather than make inquiries through the resources that were available to him in the department, he was going to pay the parents of Giovanni's wife Rebecca a visit.

The drive to the Stone's residence gave Dante plenty of time to collect his emotions and present himself as an old friend of their daughters who would love to get in contact with her.

Dante pulled into the Stone's driveway, to find them sitting on their front porch enjoying the pleasant weather. Dante exited his car and walked on the sidewalk leading to the porch.

"Mr. and Mrs. Stone?"

"That's us, what can we help you with young man?" asked Mr. Stone.

"You may not remember me, I'm Dante, a high school friend of your daughter Rebecca." Dante could see from the expression on Mr. Stone's face, the name wasn't familiar. However, Mrs. Stone's eyes lit up at the sound of Dante's name.

"Yes of course! I remember you, Dante. My, haven't you grown up to be a handsome man," exclaimed Mrs. Stone.

"Thank you, Ma'am."

"What have you been doing with yourself all these years?" inquired Mrs. Stone. Dante didn't want to get into a long-drawn-out conversation. He wanted to avoid talking about his family at all cost.

"I'm a detective in Tampa Bay." Mr. Stone's interest had been piqued as he sat up in his chair.

"Detective? Rebecca isn't in any trouble is she detective?" he asked.

"No sir, not at all. I was thinking about her, and I was just curious to see if she was still around." Mrs. Stone chimed in,

"She got married you know; they are expecting their first baby too."

"No Ma'am, I didn't know. A baby! That's great! Who did she marry?"

"Her high school sweetheart, Giovanni Santoro, but he doesn't go by Santoro any longer, their last name is Davis. For some reason he changed his last name before they were married. Don't ask me why, she exclaimed holding up one hand and shaking her head. Apparently, he believed his Italian last name was keeping him from getting the kind of work he wanted."

"Yes, I remember Giovanni. That is strange about the name change," added Dante even though he already knew about it. "Are they still living in the area?" Once again, Mrs. Stone answered Dante's question,

"As a matter of fact, they are. They live just north of Tampa, a little town called Dade City. Have you ever been there?" she asked.

"No ma'am, I haven't." At this point in the conversation, Dante believed Giovanni may be alright since he was living in Florida and the Stones obviously were not mourning his death. "May I trouble you for their phone number?" Mrs. Stone was eager and willing to provide Dante with the number. She tore a nearly blank page from her crossword puzzle book she had lying beside her and wrote the number down for Dante and handed it to him.

"Thank you very much Ma'am. It's been a pleasure seeing you again. I better get going, thank you for your time."

"You are very welcome, Dante," replied Mrs. Stone.

"Be careful out there," said Mr. Stone.

"Thank you, sir, I will."

Once he was back on the road, Dante decided to go home and make the call to Giovanni from there. He began to think about what he was going to say to his long-lost friend, then decided he would just tell it like it is and hope for the best.

***

With each number he dialed, Dante's anxiety level increased. After three rings, he was tempted to hang up but chose to remain on the line. On the fifth ring, it was answered.

"Hello." It was a male. Dante assumed it was Giovanni but wasn't sure.

"Yes, hello sir. May I ask who I'm speaking with?"

"This is Steven Davis." Dante was caught off guard. Mrs. Stone never said anything about Giovanni changing his first name as well.

"Yes, Mr. Davis, I was wondering if you could help me locate someone. I'm trying to reach Rebecca Davis. Do you know anyone by that name?" Dante could hear the man chuckle.

"I should hope so, Rebecca is my wife. Who is this?" Dante took a deep breath before answering,

"Giovanni, it's Dante." There was no response, only silence.

"Dante, how…how did you find me?"

"I did a little investigating and paid a visit to Rebecca's parents, she gave me your number, call it an occupational hazard."

"Sorry Dante, I don't understand."

"I'm a detective for the Tampa Police." Giovanni snickered.

"Say it isn't so, you're a detective? That's funny D. Is this a business call?"

"I'm sorry to say John, it is." The first thing that came to Giovanni's mind as to what the call was about, was his father. "When was the last time you spoke with your family?"

"What is it D? What do you have to tell me?"

"I don't have confirmation yet, but what I've learned is that your family has been murdered in Sandersville Georgia." Giovanni stood holding the telephone receiver to his ear. The news tore through Giovanni's heart.

Over the past few years, Giovanni slowly came to the realization that one day, perhaps in the distant future, his father's life as a gangster would catch up with him and bring tragedy to the Santoro family. That day had finally arrived, but all his preparation helped him very little. Rebecca entered the room and found Giovanni holding the phone to his ear while staring off into the distance.

"John honey, what's wrong?" she asked. Giovanni slowly turned to her and said,

"My family has been murdered."

"Dear God, no!" she gasped, bringing her hand to her mouth. Giovanni collected his thoughts and asked,

"Did they catch who did it?"

"No, John. I have an idea who may have been behind it," replied Dante.

"Who's behind it D? You must tell me," he demanded.

"I believe it was my dad, John." The sorrow and pain instantly transformed into anger and hate.

"Are you going to arrest him D?" asked Giovanni.

"It's not that simple John, I need to…"

"You need to what D? You need to what!" shouted Giovanni. "You need to find your old man and arrest him!"

"John please, I…"

"No Dante! No please John. I've heard enough. I'll find him, and when I do, I'll be making a phone call to you, to let you know where you can find his body! One last thing Dante, in Italy they have a word for what I'm about to carry out. The word is vendetta. You might find the meaning of the word interesting. Goodbye Dante."

Giovanni ended the call and looked at Rebecca's tear drenched face. He pulled her close and wrapped his arms around her.

"What are you going to do John?" she asked. Giovanni held her tightly and said,

"I'm going to kill them; I'm going to kill them all." Rebecca gently pushed herself away from him.

"Listen to yourself! You must let God punish these people not you!"

"I can't wait an entire lifetime for God to do anything. I'll save him the effort and take care of this myself." Rebecca couldn't believe what she was hearing.

"You must put your faith in the Lord John!' she pleaded.

"I did Rebecca, look at what it got me." Giovanni placed both of hands on his wife's shoulders, looked deep into her eyes and said, "I have to do this. I want you to help and pack a bag for me. I may be away for a few weeks, but I promise you, I'll be back." Rebecca lowered her head and started to think that one day soon she would be getting a phone call informing her, her husband was killed. He placed his hand under her chin and gently raised her head.

"Trust me," he said. "Now help me pack a bag, okay?" She nodded and whispered,

"Okay."

***

Dante sat on his living room sofa listening to Giovanni's threats echoing through his mind. He glanced over toward a small bookcase he had in his living room and decided to take his friend's advice and look up the meaning of vendetta in his dictionary. After flipping through a few pages, he found the word 'Vendetta' and read the definition,

Vendetta

A feud between two families that arises from

The injury or killing of the member of one family by

A member of the other family, leading to long-lasting

Animosity and retaliatory acts of revenge

A condition of private war in which the

Nearest of kin execute vengeance on the slayer

Of a relative; a blood-feud

Dante set the opened dictionary in his lap and contemplated how far Giovanni would carry out his threat. Knowing he was a religious person; he couldn't imagine he would resort to violence. For the time being, Dante decided to wait before acting on a threat from someone who had just been informed his family had been murdered. But to be on the safe side, he decided to take a drive by his parent's house to see if they were alright and hopefully be able to confront his father about what had happened to the Santoro family.

Chapter 32

Dante began his drive to his parents' house, not only to alert his father about Giovanni, but also to make sure his mother was safe. He contemplated moving her to a hotel or even into his house, until the threat was over.

In the meantime, Giovanni closed his overloaded suitcase and told Rebecca he would be downstairs in a few minutes. "Do you want me to make you some sandwiches for the road?" Rebecca asked.

"That would be great honey, thank you." After Rebecca left the room, Giovanni went into their closet and pulled up one of the floor planks. He reached inside the opening in the floor and retrieved a .357 magnum revolver he had purchased a few years earlier without Rebecca's knowledge. Deep in his heart, he always believed he would need it one day because of his father's line of work. He often prayed that God would protect him and Rebecca from anyone who would take their lives because of something his father had done. Leaving nothing to chance, he felt more comfortable with a bible and a gun, rather than just a bible. He secured his weapon by tucking it inside of his waistbelt in the small of his back, draping his untucked shirt over it.

The time had come for Giovanni to begin his mission. He closed the lid of the trunk that contained his suitcase and slowly approached Rebecca, who began to cry once more. Although she knew what her husband's reaction would be, she attempted one more time to convince him of a safer alternative in finding justice for his murdered family.

"Giovanni, if you won't let God handle this his way, then let the police do their job."

"The police won't be able to do what I intend to do, Becky." Rebecca looked puzzled,

"What won't they do John?"

"There's no need to worry about that, just let me do what I have to do." Rebecca lowered her head feeling defeated and alone. She had a sickening feeling she would never see her Giovanni again. "I need to go honey." He gave Rebecca one last kiss goodbye and reassured her of his safe return.

***

Dante pulled into his parents' driveway. Immediately, he noticed his father's car wasn't there. Nevertheless, he still needed to make sure his mother was alright.

Dante approached the steps leading up to the front porch. He saw no movement inside the house as he glanced through the front bay window. Before knocking, he checked to see if the front door was locked.

No matter how many times his father scolded his mother about not locking the door when he was away, she didn't listen. This time was no different, the door was left unlocked. Dante removed his weapon from inside his jacket and cautiously entered. He wasn't entirely inside the house, when his mother rounded the corner from the dining room. Dante raised his weapon, pointing it directly at his mother. Linda Carducci screamed and nearly fainted with fear. Dante quickly lowered his weapon and called out,

"Mom! It's me, Dante."

"Jesus Christ son, what's wrong with you? You practically gave me a heart attack!"

"Sorry mom, why was the door unlocked? You must remember to keep it locked when Dad's not home."

"I have been, I guess when I got the mail, I forgot to lock it when I came back in. Why are you sneaking in here anyway?" she asked, still trying to calm herself down. Dante holstered his weapon and approached his mom with open arms.

"I'm sorry mom, I didn't mean to frighten you." He held his embrace of her and asked, "Are you alright?" Before she unwrapped her arms from around him, she slapped him on the back of the head,

"Don't ever point a gun at me again son! Why are you here?" Dante had decided not to tell his mother what his father had done to the Santoro family and made up a flimsy excuse for his presence.

"There was a bulletin issued about a dangerous escapee possibly in the area and I thought I would stop in since I was nearby."

"Well, thank you honey, as you can see, I'm fine," responded Linda. "I just finished making some sun iced tea, would you like some?"

"Sure mom, that sounds great." He followed her to the kitchen. Dante sat at the breakfast table while his mother retrieved two glasses with ice and a pitcher of tea, then joined him at the table where a prescription bottle of tranquilizers had been placed. Dante picked the bottle up and read what it was and whom it was prescribed for.

"Why are you taking tranquilizers mom?" he asked with a voice filled with concern. Knowing his mother well, Dante expected how she would react to the question about her health. She didn't disappoint him,

"Those? Oh, there nothing sweetheart," she replied trying her best to dismiss her son's inquiry. She took the bottle of pills from Dante and quickly placed them on the counter next to the sink.

"Tranquilizers are serious medicine mom. Why are you taking them?" Reluctantly, Linda thought it best to inform her son of the need for the medication.

"I guess it stems from the professions of the two most important men in my life. Who knows what your father is into, and I don't want to know. I'm certain it's not legal, then there's you, being a police officer…"

"Detective mom, I'm a detective,"

"Fine. A detective, who is my son, and who I worry about every day. I read in the paper how violent and dangerous the criminals are these days and I don't think I would be able to cope with losing you." Dante could see his mother's eyes beginning to well up. He held her hand and said,

"Mom, there's no need to worry, I'm always careful. I don't try to be a hero and do all these things you see on those television shows. Me and the other detectives watch each other's backs. All of us want to go home at the end of the day. We are trained to be safe.

The heartfelt assurance from Dante helped ease his mother's worries for the time being. She assured him that she would do her best to ween herself from the medication. Dante knew better, and if the medication helped her get through the troubling times, then so be it. He would not press her anymore about the subject.

Dante spent the good part of the afternoon talking to his mother and drinking iced tea. Before either of them realized, it was nearing the dinner hour.

"Would you like to stay for dinner honey?" asked Linda. Dante looked at his watch and replied,

"Sorry mom, I would love to, but I should have been back at the station an hour ago. They are probably wondering if I quit!"

"That sounds like a wonderful idea son!" responded a smiling Linda.

"Stop it mom," he replied. Dante and his mother stood from the table and embraced each other.

"I love you, Dante."

"I love you too, mom." The two walked to the front door with Dante leading the way.

"Lock the door after I leave and tell Dad to give me a call when he gets home."

"Yes, sir detective," playfully answered Linda. He stepped out onto the porch and closed the door behind him. Before taking another step, he listened for the door to be locked, he heard nothing and was about to turn around until he heard the deadbolt being engaged. That a girl he thought to himself.

***

During his drive to Sandersville, Giovanni was able to clear his mind long enough to begin his plan on how he would execute his plan of revenge. Each mile that passed, his heart hardened. He envisioned himself pointing his gun at Sal Carducci and pulling the trigger repeatedly. He saw himself face to face with Dante. The loss of his friendship with him years ago, enabled him to see himself shooting him on site. There was a problem however with how he would approach dealing with Dante's mom, Linda. In his heart, Giovanni knew she had nothing to do with any of it. He couldn't imagine shooting her or hurting her in any way. Then he came to realize he needed to carry out the vendetta to its fullest. Leave no one alive. Make them suffer, inflict pain, make them beg for mercy, then kill them. The thoughts he had, seemed concise and unyielding to any biblical scripture he knew.

Giovanni looked on top of the dashboard of his car and saw the small plastic figurine of Jesus that was attached by a magnet, and a crucifix that dangled from the rear-view mirror. He rolled his window down, removed the crucifix from the mirror, snatched the figurine from atop the dash and tossed both out. The gesture rid Giovanni of conscience and guilt for what he was about to do.

***

Giovanni reached Sandersville in a short amount of time. As he entered the city, he slowly approached the family's hardware store. As he drove past it, he saw the closed sign hanging in the window. There was no sign of police activity inside, nor were there very many people walking about on the outside of the building. He circled around the block and parked across the street from the hardware store on his second pass by. He stepped out of his car and looked at the windows facing the street in the upstairs apartment. The drapes were closed. The building looked deserted. It was difficult, but he knew he had to go inside, he had to see for himself that his family were no longer there.

He walked across the street and approached the large window on the store front. As he peered inside, he saw that the store's shelves were still stocked. Nothing had been removed. It looked as if it were ready to open.

"It's a goddamn shame, isn't it?" commented someone who stood behind Giovanni, startling him. Giovanni turned and saw an older gentleman and asked,

"I'm sorry, what did you say?"

"The family, it's a goddamn shame the whole family was murdered." Giovanni realized the gentleman did not recognize him.

"Murdered?"

"Yep, all three killed in broad daylight."

"Did you know them?" asked Giovanni.

"Not personally, but I've been here several times. Really nice people, but some are saying it was gangsters that killed them."

"Gangsters?"

"Yep, they say the father was one of them."

"What do you say?" asked Giovanni.

"I say that's a bunch of bullshit, Mr. Davis and his wife were good people. Well, I best be going, got to pick up a few things from the grocery for the Mrs. Take care young feller."

"Thank you, you too." As the old man walked away, Giovanni made his way around to the side of the building and up the flight of stairs that led to the apartment. Once he reached the landing at the top, he reached into his pocket and retrieved the key his father had given him to the apartment when he lived there. He had hoped his father never changed the locks and the key still worked. He inserted it into the dead bolt lock and turned it to the left. The sound of the bolt sliding back brought a sigh of relief to Giovanni. He now needed to muster the courage to enter his family's execution chamber.

As soon as Giovanni walked in, he spotted the bloodstained outline of where one of his family members fell dead. He took caution not to step anywhere near the outline and entered the doorway that led to the staircase to the hardware store below. He looked down the stairwell and spotted another bloody outline on the landing below. With a clenched jaw, Giovanni descended the stairway slowly and tiptoed his way over the outline. The daylight streaming in through the store-front window revealed the last body outline.

Giovanni clenched his jaw and held off the urge to cry. He resurrected the hate and anger he felt before. It was at that point he decided he would cry for his family when what he had to do was accomplished.

Before he left, he went back up to the apartment, to retrieve a few more weapons he knew that his father had stashed away, providing the police didn't find them. To his delight, they didn't. He was now well armed and ready to render mob justice.

Chapter 33

Despite the images etched into his brain of seeing where his family had been murdered, Giovanni had the presence of mind to seek professional advice on how to kill the person responsible.

Based on what he had observed when he accompanied his father in Savannah four years ago, Denny Burke was a man he believed he could trust in guiding him in carrying out his mission. Giovanni vaguely remembered how to get to Burke's house. Once arriving in Savannah, it took a few hours just to find the street.

Giovanni parked across the street from Burke's front gate. He wanted to see who came in and out of the residence, but also observe anyone loitering as well. An hour passed. He saw no one until Burke's front gate opened. It was Denny Burke. Giovanni quickly opened his car door and called out,

"Mr. Burke!" The retired assassin slowly turned in Giovanni's direction.

"Yes?"

"I don't know if you remember me, I'm Giovanni Santoro, Michel Santoro's son." Without saying a word, Burke took a quick survey of the street and sidewalks nearby. He opened the gate and gestured for Giovanni to enter. He glanced at the street once more before closing the gate behind him.

Once inside, Burke offered Giovanni a chair and said,

"I heard what happened to your father, I'm terribly sorry."

"My mother and sister too Mr. Burke."

"I'm sorry, my apologies. Why are you here, Giovanni?"

"I know who murdered my family, I was hoping you could give me some advice on how I can kill the man who did it." Before responding to the request, Denny Burke could see the rage and determination in the young Santoro's eyes.

"You want my advice?" Giovanni nodded. "Let the police handle it." This was not what Giovanni expected to hear from Burke. "You will get yourself killed. Sal Carducci is an experienced killer; besides, you have probably never fired a gun in your life, have you?"

"How did you know that?" asked Giovanni.

"Lucky guess," responded Burke. Giovanni was embarrassed. He understood that Burke was looking out for him and needed to bring his lack of experience to the forefront.

"Look son, I can't teach you what you need to know to kill, what I can tell you, is when and where you need to kill them." Giovanni looked confused and Burke read the expression on his face. "What's wrong?" he asked.

"You said them, who else did it?"

"In this business, there is a rule that must be followed, or you'll get wacked. No one kills unless they are given the go ahead by someone higher up in the family. In this case, Thomas Califano gave Carducci the go ahead to kill your father." Giovanni was taken by surprise to hear that the man he and his sister considered an uncle would bless such a thing.

"Why did Thomas allow my mom and sister to be killed? It doesn't make any sense."

"Nothing in this business makes too much sense kid. It's a Sicilian thing. The Italians take their vendettas to an extreme. If you are wanting to take an eye for an eye, you will have to kill Thomas for giving his consent, then you will have Sal and his family to kill as well. Once that is done, hopefully, that will be the end of it.

"Are you saying it might not end?" asked Giovanni whose anxiety level began to increase and was recognized by Burke.

"It all depends on the families involved."

"How so?"

"Depends on how many are in the family."

The reality of the situation wasn't as cut and dried as Giovanni had hoped. He had no idea how large the Carducci family was, nor did he know how large his own mother and father's family were for that matter. He did know his father's brothers still lived in Italy but wasn't sure what they did for a living. It became increasingly apparent that he was going to fight this battle alone.

Giovanni refocused and asked,

"You said you could tell me when and where I would be able to kill them, you have my complete attention."

"Very well, first let me ask you, what weapons do you have?" Giovanni immediately reached around behind him and pulled out his .357 magnum revolver and held it up with the barrel pointing to the ceiling. ".357?"

"Yes sir."

"What else?" asked Burke.

"I took another pistol my father had and a rifle."

"What are they?"

"The rifle is a shotgun, I'm not sure what the pistol is." Burke stood up and held out his hand,

"Give me the keys to your car, are they in the trunk?" Giovanni stood as well and pulled the keys from his front pocket and responded,

"Yes, they are in the trunk wrapped in a blanket."

"Stay here, I'll be right back."

Burke returned within minutes, carrying the weapons wrapped in the blanket.

"Your father always kept the best guns," he said as he set the weapons on the table. "Do you know how to use these?"

"No sir," embarrassingly replied Giovanni.

"Come over here and I'll show you," offered Burke. After thirty minutes of training, Giovanni became much more comfortable and confident in the use of the weapons. "Alright, here's where and when you should make the hit," continued Burke. "Do they still meet at that shitty little grocery store?"

"Yes sir, their office is in the back of the store."

"Alright, if everything is the same from when I was there, they always hold a meeting on Friday night. After the meeting they usually play cards until two or three in the morning. What I want you to do is park your car on the street out in front of the store around 9:00 p.m. It's important that you take note of who and how many go into the store. If you can, park where you can keep an eye on both front and back doors. Like I said, they usually end the card games around two and three. Thomas and Sal like to be the last ones to leave the building. Sal always lit a cigarette before getting into his car. That will help you determine who is who. Most likely, Sal will be the one who will have his gun drawn first, he's the one you shoot first. How long has it been since you've seen either one of them?"

"It has been at least four to five years or more, why?"

"Because not recognizing you, will buy you a few seconds. Those seconds will determine if you live or die."

"I'm not quite sure I'm following you, Mr. Burke."

"Let me finish. When they come out you need to pull up in front of them, but not too fast. If you're too fast, they may think it's a hit, and they will be reaching for their guns, just drive normally. Stop the car, put it park, grab the shotgun, and get out of the car. Keep the car between you and them. Use it as a shield but don't try and shoot over the roof of the car. Move to the rear of the car and shoot over the trunk. Understand?" Giovanni only nodded his head.

"What did you say?" asked Burke. Giovanni cleared his throat and replied,

"Yes sir."

"One last thing, you're not going there to give some speech about revenge or curse them before you shoot. That shit only happens in the movies. You are going there to kill two men. Don't think of them as human beings. They are pieces of shit that are a threat to you. You are there to eliminate that threat. Any questions?"

"What do I do when it's over?"

"You go home and live with it." Giovanni was expecting a more detailed answer, but the more he thought about it, the short simple answer was all that needed to be said.

"Thank you for all your help, Mr. Burke," said Giovanni as he extended his hand. Denny Burke shook his hand and said,

"When it's done, don't be writing me any fucking letters to tell me all about it. If you're successful, I'll read it in the papers. If you're not, I'll read about your body washing up in the bay. Don't worry, you'll be fine. Just don't hesitate. Good luck to ya kid." Giovanni wrapped the weapons back up into the blanket and returned them to the trunk of the car.

After leaving the city limits of Savannah, Giovanni started to give his plan of revenge a second thought. He needed to hear words of support from Rebecca that he was doing the right thing. The first gas station he came to had an outside telephone booth.

He pulled up to the pumps and decided to fill the tank while he was there.

"Fill it up?" asked the attendant who seemed to come out of nowhere as soon as Giovanni climbed out of the car.

"Yes, thank you," responded Giovanni. "Does the phone work?" he asked pointing at the booth located on the corner at the end of the station.

"It did yesterday," replied the attendant as he proceeded to clean the windshield of the car while it was filling. Giovanni reached deep into his pocket to retrieve change for the call, his thoughts were racing through his mind. He wasn't sure what he was going to say to his expecting wife. He just wanted to hear her voice perhaps, for the last time. After dialing the last number, he wanted to hang up. He didn't want to inflict more heartache upon the woman he loved.

"Hello honey, it's me." Rebecca was so relieved to hear her husband's voice.

"John? I've been so worried about you. Where are you?"

"I'm still in Georgia, but I'm on my way home."

"When will you be home?"

"I'll be home day after tomorrow, are you alright?"

"No John, I'm not alright. Why would you even ask me that? My husband is gone for three days on a hunting expedition to kill people. Do I seem alright to you?"

"No, Rebecca, I'm sorry. Look, I've been having thoughts about whether what I'm about to do is wrong…"

"Of course, it's wrong John, murder is wrong. You know that. God will help you get through this. All you have to do is pray to him and ask him to heal your heart, and I will be there for you too!" exclaimed Rebecca.

Giovanni knew his wife was right, but somehow the fire of hate still burned strong within him. It was something he could not ignore. At that moment, he was one hundred percent committed to the execution of the Carducci family.

"I have to get going Rebecca."

"So, I'll see you tomorrow?" she asked, hoping he had changed his mind.

"You'll see me when it's finished," he replied more determined than ever. "There's one more thing, pack a suitcase for yourself and have it ready when I get home."

"I'll pack Giovanni, but I can't guarantee I'll be here when you get back." Rebecca hung up. Giovanni slowly hung the receiver up on the pay phone and stared at it for a moment. Suddenly, someone started banging on the booth door startling him. It was the gas attendant.

Giovanni pulled the booth door open.

"Will that be all sir?" the attendant asked. Giovanni nodded. "Then that will be six dollars seventy-five cents." Giovanni pulled out his cash and peeled off a ten-dollar bill then handed it to the attendant and said,

"Keep the change." He folded the wade of cash and slipped a rubber band around it. After sliding it back into the front pocket of his trousers, he realized he was handling his cash the same way his father did, but more frightening, the way a mobster would.

***

Giovanni reached the suburbs of Tampa in the middle of the afternoon the following day. He took his time getting there, because he wanted to play scenarios over and over in his head on how he was going to carry out his revenge. His first stop was the home of Salvatore Carducci.

Chapter 34

Giovanni parked his car on the curb, three houses away from the Carducci's home. There were no cars in the driveway, or signs of any activity on the outside. He assumed Sal may not be there, which might be to his advantage. If he were already inside the house, he could catch Sal off guard and kill him there. Before he got out of the car, he checked the chamber of his handgun to make sure there was a bullet loaded and ready to be fired. After he stuffed the weapon inside his waistband, Giovanni sat for a moment focusing on what he was about to do and give himself ample time to build his courage. It's time, he thought and climbed out of the car and headed straight to the front porch. He stepped onto the porch and stood at the door for a moment listening for anyone inside. He heard nothing. He opened the squeaky screen door, then grabbed the door handle to the main door and turned. To his surprise the door opened.

Silently, he stepped inside and gently closed the door and locked it. It appeared no one was home. As Giovanni took one step further into the house, Linda Carducci began her descent down the stairs from the upper bedrooms. Giovanni lifted his shirt which covered his handgun and placed his hand on the weapon.

"Oh my God!" the startled Mrs. Carducci shrieked. "Who are you? What do you want?" she asked. Giovanni said nothing and continued to listen for anyone else who may be in the house. After having a few moments to look at the intruder standing inside her house Linda said,

"Well, I'll be damned, you're John Santoro, aren't you?" He smiled, removed his hand from the weapon, which went unnoticed by Mrs. Carducci.

"Yes Ma'am, he replied." Linda was suddenly at ease, making it easier for Giovanni to talk to her. "I'm sorry for just walking in, but the door was unlocked, and I didn't know if anyone was home.

"Please don't tell Dante, he's always reminding me to keep the door locked when I'm here by myself."

"I won't Ma'am."

"Have you seen Dante? Does he know you're here?"

"No, I haven't, and no he doesn't know I'm here." Linda took a few steps toward the telephone in the living room and said,

"Well, I'll give him a call right now and tell him you're in town," Giovanni pulled out his handgun from under his shirt, stopping Linda Carducci in her tracks. "What are you doing Giovanni?" she asked as her smile quickly disappeared from her face.

"There's no one else here, is that correct Mrs. Carducci?" She hesitated to answer then began to stammer, "Ah, no I, yes, I think…"

"You're here alone," confidently stated Giovanni. He walked up to her, gently grabbed her arm, and led her to the kitchen. He pulled a chair out from the kitchen table,

"Have a seat please Mrs. Carducci," directed Giovanni.

"What is all of this about?" asked Linda. Giovanni turned his back to her as he stood in front of the sink. He opened a cupboard door and took a glass from the shelf, filled it with water and took a large drink.

"Apparently, your husband hasn't told you, or your son for that matter."

"Told me what?" she asked.

"Your husband killed my father, my mother, and my sister in Sandersville Georgia a few days ago." Linda's first reaction was one of disbelief,

"No, no, that can't be possible. Sal wouldn't do such a thing."

"Believe it Mrs. Carducci, your husband is a psychotic killer and I'm here to make things right."

"What do you mean by that?" asked Linda. Giovanni detected a sense of fear creeping into her voice. He turned around once more to refill his glass with water. As he did, he noticed the bottle of tranquilizers sitting next to the sink. He picked them up and read the label, then turned to Mrs. Carducci and asked,

"Are you taking these?" she nodded. He placed them back on the counter and said, "I can see why with a piece of shit husband you have."

"What do you want from me?" asked Linda, only this time, anger substituted fear.

"I want you to die as my mother did, Mrs. Carducci. "However, my mother was shot, I don't have it in me to shoot you, unlike your murderous husband."

"What are you going to do John?" He stood silent for a moment and looked around the room to see if there were any implements, he could use to kill her without being cruel. His eyes were drawn to the tranquilizer bottle once again and noticed a six-inch granite mortar and pestle just to the left of it. His dilemma had been resolved.

Giovanni reached back into the cupboard and grabbed another glass, filling it with water. He placed the glass of water in front of Linda. He removed the cap of the tranquilizer bottle and poured approximately twenty of the pills into mortar and proceeded to crush them into a powder. He opened a drawer directly in front of him and retrieved a small spoon and brought it to the table along with the mortar of powdered tranquilizers. Linda remained silent, watching every move Giovanni made. She began to see what he had planned for her and started to squirm in her chair.

"It's not time to take a pill," she said. Giovanni did not respond, rather he took the glass of water he had placed in front of her and poured the powder into the glass. He picked the spoon up and stirred the mixture until the powder eventually dissolved. He removed the spoon, placed it on the table then slid the glass closely in front of Mrs. Carducci. Giovanni walked around to the other side of the table and sat down directly across from Linda and placed the handgun on the table, pointing directly at her.

"I don't want you to take a pill, Mrs. Carducci, I want you to drink all of that." A stream a tears flowed down Linda's cheeks. She knew she did not have a choice, but she managed to display one last act of defiance.

"No. I will not do that."

"Your only other choice is getting shot in the head," he said as he picked up his gun from the table and pointed it directly at her forehead. "Imagine Dante walking in and seeing his mother brutally murdered. Or he could walk in and see you sitting in that chair looking as if you were sleeping. That would be less traumatic, don't you think? Let's get started, shall we?"

Linda's tears continued to flow. She was so upset, she found it difficult to even reach for the glass. Giovanni sat quietly watching her agonize over what she was being forced to do. He picked the glass up and held it in front of her. With a soothing and calm voice, he said,

"It will be alright Mrs. Carducci; you won't feel a thing. You'll just fall to sleep." Linda's display of courage impressed Giovanni when she picked the glass up and drank the entire lethal mixture without pausing.

After about ten minutes, the effects from the overdose were beginning to take its toll. She sat back in her chair with her arms remaining on the table and her hands folded. Her breathing became shallow and weak. Her eyes closed. Moments later, she lowered her head and quietly passed away.

Giovanni stood from his chair and proceeded to wipe down everything he had touched in the kitchen with a damp cloth from the sink. After wiping the doorknobs and handles to the front door as he exited, he dropped the rag behind the bushes in front of the porch. At a leisurely pace, he returned to his car. Before driving off, he retrieved the shotgun from the trunk and placed it on the front seat next to him. His next stop was the grocery store to kill Sal, and Thomas.

***

As Denny "The Blade" Burke instructed, Giovanni arrived at the grocery store at 9:00 p.m. He parked on the street, giving himself a good look at both the front and back doors of the building. All he had to do now was wait and keep his nerve sharp.

The hours passed slowly. Giovanni watched a few of the crew members come and go. The lighting by each door was minimal but gave him a fair look at them. He had worried if he would be able identify Sal and Thomas when they emerged. The last thing he wanted to do was kill the wrong men. He continually told himself to trust and follow Denny Burke's instructions. He had no choice; it had all come down to kill or be killed.

It was 2:13 a.m. Several men had left alone. There were only two cars left parked in front of the store. A light glowing from a small window near the rear of the building faded. Giovanni's heart felt like it was about to pound out of his chest, he started his car and put the car in gear, keeping his feet on the clutch and break. Judgement day had arrived.

The front door to the grocery store swung open. It appeared Thomas was the first one to step out followed by Sal, and just as Burke predicted, Sal lit a cigarette. Giovanni took his foot off the brake and eased off the clutch, moving the car cautiously toward the men. Giovanni's eyes never left them. They stood a couple of feet apart having a conversation. Neither one noticed the car until it was directly in front of them. Giovanni activated the parking brake, grabbed the shotgun from the seat next to him and climbed out of the car holding the gun down behind his car out of view from his targets. He walked to the rear of the car and stopped once he reached the trunk. He saw Sal reaching for his weapon inside his jacket. Giovanni raised the shotgun and pointed it directly at Sal's chest and squeezed the trigger. The thunderous boom from the 12-gauge shotgun caused Thomas to flinch while the buckshot pellets that struck Sal threw him backward against the door of the grocery. Thomas had his weapon in hand and pointed it at Giovanni.

"Don't do it Uncle Thomas!" shouted Giovanni. The voice of the assassin was familiar to Thomas, and the shadowy figure that stood before him was now visible. He paused and asked,

"Giovanni?"

"Yup," was his reply. He racked another round into the chamber and pulled the trigger. The force of the blast hitting Thomas in the upper right chest, launched him through the storefront window.

Now that both men were down, Giovanni carefully walked out from behind the car and approached Sal who was moaning in agony. He stood over Sal and racked another round into his weapon. Sal looked up at him and asked,

"Who the fuck are you?"

"I'm the avenging angel, Giovanni Santoro." Sal began to chuckle and said,

"Fuck you Santoro." The shotgun was pointed at Sal's chest. Giovanni slowly moved it up to Sal's face, smiled and replied,

"No, fuck you, Sal." The close-range blast busted Sal's skull open like a ripe melon. Giovanni glanced over at Thomas who was lying motionless and presumed he too was dead.

He found it difficult to walk away from admiring his work but could hear Denny Burke in the back of his mind, shouting and urging him to leave.

However, there was one thing Denny Burke did not mention to Giovanni. He didn't tell him after killing your first man with a shotgun and the extreme rush of adrenaline through your body, it wasn't uncommon to vomit when you witness firsthand the damage a close-range shotgun blast will cause. Before Giovanni took his first step back to his car, he vomited all over Salvatore Carducci's corpse. He pulled a handkerchief from his pocket and wiped his mouth then, hastily made his way around his car and looked up and down the street to see if anyone was nearby that might have seen what had taken place. He was relieved, not because no one had seen him, but because he would not have to kill anyone that did.

Giovanni needed to rest. He drove around searching for a motel suitable for maintaining a low profile. Within a few minutes, he found the perfect location appropriately named, 'The Getaway'. After grabbing a shower, he watched the local news stations to see if there were any reports about a mob hit. To his delight, there were none. He crawled into bed and stared at the ceiling. His final thought before going to sleep was, I'm coming for you next, Dante.

Chapter 35

Dante took his first sip of morning coffee while sitting at his desk thinking about his last conversation with Giovanni. Knowing his lifelong friend was a complete amateur when it came to the crime world, he found it difficult to anticipate what Giovanni would do. Deep down he couldn't imagine Giovanni doing anything against the law. He had threatened to enact revenge on the Carducci family, but Dante believed he didn't have what it took to kill anyone. His only hope was that his friend's anger would subside and that he would lean on his belief in God to help guide him through this troubling time.

Dante's train of thought was suddenly disrupted by the precinct captain who had approached the detective's desk next to his. The captain handed the detective a photo and the latest report of the shooting that had taken place in front of the Bay Street Grocery.

"You're going to love this," commented the captain. The detective looked at the photo and responded,

"Who's this poor bastard?"

"Read the report," replied the captain. A quick scan of the report brought a smile to the detective's face.

"No shit, it's Salvatore Carducci!" Upon hearing his father's name, Dante's heart sank but he maintained an attentive ear to what was being said between his two colleagues. The detective noticed Dante's sudden interest.

"Want to see what a pile of shit looks like rookie?" asked the detective as he handed Dante the photo. He took the photo from the detective but couldn't look at it.

"You better get used to looking at this kind of thing kid if you want to work in homicide," commented the captain as he waited for Dante to look at the photo. He had no choice, he had to look, or he would be back to writing traffic tickets next week. He tightened his jaw and turned his eyes to the photo. While he gazed at the bloody image, his mind told him this wasn't his father, it was someone else. He found this was the only way he could keep himself from bursting into tears. After viewing it for a few seconds, he handed it back to the captain and said,

"Lovely." His colleagues took advantage of the situation to have a good laugh at Dante's expense.

The detective read more of the report and said,

"It looks like Thomas Califano was hit too, but it looks like he's still alive in the ICU at the hospital. Hell cap, whoever's responsible is sure doing us a favor. I wonder who's next?" asked the detective.

Dante's mind was racing. It appeared that not only Giovanni carried out his threat against his father, but he also tried to kill Thomas as well. His thoughts turned immediately toward his mother. He needed to get to her as soon as he could.

"Hey rookie! You listening?" bellowed the captain, bringing Dante out of deep thought.

"Sir?"

"I said I want you to go to Saint Christopher hospital and see if you can get anything out of Thomas Califano."

"Yes sir, I just need to make a call first."

"Hurry up, we don't know how much time Califano has."

"Yes sir." The captain and detective finished their conversation in the captain's office, leaving Dante to his phone call.

After the fourth ring to his mother's house, Dante tried to convince himself that she was too far away from the phone to hear it. His gut told him something else and it wasn't that she was outside picking flowers for a table centerpiece. He hung the phone up and sprung from his chair, dashing out of the office, and making his way to his car. Once inside, he remembered that he needed to go to the hospital first before driving to the northern suburbs of Tampa to check on his mother.

***

The roads on the way to the hospital were unusually congested with traffic, adding more anxiety to Dante's worried disposition. Once parked at the hospital, he sprinted to the front desk and obtained Thomas's location. Dante entered the intensive care unit and found Thomas unconscious, hooked up to an IV and oxygen. He stood next to the bed looking at Thomas, remembering meeting the man for the first time when he was a child.

Thomas never took to him the way he did with Giovanni and Angela. Perhaps it was because Dante feared Thomas. He remembered his father telling him that Thomas was his boss and that he did what Thomas told him to do. Young Dante thought that this man needed to be feared because he was telling the man who he thought was the strongest in the world, his father, what to do.

"Thomas, can you hear me?" Dante waited to see if his verbal attempt to wake him worked. He tried again, "Thomas, it's Dante, can you hear me?"

"He might be able to hear you, but he can't answer." stated a doctor who had just stepped in behind Dante. "He's in a medically induced coma. Are you a family member?"

"No sir, I'm a detective investigating the shooting," answered Dante as he flashed his badge. "Why did you have to induce a coma?"

"Apparently, the shotgun blast that sent him flying through a window, caused him to hit his head on something very solid. It caused swelling on the brain, that required us to take such action."

"How long will he be out?"

"That depends."

"On what?"

"How strong he is. He has suffered severe injuries, as long as he keeps breathing, he'll have a chance."

"What is his chances doc?"

"Twenty-five percent, considering his age, fifteen. Is there anything else detective?"

"No, thanks doc." Dante realized that he, nor anyone else would be getting any information from Thomas any time soon. He stepped out into the hallway and went to the first phone that he saw, which happened to be at the nurse's station. He placed a call back to the captain and reported what he had been told. His focus now was to get to his mother's house as soon as he could.

***

Dante pulled into the driveway to his mother's house and turned off his car. He sat there a moment looking to see if his mother would come outside and onto the porch to greet him. She didn't. There looked to be no activity around the outside of the house, nor inside from what he could see through the windows. He reached inside his jacket and removed his pistol from its holster. He quietly stepped out of the car and carefully closed the door. Using caution, he ascended the short flight of stairs to the front porch, glancing at the front door and the large bay window at one side. He opened the screen door hoping it wouldn't make any noise. He may as well have beaten the door down with a sledgehammer, because the door creaked so loudly, the element of surprise was eliminated. He grasped the door handle to the main door

297

and turned it quickly. To his disappointment the door was not locked despite his pleading to his mother to do so. He readied his weapon and swiftly swung the door open. The house was quiet.

"Mom!" he called out. There was no reply. He cautiously entered further into the house checking every corner. With his weapon pointed out in front of him, he stepped into the kitchen. He lowered his weapon when he saw his mother sitting at the kitchen table, with her arms resting on the table in front of her. Her eyes were closed, and her head tilted to the left. Dante placed two fingers on the carotid pulse on the side of her neck. It was confirmed that his mother was dead. He sat down next to her and observed the tranquilizer bottle of pills sat open near the sink, a mortar with a powdery residue on it, along with an empty glass on the table in front of his mother.

"She went peacefully Dante." Dante slowly stood up straight with his weapon still in his hand hanging down to his side.

"Don't turn around, I have a gun pointed at the middle of your back."

"Looks like you didn't fall far from the tree at all, did you John, I didn't think you had it in you being a God-fearing man and all," stated Dante.

"I surprised myself D, amazing what a human can do to another when he's pushed. Now, if you would, please set your gun on the table with your left hand holding it by the barrel." Dante lifted his right hand bringing the gun in front of him. He grabbed the barrel end of the gun with his left hand and lowered it slowly to the table. As he placed the gun on the table, he simultaneously reached inside the front of his waistbelt and pulled out his back-up revolver. He whirled around pointing the gun at Giovanni. Before he could squeeze the trigger, Giovanni fired one shot from his father's 9mm pistol, striking Dante in his lower left abdomen. Dante dropped his revolver and bent over in pain holding his hands on his stomach.

"You son-of-a-bitch, you shot me!"

Those words spoken by Dante suddenly pulled on Giovanni's heart strings. Never in his life had he ever thought about killing anyone, especially his best friend. The compassion he felt nearly prompted him to drop his weapon and rush to Dante's aid, but the flames of revenge still burned hot inside him. He cautiously stepped closer to Dante, keeping his pistol pointed at him. He pulled a chair out from the table and placed it in front of Dante.

"Have a seat D." Dante gently eased himself onto the chair continuing to hold his stomach. Giovanni couldn't help but wonder how his friend was feeling. "Does it hurt D?" Dante looked at him and replied,

"Are you fucking kidding me? Yes, it hurts, but I must admit, I thought it would hurt more than this." Giovanni walked around behind him to see if the bullet had passed through. It did. He grabbed a couple of kitchen towels that were near the sink and handed them to Dante.

"It went straight through D, I've been told if a bullet hits bone, it hurts a lot more. Hold those towels on the wounds. Do you think you can walk?"

"I don't know."

"I have to get out of here, I can't stay here much longer, D."

"You just go ahead and leave, I'll be fine."

"Nice try, but I can't leave witnesses behind. You're coming with me." Giovanni was through talking. He placed one hand under Dante's right shoulder and helped him to his feet. "You okay?" asked Giovanni, still concerned for his friend's wellbeing.

"No dumbass, you fucking shot me!"

"So, I did, come on, let's go." The two made their way across the kitchen to the back door. Just before he stepped out of the door onto the steps, he gave one last look at his mother. I'll see you soon mom. He thought.

Once they reached the bottom of the small back porch, Giovanni asked,

"You want to stand or sit? I'm going to get my car; I won't be long."

"Let me stand, I'll have an easier start when I take off running." Giovanni knew damn well his friend wasn't going anywhere. He admired his friend's courage while staring into the face of death.

"Don't make me chase you or else I'll make sure the next bullet hits bone." Dante managed a defiant smile despite feeling a bit weaker.

"Why don't you just finish it here and now?" asked Dante.

"It's not going to be that easy D; you're going to suffer the way I did. The only difference is you're going to die." Dante could see the look of a determined assassin in Giovanni's eyes. His thoughts of surviving this ordeal began to fade. "I'll be right back," said Giovanni.

While Dante stood holding the kitchen towels against his wounds, he felt his body temperature slightly drop giving him chills. At that moment, the sun fought its way through the stubborn clouds. A warm bright ray of sunlight covered him. He lifted his head toward the sky and closed his eyes welcoming the comforting warmth of the sun.

His moment of meditation ended when Giovanni pulled into the driveway and stopped near the rear of the house. As he hoped, he saw Dante standing in the same spot where he had left him. He was now convinced he didn't have to worry about Dante running off.

Giovanni left the car running as he helped his friend into the back seat.

"Let me lay down, John." Giovanni obliged his suffering friend and helped him get as comfortable as he possibly could. He backed the car down the driveway. Once he reached the road, he looked to see if there were any cars coming. His stomach sank when he saw an approaching black and white police car patrolling the neighborhood. The cruiser passed by slowly. Giovanni kept his eye on the patrol officers inside the vehicle. Neither one looked in his direction. A sense of relief ran through his entire body. He eased out into the street and pointed the car in the opposite direction of the patrol car.

***

Giovanni had no idea where he was going. He got on the nearest highway and headed north. Having Dante lying on the back seat of his car, wounded by a bullet he put through him was not part of his plan of revenge. He had hoped he would be on his way back home to his pregnant wife by now. That is if she were still there. The last words she spoke to him presented the possibility he would be returning to an empty house. The thought of losing Rebecca sickened him. He knew he would need her more than ever once all of this was over. All he had to do was make it home alive.

The sun was beginning to set. Giovanni found himself on a lonely stretch of highway and still had no plan as to what to do with Dante. The thoughts of everything that had taken place, the loss of his family, the lives he took, the possibility of losing his wife and having his lifelong friend slowly dying in front of him became more than he could endure.

He pulled the car over off to the side of the highway and turned off the engine. He placed both hands on top of the steering wheel, leaned forward resting his head against his forearms and began to cry. He wanted no more of the madness. He poured his heart out to God asking his forgiveness. When he regained his composure, he felt hollow. Void of hate and vengeance and truly lost. He dried his tears and was afraid to look in the back seat. He looked in his rearview mirror and called out,

"You still with me Dante?" There was a moment of silence then came a weak verbal response,

"Fuck you." Giovanni chuckled. Not at the response, but that his friend was still alive. He looked off to the side of the highway and noticed a lone Florida dogwood tree, halfway up a grassy, gentle inclined embankment. The sight of the tree brought back a memory of Dante quoting one of the civil war generals he studied and admired in high school. Unfortunately, he couldn't remember the quote nor which general. The only thing he remembered was how moving the last words of the general were.

Giovanni decided not to inflict any more injury on his friend. If he had to do it all over again, he would have let Dante kill him, so he could be with the rest of his family in the afterlife. He went around to the back of the vehicle and helped his friend out of the car. Amazingly, Dante still had strength enough to make it up the gentle slope to the large shade tree. Giovanni helped him to the ground enabling him to lean his back against the tree. It appeared the bleeding from the bullet holes had slowed. Giovanni removed his lightweight jacket, rolled it into a ball and stuffed it against the exit wound in Dante's back, then sat on the ground next to his wounded friend.

"So, why have we stopped here John?"

"Remember when we were still in school, you were drawn to history, especially the civil war?" Dante nodded. "You told me what one general said on his death bed just before he died. Do you remember?"

"You calling this my deathbed John? That's a bit morbid, don't you think?"

"Sorry D, I didn't mean for it to sound that way. I just remember how I felt at peace after hearing it. I would imagine it brought piece to the general that spoke those words, that's all." The two sat quietly for a moment admiring the colorful sunset. Then Dante spoke,

"Let us cross over the river and rest under the shade of the tree."

"Yes D, that's the one!" exclaimed Giovanni.

"General Stonewall Jackson's final words," stated Dante. "I have to say I've always liked that one myself. Seems quite appropriate don't you think?" Giovanni didn't say anything. He didn't want his friend to die, but he believed he still needed to maintain his 'cold blooded killer' persona to honor his father.

"I have to go D. With any luck you'll make it through the night, and someone will see you in the morning." Dante was too weak to respond. Giovanni stood up and dusted off the seat of his trousers, looked at his friend one more time and made his way back to his car and slowly drove away.

Within a few miles from leaving Dante, Giovanni's focus was now on getting back to Dade City Florida, and his wife Rebecca, who he prayed was still there.

***

A late-night call came into St. Mary's hospital. The anonymous caller spoke clearly and specifically,

"Northbound on route 441 before the Orange Lake exit, you will find a man on the embankment sitting under a tree. If you don't get to him soon, he will die." The man said nothing more and ended the call.